WE LIVE H

ALSO BY C. D. ROSE

Walter Benjamin Stares at the Sea

The Blind Accordionist

The Biographical Dictionary of Literary Failure

Who's Who When Everyone Is Someone Else

We live here now

C.D. ROSE

MELVILLE HOUSE
brooklyn • london

We Live Here Now
First published in 2025 by Melville House
Copyright © 2024 by C. D. Rose
All rights reserved
First Melville House Printing: May 2025
Distributed by Penguin Random House LLC, 1745 Broadway,
New York, NY 10019 USA. www.penguinrandomhouse.com

Melville House Publishing
46 John Street
Brooklyn, NY 11201
and
Melville House UK
Suite 2000
16/18 Woodford Road
London E7 0HA

mhpbooks.com
@melvillehouse

ISBN: 978-1-68589-201-2
ISBN: 978-1-68589-202-9 (eBook)

Library of Congress Control Number: 2025934636

Designed by Beste M. Doğan

Printed in the United States of America
10 9 8 7 6 5 4 3 2 1

A catalog record for this book is available from the Library of Congress

The authorized representative in the EU for product safety and
compliance is Easy Access System Europe, Mustamäe tee 50, 10621 Tallinn, Estonia.
gpsr.requests@easproject.com

> I think where I am not,
> therefore I am where I do not think.
> —JACQUES LACAN

> Most important things
> want to remain invisible. Love is invisible.
> War is invisible. Capital is invisible.
> —HITO STEYERL

> Every something is an echo of nothing.
> —JOHN CAGE

CONTENTS

We Live Where Now? • *3*

It Is What It Isn't, We Are Where We Aren't • *22*

Every Echo Is a Leak • *43*

Manifest • *70*

Death #47 • *97*

Commission • *121*

Six Versions of Thomas Vyre • *153*

Ich Verstehe Nur Bahnhof • *178*

Crazy Russian Kids Climb Old Soviet Tower • *193*

Available Light • *209*

Contract • *244*

Aleatoric Outcomes from an
Interaction of Conflicting Forces • *260*

Chicago Typewriter • *274*

Klein Bottle: The Comeback • *293*

Acknowledgments • *311*

About the Author • *312*

WE LIVE HERE NOW

WE LIVE WHERE NOW?

Che Horst-Prosier takes a look at the work of Sigismunda Conrad, and the controversy that still surrounds her 2015 installation We Live Here Now.

It's difficult to know where to begin with a piece like this. Let me propose a question: What do you remember, now, about Sigismunda Conrad? It seems straightforward enough, doesn't it? But try answering.

You might recall something about 2011's *The Red Thread*, or—more likely—remember her breakthrough piece 'Guest/Host,' the Serpentine summer smash of 2012. You could try to impress by showing off a discreet knowledge of her early work, the smaller drawing-photograph hybrids recently coming onto the market again. You might be able to say something intelligent-sounding about her work with space, or architectural form, or note that she was one of the first British female artists to show at MOMA. You might vaguely remember her as the woman who built houses, or rooms, or spaces. Most likely, though, is the question that would arise on hearing her name: 'Didn't she . . . ?,' 'Wasn't there that thing in . . . ?,' 'Whatever happened about the . . . ?'

That said, it is quite possible you do not remember her at all: when I told my partner I'd been commissioned to write a piece on Sigi Conrad, I got nothing but a blank stare. Reputation is a fickle maestra.

Unique in being the only major contemporary artist who has no

Wikipedia page, Conrad (originally from 'somewhere in Oxfordshire' according to friends) first emerged in the late 1980s, alongside but quite definitely not with the feted YBAs. Her work, at that time intentionally introspective, quiet, minor, would clearly find little space alongside the pickled sharks in vitrines, unmade beds and self-portraits in frozen blood. Conrad was never one for being seen at the Groucho Club or the Met Bar, preferring to spend time alone, reportedly wandering less modish parts of London with sketchbook or camera in hand, recording things others would miss.

Friends from Central St Martin's remember her as affable but unclubbable, occasionally evasive or even aloof. 'She always gave off the sense that she had somewhere else to be, or something else—perhaps something better—that she could be doing,' recalls Carolynne Fox, now a senior curator at the Royal College of Art.

It wasn't only a question of character which marked her out from the Sensation group, though: while Hirst, Emin et al. were arguably making their best work at the beginning of the 90s, there is also the brute fact that much of Conrad's early work simply isn't that good. The catalogue for her first solo show (at the long-defunct Tobacco Factory space in Clerkenwell) includes a few interesting architectural sketches which linger ambiguously between drawing and photography, and some small but striking composite pictures of 'impossible' spaces, but ultimately they are the work of a talented but derivative, upper second Fine Arts student. They suggest promise, but are yet far from delivering it. Over-exposure at this stage would surely have done her more harm than good; she'd have ended up as one of the unnamed hangers-on in Johnny Shand-Kydd's photos of the time, slightly out of focus with a B&H in one hand and a G&T in the other.

It was perhaps to her advantage, then, to become known in mainland Europe before the UK or the US. The untitled piece (now listed as 'Wardrobe') at the Leipzig Kunstverein collective show in 1994, a solo exhibition at T293 in Naples a year later, then a few of her installation pieces at a Krakow Biennale, all show an artist who needed space to develop and take risks far from the harsh glare of the horribly parochial Anglophone critical sphere. So when *The Red Thread* opened at the Whitworth in Manchester (as part of the MIF), and then later, the briefly famous *Guest/Host* at the Serpentine, it was little surprise that some less attentive observers thought she had emerged, fully formed, blockbuster exhibition ready.

It was during this gestational period that I first experienced one of Conrad's works—'Camera, Camera' at the Kunsthistorisches Museum, Vienna. This was one of those fashionable-in-the-noughties 'takeover' projects, in which an artist—following some supposed curatorial principle—was given free rein to re-organise the museum however they liked. I later found out the process had not been an easy one, and contrary to what she believed she had been promised, Conrad had only been granted the freedom of some of the minor galleries towards the back of the main building. The impressive banners on the lead up to the museum's main entrance were therefore somewhat misleading: on entering, you'd have noticed hardly anything different, and would perhaps wonder what kind of miniscule intervention the artist had made on the museum's continuum. A viewer may have spent fruitless hours looking for the tiniest exhibit that had been moved or modified, a small picture placed where a large one should be, or a text description that had been subtly altered, before only then noticing the signs directing visitors to the *Conrad Ausstellung* which was situated far to the back of the main museum space. When you eventually found your way there, instead of a creative reimagining of the gallery space or the rehanging of a few neglected classic paintings, now strikingly juxtaposed with, say, a relic from the museum's notable collection of Hapsburg armour, or a gilded salt cellar, or indeed one of Conrad's own works on paper, all that she seemed to have done was open up the back stairs, an emergency exit and one of the junk rooms leading down into the car park beneath.

This might sound cynical or snide, but it's not meant to be. It was genuinely one of the most affecting experiences I've ever had in a gallery space. Being unable to tell where the work ended and the world began was disorienting in a remarkable way, forcing the viewer to genuinely see the world anew—a much-vaunted but rarely achieved aim of art. It marked me as a Conrad fan, if not quite devotee, from that moment.

(That said, there is an odd coda to this story. When researching this piece, I tried to find the catalogue for the show, and cannot. Moreover, there is no record of it on the museum's website. Nor can I recall quite why I was in Vienna in 2008.)

Though the show was coolly received it didn't set her star back and over the next couple of years she managed to do larger or smaller installations for the Museum für Moderne Kunst in Frankfurt, the Kuenstlerhaus Bremen, the Kunsthalle in Bregenz, the Kunstmuseum Liechtenstein in Vaduz, and the Moderna Museet in Stockholm.

UK commissions for *The Visitors*, *The Open Door*, *Flow* and *The Red Thread* followed. 'It was a busy time for her,' says Fox. 'Up until then she had always approached her work methodically and sequentially, like a novelist might, one project on the go at a time, a new work to appear every three to four years. But by the late noughties she had several things running at once. Her older shows were still touring and she was trying to get newer ones off the ground.' It was around that time, Fox also recalls, that Conrad had begun to lose touch with her old friends. 'Her mobile went straight to voicemail. She didn't reply to texts. If I ever saw her she'd claim she'd lost her phone and now had a new number. The last time I saw her was some time in 2012, I think.'

It was this run of work which consolidated her style, with comparisons to Rachel Whiteread, Mike Nelson and Ilya Kabakov abounding, as well as to the then modish work of immersive theatre companies such as Punchdrunk or choreographers like Beata Baum. To me such equivalences seemed facile. The epithet 'theatrical' suggests a sense of play, or an awareness of the artifice of the work, if not both of these things. Conrad's works had neither of those. There was nothing theatrical about them in the least. They were deadly serious.

'Through the 90s and into this century, art underwent this massive growth in scale,' says art historian and curator Dan Herman, another former friend of Conrad. 'There was the gigantism of people like Richard Serra or Anish Kapoor—artists whose work necessitates a huge team of engineers and architects to help put up those rusty metal hulks or the colossal red things—but there was also that of the serial producers, artists who were flooding markets with sheer quantity. A surprising number of people still seem to think that Damien Hirst does all those spot or spin paintings himself, or that Anthony Gormley spends his days casting every one of those figures.' We still want to believe in a lone Romantic genius, chipping away at a marble block, sketching furiously into the night by the flicker of a single flame or grinding their own pigments from pig bones and beetle's blood, but the market demands numbers, sales-ready objects, never-ending product.

Conrad didn't offer that, but did have the potential for scale and spectacle, undoubtedly one of the things which brought her to the attention of the increasingly avaricious early 21st century art-industrial complex. But to meet that demand she needed more people, even as she seemed to be shedding friends. As well as the emerging artists and grad students who often make up such a crew, Conrad had always employed craftsmen too, people who had worked and continued to work other jobs—builders, decorators, mechanics, anyone who had the skills to do what she wanted for any particular project. Now she started taking on more of them. Howie Brennan worked in a garage that repaired her car after a minor crash—she liked the way he'd done the spray paint, and got him in to work on *The Red Thread*. Ryan Vaunt was a photographer who'd done a portrait of her, Kev Hewes had been her gardener, and Lewis Nardone was a gobby Glaswegian who had an NVQ in electrical installation engineering and a massive amount of self-taught (and self-proclaimed) knowledge. There was a brickie whose name no one seems to remember, but who'd done a job removing a supporting wall in her kitchen. And then there was Oreste Lauro, an untrustworthy Neapolitan who is telling me most of this.

A turning point came with the invitation to show at London's Serpentine Pavilion, a space usually reserved for architects, or at least those of them ready to do the dance moves of contemporary art. In 2012, when the rest of the city was engaged in the quadrennial hoopla surrounding the Olympics, *Guest/Host* became the feel-bad hit of the summer, a counterblast to the manufactured euphoria. Queues stretched around the park but cameras were strictly banned: the very fact that the experience wasn't Instagrammable added to its attraction.

Not everyone fell for her. JJ Wilson, still one of the British broadsheets' more pugnacious critics, reflects on the savaging he gave *Guest/ Host*. 'I don't regret it,' he tells me via email. 'They were just fucking film sets, stage sets, you know? Nothing more than that. It was theme-park shit.' Carolynne Fox has a kinder view: 'It was the peak of relational aesthetics, for me. It was, finally, where the world became the work, and vice versa,' while the piece left Dan Herman perplexed, though 'not unpleasantly so—I was never quite sure of the role I was supposed to be playing, or what I was supposed to get from any of this. It was very hermetic in its way, although at the same time strikingly obvious.' I myself was undergoing some severe emotional distress that summer, and cannot quite remember if I saw the show or not, which—I suppose—was ultimately part of its intent. Despite this, the popular buzz around the show and its eventual appearance on many influential best-of-year lists led to an inevitable controversy when Conrad yet again failed to even be nominated for the Turner Prize.

'I'm not sure that was as much of a knockback for her as has been made out,' says Fox. 'She was notoriously uninterested in prizes and all the attendant carnival.' Herman is more pragmatic: 'The Turner doesn't mean so much these days, anyhow.'

The prize snub may also have been caused by the growing rumour that Conrad was somehow 'difficult' to work with. The accusation, often tiresomely levelled against female artists as meticulous or attentive to every aspect of their work as a male artist might be, is unsurprising given that Conrad's work is, in parts, intricately detailed, and she insists on getting each and every one of those details exactly how she wants it. With Conrad, it may have been more of her by now well-established elusive personality and the tendency to go AWOL at crucial times. It was rumoured she'd just take off for weeks at a time, perhaps when the stress got too much, or when she wanted to work alone. 'Everyone knew that she had a house on an island somewhere in Scotland,' concurs Oreste Lauro. 'Sometimes she'd just up and go there. No phone, no internet, nothing.'

Conrad not being around to do any of the glad-handing fundraising often necessitates meant that the larger sums of money now needed weren't easy to tap. Big donors and sponsors weren't willing to shell out for an uncertain return, and one over which they had no say. Lauro remembers getting paid haphazardly, a wad of notes appearing in a brown envelope at irregular intervals. 'We weren't salaried. Some of the boys were doing it as a nice little extra. The art school kids were all working for free.' That said, Lauro does remember Conrad having 'some kind of business manager, someone doing the money thing for her,' though he has no name (or, at least, is unwilling to divulge one).

This, combined with the ongoing shedding of friends in the art world, and the growing reliance on that inner circle, had the effect of further isolating Conrad. 'She was always a step away. Never quite there, never quite with you. I just thought that's what artists were like,' says Lauro. 'The team worked closely, but we were never a clique. Plenty of people came and went. She was just picky about who she worked with. You have to respect that, don't you?'

Lauro was Conrad's fixer, finder, sourcer, the man who brought things to her, the man who found what was needed. He doesn't remember how he got to know her—'Someone knew someone who knew someone,' is all he will say. 'I got a call, this must have been when she was working on *The Red Thread*, I think. She wanted some kitchen tiles, they had to be late 60s, Gio Ponti, very specific. I told her it was no problem. It wasn't. After that, I started to get calls more frequently, asking if I could get hold of coral jewellery, 18th-century silhouettes, sheet music from the 1900s. She asked if I knew someone who could make pinhole cameras, or bind books using 16th-century techniques, or recreate the smell of autumn. I usually did. She paid well.'

Once, she needed a chair. 'She told me about a room, and this room was completely empty, apart from one chair. "I want you to find that chair," she told me. That was all, nothing else, no description, nothing.'

I remember the chair. It was part of *The Red Thread*, an exhibition which was a house turning itself inside out, spilling its guts and its secrets, inviting you in then casting you out. Viewers (Conrad always preferred to call them 'participants') entered by walking into a room which was empty apart from that chair, then passed through, finding their way through the whole experience. (I walked for what felt like miles, up and down stairways, along narrow corridors and through wide hallways.) Then, inevitably, whichever path you'd taken, you'd find yourself once again in that room, now entering it from a different angle. By now, the chair looked totally different—replete, filled with purpose. People would just know: they'd sit down in the chair and start to tell a story. They didn't even have to be prompted. It was amazing, it worked nearly every single time.

'Yeah, weird, huh?' gargles Lauro. 'Fucking weird. I found that chair: it'd been mine, at least, it had passed into my possession. I'd got it from my grandmother. Though I'd never told anyone that. I told Sigi I'd got it from an old furniture store.'

It was the chair that was the striking incident of the piece, though in popular memory there is another story. The troubles that eventually characterised *We Live Here Now* weren't unprecedented. Lauro laughs at the mention. 'Sigi got trapped in there one night. I don't know what she was doing in there, no. Who'd question her? She sometimes went looking around her work on her own, adjusting things, y'know? It was the kind of thing artists do, I guess.' She managed to set an alarm off, and somehow (again, no one will say exactly how), could not make her own way out. In order to free her, the fire brigade had to be called. The headlines were predictable only in their banality, as well as the claims it had been a publicity stunt.

Around that time, Conrad was already beginning to conceive what was to be her biggest project yet, the work which would become *We Live Here Now*. It was to be this work which would effectively lift her from the status of being a respected but in some ways undervalued artist, to that of being a recognisable luxury brand, a member of the international super league. It was, in the end, a work which certainly transformed the lives of everyone who encountered it, in one way or another. Conrad had clearly outgrown the now distinctly tired-looking YBAs who were endlessly repeating the same gestures, stuck in an eternal 1990s, and was up there with Richter, Kapoor, Gormley, that Icelandic guy.

'*WLHN* had been in the works for a while, at a preparatory level at least,' says Fox. 'It wasn't a huge thematic departure for her, or a stylistic one, but by the time she really got to work on it, it became apparent to her that she'd need more scale.'

There had been talk of Tate Modern's Turbine Hall, and according to some she was pencilled in there for 2014, but this fell through after what may have been a row with Nick Serota, then Tate director. 'That was the public story,' says Lauro, 'but I don't think it was that. There was other stuff happening.' Serota himself has always refused to comment on the story. The failure to do one of the extremely high-profile series may have been a failure of nerve, or—for an artist whose work had in so many ways been so intimate, so personal, so up close—a refusal to make that massive leap, a challenge to those accusations of gigantism and lust for fame.

With no Tate (or any of their sponsors), and the brief collaboration with Artangel (an organisation that specialises in staging large-scale non-traditional art events) also terminated due to another non-specific row, money continued to make the location question a gnarly one. A disused office building next to Paddington Station was primed, but fell through at the eleventh hour. A brewery at Hackney Wick, same story. A former Lloyds Bank and a closed-down Woolworths were considered, but Conrad wanted nothing that came with its own aura or too much of its own history. The space had to be as neutral as possible. A move out of the capital was considered.

'We rented an old aircraft hangar on a disused airfield in Norfolk,' recalls Lauro, 'miles from anywhere. At first we thought that was where we were going to put the piece together, then Sigi started saying she wanted to do it here, I mean, like, the whole show. Someone must have kicked off somewhere, because that never ended up happening.'

I try to pin Lauro down on the details of this place, and do some more research later. It turns out that the hangar (a former RAF base at Blackbriggs) is still registered in Conrad's name, and is kept there, completely empty.

Conrad ended up being one of the tangential benefactors of the 2008 financial crash. The space eventually used for *WLHN* covered three floors of a curious relic of that era of collapsed PFI initiatives and market panic. While other such colossal builds were stopped in their tracks by bank collapses and lending dry-ups, or never got further than blueprint and hefty grant stages, work on this place had advanced so far by the time the bottom vanished from the market that it could no longer be abandoned. It had acquired too much momentum. They kept on building, full-knowing the place would remain empty. It's still there, way less flashy than the Gherkin or the Shard, an office building as anonymous and familiar as those like Aldgate Tower or 5 Broadgate, the kind of place you could—and still can—walk past every day and not notice. Like those buildings, it is ubiquitous, and invisible.

'I remember walking in for the first time,' says Lauro. 'There were carpets, plug sockets, even lightbulbs in. Paint still drying on the walls. That smell of newness. It was like it had been waiting for us to come.'

While it is possible Conrad secured use of the space for nothing, or fairly close to it, a quick enquiry shows that renting even a few square metres of this building now is nose-bleedingly expensive. When I ask if they were paying for the space, Lauro returns to his characteristic vagueness while Carolynne Fox thinks Conrad had set up, or had access to, some form of ghost corporation, a zombie company, a shell. 'With Sigi, nothing was ever quite real,' she says.

After the false start/dry run of the aircraft hangar experience, work should have begun smoothly, but personnel problems skewed things from the start. 'Lewis, the Glaswegian guy, decided he wanted more money. They were paying us but it was still pocket money, y'know? Peanuts. A nice gig for the students, but—like he said—he was a skilled labourer, and wanted union rates. He wasn't wrong, I guess, but it didn't make him popular with Sigi.' Money wasn't the only problem. 'There was this other guy she brought in; he did work with old furniture, distressing it,'—Lauro says the word with notable distaste—'making it look old and worn. We'd all become really tight-knit by then, you know, and someone new upset the balance. Lewis hated him, some of the others too, no reason other than they thought it was just some bougie shit he was doing. I'd've thought so too, but this guy was good, you could see it. It was more than tea stains, more than just making things look old, a bit of wire wool, scuff up the old paintwork. Way more than that.'

Lauro isn't wrong. I've since had a chance to look more closely at the work (a few pieces made it out), and it is extraordinary. The man in question—who, tellingly, no one seems to be able to locate now, and only remembers by the name of 'Sweeney'—created lives where there had been none. A knife cut on a stair rail, a red wine stain on a carpet—each of these was imbued with something else, with so much more. He evoked presences, gave things auras. He created lives and memories where none had existed. There is mist on a mirror, as though the same breath had touched it, every morning and every evening for years. Any object, once touched by him, became alive, and uncanny.

Lewis Nardone's unrest and the newcomer's intrusion weren't the only problems, however. 'I'd got hold of some of that black, the one they've patented now and you can't get anymore,' Lauro tells me. (If anyone had the ability to do this, it would be Lauro.) 'Lewis got hold of it, and painted everything, I mean everything in one of the rooms. He did it as some kind of protest, I think. It was more than that. It was as if the whole space had disappeared. Or rather, gone into a black hole, and stayed there. If you walked in, you could almost feel it sucking the light out of your eyes. It was upsetting. I think he meant it to be, though he claimed it was a joke.'

Conrad didn't see the funny side and sacked Lewis immediately. She'd probably been waiting for an excuse to do so. 'Looking back on it, we should've unionised or something. Supported him,' says Lauro. 'Especially given everything else that happened.'

Lauro saw Nardone one more time.

'We normally knocked off around seven, or eight, sometimes later, then went out drinking. It had become my job to lock up. Everyone else had gone and I was there with the keys, and the emptiness, and there he was. He'd waited till everyone had gone, he knew our rhythms, then just slipped in. He walked right past me, knew I was watching him, didn't care. He went in, and I didn't think too much about it, thought he'd let himself out, he was canny like that. I thought, yeah, he's probably up to no good, but just some messing around, you know? But I never saw him again.'

Lauro claims not to have been too worried initially. 'It was no great surprise, we weren't really close friends or anything. And he'd always been the kind of guy who'd brag about what he was up to, his dodgy mates, that kind of thing. I had a feeling he'd show up somewhere or other, but later I wasn't so sure.' Seeing as Nardone was no longer working on the project, no one really thought much about him. 'Nobody seemed to have noticed him missing or anything. It's easy to disappear, I guess.'

Looking at it now, I wonder if the story of Nardone may have somehow caused what happened later on, but have no way of knowing this.

Lewis Nardone wasn't replaced, the others worked more, nothing was said, as if the waters simply closed over his head. They were behind schedule and now a person down. The tensions in the group were rising.

'Sigi decided she wanted to use the chair again, my chair, the one from *The Red Thread*. I thought this was lazy, I told her so. She didn't like it, but she wouldn't have sacked me. She got that guy, Sweeney, or whatever his name was, in on it.'

Sweeney hardly touched the chair. He placed it in a room empty but for banks of piled dust around its edges, then had it lit by one narrow, intense beam, from above. 'It was like that gameshow, you know the one?' says Lauro. (I believe he's referring to *Mastermind*— the BBC quiz in which a single contestant is placed under a single white spotlight.) Others who saw the show, or at least that part of it, disagree. 'It was so much more than that,' says Fox, who was present at the opening. 'There were presences in that room. There was someone sitting in that chair, even though there wasn't, if you know what I mean,' she says, and I—almost—do. Dan Herman remembers sound design: 'There was a deep hum, or a kind of intense whispering in the room.' Others remember nothing but deep, thick silence.

'I wasn't impressed,' continues Lauro, 'but there is a story about it. I dreamed about that chair, that room, every night for a week, and each night the dream was the same. The chair was covered with flowers, really intense flowers, all sizes, shapes, colours, orchids and sunflowers, and roses, and everything, y'know, little ones too, daisies and buttercups, all that. And I can't explain it, but, like in a dream, you kind of know things—even though the chair was empty I knew there was someone sitting in it. Then I look at myself, and I'm on fire. There are blue and green, and then yellow and red flames leaping from my arms, all over. My head is on fire! But I feel nothing. So I start running, and I run and run, faster and faster and faster, and then, I'm just about to turn a corner, and I wake up. Every night I had that dream, for a week.

'And then, y'know what? Next time I see Sigi—she's already starting to come less and less by now—next time I see her, I tell her about this dream, and you know what she does? She just looks at me and says, "Yeah, of course." I mean, that's it, that's all she says. "Yeah, of course."'

What Lauro might not know is that everyone who worked on the project had exactly the same dream, and, now that I have begun writing about this piece I, too, have dreamed this dream, each night for the past month. I expect I shall dream it tonight, too.

By this point, with only a few weeks to go until the opening of the show, Conrad had practically abandoned the project. The team ended up working on it alone, often making their own decisions as they went on. She was not completely absent, however.

'One night late, getting close to opening, only a couple of days, maybe,' Lauro tells me, 'I was locking up. I heard a noise. I thought about Lewis. I walked in, and there she was, Sigi. Just sitting there, looking at something. I don't know what—there was nothing to look at. I hadn't heard her come in, didn't know she was around. I called her name but she didn't look up, as if she couldn't hear me, or see me. So I called again, slightly louder, and this time she turned round and looked at me, but, blankly, you know? As if she didn't really see me, or recognise me. Something about her was telling me to be quiet, not to move, as though I would disturb something. I stood there a moment and then, I just got a bit freaked out, y'know? There was nothing there, I swear. But, at the same time, there was. I took her by the hand, very gently, and slowly led her out of the place. We never talked about it again.'

Though the story seems entirely plausible to me, when quizzed about it Lauro becomes defensive, almost second-guessing himself. 'It was never easy to be sure of anything from around that time. It was only a few years ago, yet it seems much longer already. It was a pretty fuzzy time even when it happened. We were drinking a lot. There was always that feeling in those spaces. It was impossible to feel alone. There's that thing from psychoanalysis, y'know? "Wherever there are two people, there's always a third." I thought about that a lot. Polar explorers—it happened to them. Jesus or something—didn't it happen in the Bible?'

Lauro's observation, vague and confused as it may be, is not quite right. I have had the opportunity to see what remains of Conrad's work, and the effect he describes isn't exactly what happens. In fact, it's the opposite. You can walk in, and it seems as if there are fewer of you, as if the person you are with isn't really there. Or, perhaps, keeps blinking, on and off, on and off, sometimes present, sometimes not. And if you go in on your own, then it will happen to yourself. Sometimes you feel yourself there, and other moments, not.

When it came, the opening was muted. Reviews varied. JJ Wilson had been blacklisted but came anyway, and now refuses to talk about his experience. Dan Herman says it left him feeling blank. 'It was similar to Miroslaw Balka's piece from around the same time,' he says. 'Only there was more to it than that, much more. That said, I'm not quite sure what though. It's not something I'd try to describe, really. Or want to.' Carolynne Fox didn't make it. 'I got stuck in the Tube on my way there. Given everything that happened, I'm quite glad.' Conrad herself didn't attend.

Those who did go were made to sign a waiver allowing the CCTV images made in the installation itself to be used. ('A ridiculous gimmick,' says Fox. 'Yet another thing that put me off.') Small sequences of the footage have leaked and show little that is notably striking—

some people glance, some linger, some smile, others are nonplussed—but the strange jumps in the sequences are probably down to editing or equipment blips, nothing more. Most of the footage is no longer available, having been taken in evidence, and now lies buried and inaccessible in some lawyers' safe or police archive.

(I imagine them there, mouldering slightly, giving off gases as their secrets evaporate, another part of their transformation, into a different kind of installation. Works of art are a form of energy—never dying, only transforming.)

It was a cleaner who went first. She didn't show up for her shift. The company responsible didn't think twice about it. Their zero-hour employees were often unreliable, had complicated lives. She was replaced. This may have happened more than once: Swiftkleen won't reply to my emails.

Then there were those people you sometimes see around art galleries, the ones who come in on their own, poke about for a bit, look a bit too carefully at one or two works in particular, then slope off. They never seem to have any friends. No one would really notice if they were there or not. The last place they'd been seen, it was, but there was nothing much to go on.

No one made a connection until Seagram Lynne was over from New York, doing a piece for *White Jesus* magazine. She'd gone with a group of people who all split up once inside. Everyone thought Lynne had left with someone else, that's how she was, after all. It was only when she stopped posting on her Instagram that questions started being asked.

By that time though, the show's run had ended. It had been scheduled for another month, but the take-up had been poor, and it was probably haemorrhaging money. There were no sponsors to keep the cash pumping in, the reviews had been scarce, the crowds few, and Conrad herself was long gone.

Nothing was ever proved, of course. There was nothing to prove. They were there; they weren't there. A correlation maybe (vague at best), no connection. There was no inquest or anything.

The few shows Conrad had scheduled (Stedelijk, Jeu de Paume, Neue Nationalgalerie) were all cancelled. The piece rumoured to involve a large ship, or to be about the sea, or to be in the sea, or something like that, seems to have sunk. Others said she was working on something inspired by the work of the philosopher Lukas Lemnis, or was working with the scientist Thomas Vyre. Conrad herself no longer gives interviews. No one seems to know where she is: Fox thinks she's in Berlin, Herman on her Scottish island, and Lauro won't say for definite but concurs with Herman and thinks she's still at work on the sea project. 'I can see that,' he says as he gets up to leave. 'It'll have taken her over. Swallowed her up.' He laughs, puts down his empty glass, rolls a cigarette and leaves.

I tried to get in touch with him later, to corroborate some of the things he said, and ask a few further questions, but his phone wasn't working, and no one in the bar where we'd met had any recollection of the man.

This article was originally commissioned by Ogive for their 2020 special issue, but not published. It was subsequently refused by Frieze, Abîme, Apollo, 3:AM, Grey Noise and the London Review of Books, and is published here for the first time.

IT IS WHAT IT ISN'T,
WE ARE WHERE WE AREN'T

Chloe from Brown's mentioned to Kasha that she had someone looking to invest. 'Thought it might be your thing. Would it be OK to put in touch?' 'It would,' Kasha wrote back. 'That's what I do!' 'Great,' said Chloe. 'I'll ping you the deets and you can set up a meet somewhere. Tbh I don't think they give a flying fuck about what it is, just as long as, you know, it's safe.' 'That's what I do,' Kasha wrote back. 'I make sure everything is safe.'

A PA or assistant or flunkey of some kind WhatsApped her (no name, just a number), hoped she didn't mind an informal approach, just for a chat. 'Np,' she wrote. Kasha never minded. That was one of her strengths: she never minded. Her approachability was a good quality to offer clients who might be uncertain, or new, or nervous. Kasha could always make them feel safe.

They wanted to meet in a Costa, which was weird, and made Kasha wonder if they were serious at all, or if it was just someone pulling her chain for some reason. There were a good few out there who'd do that. She wondered if it was Silas still dicking her around.

More likely it'd be a standard job, straightforward enough: they'd be after some big names—Kasha could hardly remember how many Hirst spin paintings, Emin neons and dubious Banksies she'd palmed off to bankers or traders who wanted something shiny for their buy-to-let places in Park Slope or Ancoats, their new brasserie venture in

Neukölln or Shoreditch, or to hang in the foyers of blocks shooting up in Vancouver or Delhi. All it had to have was some kind of cachet ('Kasha's cachet' her friend Tye called it). She'd have loved to work with more emerging artists, she really would, but they weren't easy to sell to the people she usually worked with who didn't care if a piece had any integral value of its own. All that was needed for solid investment rather than wild speculation was a validation from someone else.

Kasha knew her job was to blow the smoke and polish the mirrors. If asked, which she occasionally was, Kasha told people she was an art consultant. Most knew to shut up at that point but a few more intrusive questioners might continue, what does that mean, then? If they insisted, Kasha would tell them that she put people in touch, that she offered advice, opened up opportunities, made connections.

Sometimes, though, especially with those who had more money, and now that physical space was looking less of the safe bet it always had been (and with tech providing so much more in the way of speculative investment), there were those who wanted something they could stash, keep safe somewhere, out of view. If it accrued, so much the better. Kasha knew that art was money and that money, too, in its way, if it had to be, could be art.

She made sure she was early (so she'd look reliable, trustworthy, safe) but when she got there the guy was already waiting for her. She stood at the counter, ordered her flat white, and eyed him while she waited. It had to be him: apart from a family of four and a bickering couple he was the only other person there. Thing was, he had no laptop set up, no phone visible, not even an old-fashioned notebook. It seemed as if he really did just want a chat.

She thought she should text Tye, just to be on the safe side. 'At

Costa in Victoria with a strange client in case you never hear from me again.' She put in a horror-face emoji, then took it out again.

'Hi, I'm Kasha,' she said, and the man said, 'Yes, you are,' which was weird, too, and then she put her hand out and so did he and they shook hands and his hand, Kasha noted, was curiously cold. 'Brsh,' he said, or 'Vzh' or 'Tch.' 'Sorry?' she said, and he repeated, 'Asch,' or 'Chz' or 'Kidj,' or something, and Kasha didn't want to ask again so just said, 'That's an unusual name!' and he said, 'Yes, it is,' then sat down.

She heard her phone ping, probably Tye getting back to her, but couldn't check it right now.

He had an accent she couldn't place and a very well-cut dark-blue suit, a shirt buttoned up to the top but with no tie, which always made her feel a bit suspicious, though it wasn't uncommon in the art world. Maybe he was trying to blend in, she thought. He had hair that was brown with bits of grey turning to white, and which didn't quite match his skin: he looked too young to have hair like that. His face was too young for that hair. She felt like she was on some awful Bumble date.

Twenty minutes later, when he'd gone, Kasha wasn't sure she'd met him at all. She sniffed her hand to see if the second, even briefer, parting handshake had left any smell, then realised what she was doing, and in public, and quickly stopped. (There was no smell.) They hadn't exchanged pleasantries, none that she could remember, anyhow. He'd told her what he'd told her, then gone. She looked around to see which direction he'd headed off in, but it was too late.

She'd got some bare details, though: they weren't not serious, but she wasn't sure they were serious either. Chloe from Brown's had

IT IS WHAT IT ISN'T, WE ARE WHERE WE AREN'T

been right—they (and Kasha could use this word now, because Tish or Chudj or Usch or whatever his name was, was clearly representing someone else) really didn't seem to give a flying one about what it was they got. One thing was clear: he hadn't mentioned numbers, and that was a good sign—it always meant there was money, and a lot of it. Something which would accrue, and needn't necessarily be for decoration, they wanted. Something discreet, and which could be stored if necessary. 'Can you do this for us?' he'd asked, and Kasha had replied, 'Yes, I can do that,' because that was what she did. She made people feel safe, and their money, too, no matter how that left her feeling. Kzh or Brzh or Tchr or whatever his name was had seemed to be satisfied. 'We'll be in touch,' he said, and was gone.

Kasha checked her phone. Three unread messages from Tye: 'What's he like?' 'Are you still there?' and 'You OK babe?' She sent back an emoji and walked out thinking about what she could do. Some Emin drawings, maybe, or those small Kapoor pieces she'd seen at Magaletti and Ruf's warehouse space, they'd work. She'd seen a run of some Doigs there, too, those paintings of that man in his canoe—they felt appropriate but she wasn't sure that was quite the thing. Just then—and this would show how timing was everything—Dan from Aster's called about something or other and Kasha told him about her new client, and what would Dan be thinking about in this case. Dan mentioned he had some Cornelia Parker prints, or some Gormley figurines, and a nice Ofili had just come up, but then—almost casually—said something about Sigi Conrad. 'But isn't she . . . ? Wasn't she . . . ?' Kasha began to ask, without really knowing how to finish her question, but Dan just carried on, ignoring her, 'Yeah, but there's some older stuff, a few random pieces, all back on the market now, not sure what it all is, but you could come and have a chat about it,' so Kasha said she would. Later she'd wonder about this, the timing.

Like a lot of people, Kasha had (briefly) worked for Sigi, nearly a decade ago now. The experience had been odd for a number of reasons (not getting paid was the least of it; her supposed boss disappearing for weeks at a time a bit more significant), but she'd always hung on to that interest. Conrad, she thought, might be worth a punt. She was definitely due a revival. She thought she might even have a few early Conrads of her own somewhere, in the little hoard of things she held on to or had been dumped with or hadn't managed to move. She began writing up a mental list of some names she might touch to organise something, or at least get a write up somewhere, but she might want to invest before anything happened that would put up Conrad's rep again. Yes, Sigismunda Conrad. Before she was home she was sure that'd be the right choice.

TWO DAYS LATER SHE WAS sitting with Dan in the office at Aster's. She'd done this kind of thing dozens of times. It was what she did. Deals were never done there and then, there was never any talk of sales. Things were 'acquired,' not 'bought.' There were discreet enquiries, a few nods, appointments made for clients to visit a gallery in off hours, perhaps. A dinner might be arranged. There would be a gentle nod and an avoidance of numbers. It was so smooth an outsider might not even notice it happening.

'What about the Sigi, then? Can I see it?'

'Still on that, are you?'

'You brought it up.'

'Guess I did. Thing is . . . '

'Thing is?'

'We don't actually have it here. It's in storage somewhere.'

'Pics or it doesn't happen.'

'I'll see what I can do.' He messed around with his laptop, then called someone.

'Yeah . . . that Conrad stuff . . . have we got any images? Yeah, I'm with a client now. Yeah . . . no . . . OK . . . no . . . I see. Hang on.' He put his hand over the phone. 'We don't have anything of the right quality now, but they're coming,' he said to Kasha. 'Can you hang? I tell you what, let's grab some lunch and they'll probably be there before you've finished your first negroni sbagliato.'

Three negronis in and the pictures still hadn't shown up but by then Kasha was past caring. Dan seemed to be reeling it back in, which made Kasha even keener. They ordered some food but only picked at it. They might have done a line. They might have done two. Kasha might have signed something.

When she woke up the next morning she wasn't sure but thought they'd gone on somewhere. She had to stop doing this. She'd be 30 next year. It'd be fine if it wasn't for the hangovers, the attacks of dread in particular, and they were attacking her now. She'd have to cancel her appointments for the day. She texted Dan.

'Did we settle on the Conrad?' Dan sent back an emoji. Kasha went back to bed.

Later, she tried to call Kish or Tudj again, but there was no reply. She wrote a message, telling them that she'd strongly advise a rare work by Sigismunda Conrad, and that they should move quickly as there wasn't much on the market and that Conrad was about to have a major critical upswing.

'We trust you,' they wrote back.

She relaxed. This was what Kasha did. She built trust. People trusted her. She was relieved, and decided to wait thirty minutes or so before telling them it was a done deal.

Half an hour later, that done, she allowed herself to calculate her commission. She couldn't believe how much money she'd made for little over a half a day's work (if you could call it work), but then reminded herself that this was precisely why she could make so much money for half a day's work: because people trusted her, because she was safe, because she was fucking good at what she did.

She texted Tye to tell her how much money she was about to make.

'That is unreal!' Tye wrote back.

'Ikr? Insane!'

'Cash-A! $$$$$! Unreal, babe.'

It hadn't been half a day's work, of course, it was years of building up her client base, of networking, of establishing her reputation for discretion and security that had done it. If you factored all that in, it wasn't actually all that much money, especially not compared to what some of these fuckers were making.

Her dad, who'd made his money from moving numbers around on a computer screen as far as she understood it, had told her to get into property but there was no fucking way she was going to be an estate agent walking round in a business suit with an iPad, driving one of those horrible New Mini Thugs or a little Fiat Fascist. It wasn't just that though: you couldn't move it. There was no escape from it. It just stood there, concrete and bricks and scaffolding and laminate flooring, wires and pipes plunged into the ground. It felt horribly like commitment, too too final. Silas had his chemical/pharmaceutical/

herbal side hustle (which, she knew well, wasn't really a side hustle at all, but in fact his only hustle) and while that was indeed highly mobile, there were always problems with legality and the concurrent possibility of the necessity of having to be very mobile, very quickly. Her mum was in antiquities but all that verification and history bored Kasha to tears. Dad had made his money from money, after all. That was the purest thing, only, art was better: art was respectable, no, not merely respectable, actively admirable. Art was solid. Art lasted. Art could be discreet. Art would never talk. Art had no value, and could be worth millions.

She had to factor in the aftersales service, too. That was all work. Like, where did they want the thing sending? A shipping address. Storage. It'd have to be kept in gallery conditions. She did her best for them, as far as she could. Sometimes, she knew, it'd hardly matter as the stuff would most likely as not end up hidden—from cachet to cache, all the work of Kasha.

'We're currently looking at options,' they told her. 'Tax-wise, what might be best?'

She was surprised they didn't know this. For most of these people art was a form of investment, after all, and they usually knew better than she did. Sure, she worked with money as much as art but art was her background, after all, if a half-finished degree course at the Courtauld counted, which it surely did. (She'd dropped out due to mental health issues, but knew it was really because she'd been caning it too hard. But those two things, again, were actually one and the same.) She'd spent a year living in Berlin, which practically qualified her as being an artist in itself. She'd written bits for *Frieze*, *Abîme*, *Grey Noise*, made the good connections, kept on going to the parties.

Thing was, she didn't know that much about money but knew enough: tax-wise, sending something on tour was the best thing to do.

While money didn't really exist, art most definitely did. Art needed to be put somewhere. Like money, however, art was mobile. Like money, art could be endlessly free-floating. Unlike money, however, no one even knew quite what art was. Art works needed no registration of ownership. A nice Basquiat she'd sourced for a Brazilian banker had spent at least a year travelling slowly through one tax zone, then another, then another, never staying long enough to have to pay for its stay, rarely even having to acknowledge its own existence.

She told them; they agreed. Kasha signed a few documents, and off it went. For the next few years the Conrad would sail silently, stashed away onboard a ship from Tilbury to Antwerp to Laem Chabang to Shanghai and god only knew where else, each port with a different tax dispensation, under a different jurisdiction. Its crate could be valued at a few hundred dollars, tops. Who was to say it was worth more than that?

During the pandemic Kasha sat in her flat and thought on it, from time to time, idly wondering where it may be, becalmed and belulled, and she felt she understood it, whatever it was. Silas, who had started coming over again with his supplies from time to time, and was actually helping to keep her sane despite his usual bullshit, told her that 'If we have beauty, we have everything,' and Kasha tried to take some comfort in that, knowing that beauty for her was the thought of free-flowing endless drift, of nothing being attached or anchored to anything, of perpetual motion, flow, slip, drift, slide. In her better moments, that was how she wanted to be.

SHE'D TRY AND REMEMBER THOSE moments when, eighteen months later, she was sitting by the side of busy road somewhere on the outskirts of Geneva trying, once again, not to have a panic attack.

It all seemed to have been going so smoothly. Everything was ticking quietly, calmly humming along in the background, but when the world began to circulate again, there was a message from them. 'Given current global circumstances, we are reviewing our investments.' That was always going to be bad news.

Up until then, when she thought of it at all, she thought she'd got away with it. That was what she did. She got away with things. Money (of some form) was transferred (she was always vague about the actual financial transactions—that wasn't what she did. She could leave that shit to the lawyers); documents were swapped, an art work was procured, shipped or stored (or, in this case, both).

It could have stayed there. If they were reviewing investments, fine. The thing could have been passed on to someone else. Kasha could even have done that, and taken another commission.

'But it's not that simple, babes,' she wrote to Tye.

'Why not?'

'They want to see it.'

'Can't you just organise a visit or something?'

'Again, not simple.'

'Why not?'

'I don't know where it is.'

'Fucketty fuck.'

She knew what to do, though. Of course she did. Kasha was always in control. It would be easy—the shipping company she'd worked with before, she had a tracking number, it was no more complicated than getting something via UPD or Doplodo or Deliveree or whatever.

She looked the number up, put it into the relevant box on the website. Not recognised. She tried again. Not recognised. They offered her a conversation with a bot. She had a conversation with a bot. The bot didn't know anything. It told her to try again. She tried again. Still nothing. There had to be someone, somewhere, she could speak to. There was a phone number hidden at the bottom of the webpage, she called it, managed to talk to someone who sounded almost human but did not have the first clue what she was on about. They put her on to someone else who said something about 'current circumstances' and told her they'd get back to her. They didn't get back to her. She called again, explained her story again. They said something about 'current circumstances' and told her to try again later. It was only then she had to acknowledge to herself the possibility that Sigismunda Conrad's 'Work #47' had been lost.

She needed to have a sit down, to close her eyes, think beautiful thoughts, calm. She hadn't even been on the booze much recently but she could feel the dreads lurking, ready to pounce. Silas had told her she should try meditation but she could never stop her brain from yammering long enough to even begin a mantra. Kasha always felt that the real her, the quintessence of the one true Kasha, existed somewhere between the vying poles of brain and body, as if 'Kasha' was an entity conjured by their pull and push, constantly being both iterated and buffeted by their ongoing tussle. Right now she knew the body was planning to get its own back, to do something retaliatory to the over-reactive brain, so she tried to breathe, not too much lest she should end up hyperventilating like that one time on the Tube, but enough to get her heart beating regularly, to stop every muscle in her body from tensing, just enough so that she wouldn't have an attack of the screaming abdabs again.

Meantime, and this was the problem, Tsh or Chz or Schu or his people or whoever the fuck it was kept on getting back to her, pushier every time. 'We'd like to set up a viewing and evaluation as soon as we can.' She could have got in touch with Dan from Aster's again, but to admit she didn't know what she'd even bought might be pushing it a bit. This had all started with Chloe from Brown's—perhaps she should call her again, at least find out a bit more about the people who were now chasing her.

Dan wasn't replying, and Chloe didn't know any more than Kasha did.

She tried to placate her brain, too, by telling it that she'd get away with it. She always had up until now, hadn't she? They probably wanted to view it for an insurance claim, or some form of indemnity. They could just write it off. It'd be fine. 'This is just impostor syndrome,' she told her brain, but then realised it couldn't really be impostor syndrome because that was when one falsely believed one wasn't actually up to the task, and Kasha knew full well that she wasn't up to the task. She couldn't have the syndrome if she actually was an impostor. Or maybe that was her brain doing the double-bind, though? She was, surely, just as qualified as anyone else to do the job she had niched out for herself. Nope: that was her brain tricking her into believing that it was her rational self speaking, when actually it was still her brain speaking, her brain itself being the impostor in pretending to be Rational and Reasonable Kasha.

She needed a drink. She needed something. She texted Tye. She even texted Silas.

'This is insane,' Tye wrote back. 'Unreal.'

'Want me to come over? Bring something?' said Silas.

It wasn't her own money. It was someone else's. Of course. And it wasn't money, not really. Not in that sense. Well, it was money, but not like money money. Not a suitcase stuffed with waxy, greasy, dirty, coke-stained notes. It was just credit, little lines of numbers moving from one computer screen to another. Not even their little pixels, probably—often the buyer she'd thought she was working for was actually working for someone else, who was in turn working for someone else again, who turn and turn about turned out to be working for someone else entirely. Not even some one but more like something, a bank or a corporation or some kind of colossal ultra-national organisation, so, no, not anyone's hard-earned savings.

The messages from Dash or Dazh or Dush kept coming. 'Any news on the viewing? We want to set something up before close Q3.'

What if these people were actually like properly dodgy, or something? Was this dangerous? She visualised a rapid concatenation of events ('Kashatrophising' Tye called it when telling her to stop and calm down), a few short steps which ended with her body being zipped into a cheap holdall and dumped into a black canal somewhere in Zone 5.

'Working on it! Back with you soon.'

She told Silas to come over.

A WEEK LATER SHE FINALLY got a message telling her the name of the ship it was on. She managed to track it: they'd been to Rotterdam en route for Singapore, after which it was to head back to

Europe. Even if no one seemed to know quite where it was right now, Kasha felt herself balance for the first time in ages.

'Once we locate your item, we can have it safely consigned to a location of your choosing,' the bot told her, and for that moment, Kasha loved the bot.

'Is everything OK, Kasha? We haven't heard from you.' She wondered how long she could go without responding to their message but then realised they'd have seen two blue ticks on the WhatsApp.

'All in hand.' Would that be vague enough? It seemed to work as they didn't get back to her. Three days after that she finally got a message.

'Your item has been successfully tracked.' Somehow, the thing—whatever it was—was in the Freiport at Geneva. How the fuck had it ended up there? Kasha didn't care: as long as she knew where it was, that was enough. She messaged Tish or Tush or Tazh and told them she'd located it but not where.

'Thanks Kasha. Let us know where we can see it. No need for you to come.' She couldn't take that chance. She booked a flight immediately and took a taxi straight from the airport.

SHE'D ALWAYS IMAGINED A FREEPORT to be somewhere almost romantic, on the docks somewhere, a hidden part of a bustling harbour peopled by stevedores and longshoremen who she might have to tip with a packet of unfiltered cigarettes or a pair of silk stockings to get access to what she needed. There'd be a bar with a man in a grubby linen suit crumpled over the counter, a lazy jazz trio, a few painted ladies with mysterious pasts. At least, this being

Switzerland after all, it could have lain deep in a hollowed-out Alp. But she was disappointed: this place was so bland it was as if it wasn't there. The taxi driver drove past it twice, had to throw a U to get back each time.

He eventually dropped her off on the side of the road, traffic screaming past them: there didn't seem to be an entrance to the place. She hopped over a barrier at the side of the road and walked across a small, empty car park. There was no doorway apparent. It wasn't a hangar as such, more like an extremely bland office building. All windows, smoked and mirrored. She leaned up close to one to see if she could see in, but it showed her nothing other than her own reflection, almost vanishing in the opaque glass.

A security guard (she guessed it was a security guard—some stocky guy in a vaguely military-looking uniform anyhow) appeared out of nowhere and said something to her in something that sounded like German.

'I'm Kasha Hocket-Baily,' she said, knowing that would mean nothing. 'Here for a viewing. We have something stored here.'

'Are you the owner?' She could have lied. She should have lied.

'I'm the broker,' she said, not exactly lying.

'One minute.' He pressed some buttons on his phone then gestured to a door that seemed to have appeared from nowhere. She walked over to it and heard a click as she approached. The door swung back before she even had to push it.

Inside, the Freiport looked exactly like the storage facility where she'd had to leave her possessions (clothes, mostly, plus that Eames chair that she would never part with) for six months after she'd first split up with Silas. Largely empty, slightly corporate, reassuringly bland. A corridor ran off to each side, both lined with cell-like doors identified only by a number engraved on a small brass plaque next to them. It was brightly lit, from above, but Kasha couldn't see a source of light. In front of her was a small desk with a small man behind it.

'We have nothing recorded for today,' he said. He wore the same uniform as the man outside. 'Do you have any identification?'

She handed over her passport. He typed her name into his laptop.

'Do you have an item number?'

She did: she scrolled through her emails on her phone, found the last missive she'd had and read out a number. He typed the number into his computer.

'You will be sent a one-time-only access code. Would you please be able to read me that code?'

Her phone pinged with a number. She read it to him.

'Thank you Ms Hocket-Baily. Please take a seat.'

Kasha remembered the time Silas had told her to read Kafka, 'because, actually, it's fucking hilarious.' She hadn't found it hilarious. She thought it was realistic.

Ten minutes later another man, who could have been the same one, appeared at the end of the hallway. 'Please follow my colleague,' said the behind-the-desk man.

What had looked like wall slid back to reveal a huge service elevator. The other man gestured her in and looked at an iPad with a cracked screen until he found what he was looking for. He keyed in a number on a panel by the door and they went down. He didn't look at her or say anything. They kept on going down until Kasha lost the feeling of motion, or rather, could no longer be sure they were going down, only that they were moving in some direction. Eventually the elevator bumped gently as if it had hit a solid floor.

'No further,' said the man. 'Nobody wants to go further!' He didn't laugh, exactly, but just said, 'Ha!' The door slid back. 'Here we are,' he said.

The door slid open. Kasha thought they'd gone down to a basement car park. It was dark out there, and even though everywhere else had felt thermostatically controlled, neither perceptibly hot nor cold and with air as dry as bone, Kasha was sure she felt the temperature drop a notch and the touch of moisture on her skin. Even though neither of them had moved, there was an echo.

The man raised his arm, gesturing her out. She took the step. He followed and stood behind her, like a waiter at one of those seriously fancy restaurants Kasha had on occasion been taken to.

The floor was stone, or poured concrete more probably, reinforced to withstand great weights. Kasha couldn't even see the walls, if there were walls, as the surrounding darkness disappeared everything except what stood in front of her.

'Is that it?' she asked.

The man checked his iPad.

'Yes.'

A shipping container, half-sized, stood in the middle of the room like the monolith in *2001*. It was brick red and slightly rusted. Kasha knocked on it, as if hoping someone would answer. It felt as if it were solid. A white mark like a lazy figure of eight or some kind of curvy rune but scratched and chipped beyond recognition was painted on the side.

'Can we open it?'

The man checked his iPad.

'I don't have that authority.'

'Then how do you know what's in it?'

He checked his iPad again.

'I don't.'

'I'll need to open it. I need to inspect it. That's what I came here for.'

'I don't have that authority.'

'Who does?'

'I'll need to check.'

Kasha's phone bleeped. She was surprised there was a signal down here. She'd assumed a Faraday cage, at least. She hoped it was Tye, or even Silas. It wasn't.

'We're on our way.' How had they known that? She hadn't told them, had she? Were they tracking her?

The elevator door slid open again and another man—possibly the one from the desk, or the car park, or another one entirely, yet exactly the same—stepped out. Without speaking, the two men stepped toward the container. The first man lifted the latches on the right-hand door, took both handles at the same time and lifted them, sending the lock rods up. The other man did the same thing on the left-hand door. Both doors swung open. It wasn't locked.

Kasha took a step forward. She peered in. She switched her phone's torch on and directed the beam to the back of the container. She stepped in. She walked around. The echo inside, she noted, was slightly muted. She stepped out.

'It's empty.' Both men shrugged. One looked at his iPad again, and shrugged again.

'We have no information,' he said.

'It's empty,' said Kasha.

The second man looked at the first man's iPad. He shrugged again.

'It's empty,' said Kasha, very quietly this time.

OVER THE LAST TEN YEARS Kasha had, from time to time, thought about becoming an artist herself, of cutting herself out as the middleman and simply peddling her own stuff to whoever she could convince to take it. No commissions. It was perfect, really, especially as she knew exactly what she'd produce: drawings, or sculptures perhaps, of that vast cloud which massed and whirred in her head, or that big black thing she felt right behind her shoulders, sometimes, at times like this.

Outside again, and gulping for air, Kasha felt both her brain and her body kicking in, leaving her a pummelled mess in the middle. She couldn't accuse anyone of stealing anything, not the Freiport, nor the shipping company, nor even its crew as she'd had no idea what might have been in there that might have been stolen. She had, apparently, signed something somewhere assuring carriers and storers that their cargo held no harmful or dangerous materials.

Another text: 'Hi Kasha. We're just getting in now. We can be with you in 30.'

There was a four-lane highway to one side of her, and what seemed to be a railway embankment behind her. Up the road a little there was a row of shops and she thought she could see a bright green cross outside one of them. Silas had told her that you could get anything you wanted across the counter in a Swiss pharmacy. She ran across the road and up the central divider and almost cried when she saw the place was open.

'Haben Sie Diazepam?' The pharmacist scowled. 'Xanax?'

'Rezept?' she asked. A receipt? Why would she need a receipt? 'From doctor,' said the woman. A prescription. Silas had been talking shit again. Kasha walked out and dug around in her bag to find a Lavender Kalm. They made her burps taste like an old lady's bathroom but it was the best she was going to be able to get right now.

She messaged Tye.

'Fuuuuuuuck.'

'Fuuuuuck indeed.'

'It's unreal.'

'It's insane.'

'Is it a joke?'

'It's not a joke.'

'Are they taking the piss?'

'They're not taking the piss.'

'It's insane.'

'It's unreal.'

'What are you gonna do babe?'

'Idk. Can't I just, like, dematerialise or something?'

A large black Audi Persecutor pulled up right next to her. How had they got in here? Were they regulars? Dzh got out first, then two others. One was a man so bland she'd forgotten about him even before she didn't catch his name, the other was a woman wearing dark glasses, natch, and a suit as well-cut as her straight black hair. They nodded at the security guard like they knew him. The car drove off, the door opened and then they were in the lift.

On the way down Kasha tried to rehearse her lines. 'It's a process work. We can certificate it. Clean lines. The ultimate gesture. Rich in signification and interpretative possibility. Conceptual and physical. Unique yet ubiquitous. Being and non-being.' She almost convinced herself.

The lift hit the not-bottom. The door opened. They walked out.

Kasha stood there, saying nothing as they slowly circled the empty container. They spoke to each other in low, hushed, serious voices. Kasha couldn't hear what language they were speaking. She thought she heard them say 'railway station,' but understood nothing more.

'It's a process work,' she began, but they ignored her and carried on talking among themselves. The woman clicked things on her phone. Sometimes they were asking questions of each other, Kasha thought, other times affirming things. She heard the words life cycle, then tag process, then absence, silence, market failure, speculation, laminar flow, frequency and possession.

'What is in the container?' asked Tsch, and Kasha was about to come in again with her improvised explanation but then the others replied in unison.

'The container is empty!' they said, and all three of them began to laugh.

EVERY ECHO IS A LEAK

Sixth floor, big windows, good view of trees. Recessed lighting, marble worktop, pale waxed floorboards. A rich plushness to everything. The windows had thick rubber treads through which they ploughed silently as Rachel pulled the handle, slid one open, then closed it again. Plushness. Rachel liked the word and said it out loud, hovering on that central sh and extending the closing ss. When the windows were closed any external sound disappeared. She opened them; closed them again. A hermetic seal.

She hadn't yet unpacked her bags (only two—one for equipment, the other, smaller, for a few clothes) but sat on the sofa in the middle of the open-plan living space. That's what they'd call it in a brochure or on a website: an open-plan living space. The sofa was from Ikea. Rachel had lived in enough furnished rentals to recognise one.

Hermetic was a good word and a good idea. Hermes, the messenger, but also a keeper of secrets. The god of winds and crossroads. He had wings on his heels which meant he was a god of speed too, or motion perhaps. Rachel thought she'd google it later, once she'd got the wi-fi working.

She looked around. All the furniture was Ikea. Why would that happen? Why would you be rich enough to have a place like this, put thick rubber treads on the plush hermetic windows and wax the floorboards and own open-plan living space in this part of the city, then fill it with furniture from Ikea? What kind of a monster would do such a thing?

The only interesting things were the pictures on the walls. To her left, from the grey Ikea sofa (Söderhamn, or Grönlid possibly), hung a reproduction of the Albrecht Dürer hare.

Rachel Noyes liked hares. Rachel Noyes had once miked up a dead hare to see what it would sound like. This had been the kind of thing that had got her labelled 'difficult' in art school.

There was a letter on the island in the marble-worktopped kitchen section of the open-plan living area. She thought of it as an island as she knew that's what such things were called. It wasn't a table; it had cupboards built into it. The cupboards were empty, save for two French press coffee makers with mismatching parts. The letter, Rachel assumed, was for her even though it bore no name. Herzlich Willkommen it said. Congratulations on the new job. Here's some things you'll need to know if you're planning on staying for a bit, it said.

That rug, she thought as she sat on the Söderhamn or Grönlid, the rug spread at the centre of the wide floor space in the open-plan living area, that is a very nice rug. It had a dense grey weave which Rachel found very pleasing. She could spend a week here, no problem. She almost said plush again but stopped before she began to irritate herself. She leaned down and turned up the corner of the rug to find the label. Nödebo. Top end of Ikea, but still.

The thing that struck her about the Dürer picture was that although it was dated 1502, the hare still looked very much alive. Rachel wondered how long she would have to stay alone in this flat before she noticed its whiskers begin to twitch. She had found that a dead hare didn't sound like much. Even with a good contact mic, it was still mostly silence.

The writer of the letter, whoever it had been, seemed to think Rachel could be staying here for some time, but there again the writer of the letter, helpful as they were, had also congratulated her on a job she didn't yet have.

Not that Rachel was snobby about Ikea: it was its blandness that offended her, the ubiquity. She was staying in what was regularly hyped as being one of the most vibrant cities in the world, but she could have been anywhere.

Noting that a picture of a hare was incredibly lifelike and wondering if its whiskers would start twitching was the kind of question that art critics did not ask and thus quite probably why Rachel's career as an art critic had been a very short one. The miking up of the dead hare had been towards the increasingly desperate end of a three-year degree which had left her mostly cold.

The letter was throwing her off, though that was only, perhaps, because she was being difficult again. And yet, being congratulated on a job when it wasn't a job, only a potential commission for which she'd been invited as part of some kind of interview process, seemed wrong. The first job Rachel had was stacking shelves in Tesco when she was sixteen. She'd got the sack for dropping jars of Marmite onto the tiled floor of the stockroom just because she liked the sound of it, the rich bounce and roll, the clacking echo. From there, her path had been set. Difficult.

The other picture, facing the hare, was another Dürer: the 'Great Piece of Turf.' Rachel already knew both of these pictures, and loved them both, this one for its title as much as anything else. She hoped they had been put there specially for her but on continuing to read the letter she doubted it.

Rachel hadn't told anyone about the miking up of the dead hare, not only because the results had been disappointing, nor because of the 'difficult' tag which had pretty much stuck by then anyhow, no matter what she did. She'd worried everyone would think her a goth, unnecessarily fixated on decay. Decay had become a theme and not one she was interested in. The slow degradation of sound had been done to death; it was persistence that interested her. What remained. What could be heard everywhere, if you listened carefully enough.

Perhaps the letter hadn't been left for her at all, but for someone else, someone who had come before her, perhaps, or another coming later. Apart from the mention of the job, which was inaccurate in her case, everything else was fairly generic. Perhaps the person who wrote it didn't know why Rachel was here. Rachel herself didn't know much. The whole situation was somewhat hermetic. She'd been sent an address and a keypad code and told that someone would contact her upon arrival.

There's some food in the fridge, the letter told her, but be careful as the light doesn't always work. There's internet, you'll need the password, it's written on the back of the router which is by the door, but it's a little intermittent at the moment as they're digging up some cables in the street, so it comes and goes. Rachel looked out of the window down to as much as she could of the street through the trees and saw no sign of anyone doing any work anywhere.

She opened the fridge and the light flickered an instant then went off. If she opened the door all the way it came on again. The fridge held some bacon, a packet of kornbrot, some unidentified cheese, six eggs and a bag of coffee. This would do, for a while.

In the bedroom a thick carpet and a Hemnes bed which left only a few inches' space between it and the wall to each side did the work of deadening the sound. The windows were double glazed and fixed shut. She would sleep well in there. She spent most of her life working with sound and was glad for its absence when possible. She went through the Malm drawers and they were all empty. There was usually something, something that had been left by someone or other, a bible, a broken-spined crime or romance novel, a porn mag even, back in the day, but here, nothing, not even dust or fluff. No one, she thought, had ever lived here, not really.

The choice of the 'Great Piece of Turf' then, seemed even stranger. A picture teeming with life. A picture which roared to her. She could hear the bugs moving around in it, the water mulching, the growth and—yes—decay, all at the same time. She could feel it. It reminded her of where she'd grown up.

The light in the bathroom didn't work properly either. She flicked the switch but it only turned on a fan so she left the door open and peed in the dark. The toilet was incredibly low, but she could still see the top of her head reflected in the five square inches of mirror that comprised the door to the medicine cabinet above the sink. Was this a place for short people? That was the only mirror in the place, she realised. From where she sat she could see a patch of mould on the ceiling.

Where she'd grown up had been a grit-black town in the north of England, a place of headstones, hardscrabble and rain, forever dying and being regenerated. Rain and rock. Sheep shit and mud. Rain and a high street with a Chinese takeaway, a laundrette, a Co-Op, and a fighty pub on the corner. It had been the sound of the place, she knew, which had made her. The rain hitting those hillsides and pouring into the valley; the rain hitting the slate roof of her parents' house, the rain battering the windows.

The cheese tasted of its plastic wrapper with a hint of rubber and it was not unpleasant.

Rachel stood at the window, eating cheese and watching the evening begin to invade the street. This building stood on a corner, yet there was only the one large window—where there could have been another there was a wall. Rachel had to peer out to see the crossroads. Why would you build a wall when you could have a window? This, surely, was the advantage of being on a corner: light from two sides. Bad design was one of the snares of her life. The building opposite was identical to the one she looked out from. She could see the same sixth-floor apartment with its plush windows though not past them. Did they have stuff in there? Was it noisy? Were there people in there, getting on with the messy business of living? Far from the freedom of opportunity and the excitement of the unknown that she thought she should be feeling, Rachel only felt herself stuck in a bland apartment in a fashionable part of Berlin, a city she'd visited only once before, years back, and to which she had always wanted to return, now waiting for someone she didn't know to offer her an unspecified amount of money to do she did not know what.

As it grew darker she noted light in the opposite flat. A warm low glow made everything in there look orange. She pulled back the window again and could hear some music leaking out, though it could have been from somewhere else. There didn't seem to be anyone in there.

Rachel knew she was being ungrateful, awkward, difficult again, and didn't care. Later, she fell asleep wondering what article of Ikea furniture a Dürer might be.

NEXT MORNING SHE WAS WOKEN by a WhatsApp bleep. 'Herzlich Willkommen. We hope you arrived safely, and are looking forward to meeting with you in the next few days. Before we proceed, we'll need a little more info about you and your work.' There was a link to a website, a new username and temporary password.

This had all been the wrong way round. Unusual, at least. The times Rachel had done this before she'd had to write an application before anything happened. This time she'd received a message telling her she'd been 'selected to apply,' had 500 euro advance expenses transferred to her account and had been given the address of this place. She'd asked around her few friends in the field and no one had heard of this residency, but they told her to go for it anyway. 'At the least you'll get a week in Berlin!'

Though she hadn't noticed it before, there was a tiny patch of mould on the ceiling in the bedroom too, no larger than her thumbnail, but there it was, just above the sealed window.

Rachel hadn't spoken to anyone since the taxi driver nearly twenty-four hours ago. This was far from a record. She got up and said, 'Good morning rabbit' to the hare, for the hell of it. She remembered the word Kaninchen but did not know what a hare was called in German, despite having studied the picture, so she said, 'Guten Morgen Kaninchen,' hoping the hare wouldn't mind.

The sound of her greetings had no echo, as though it had been sucked up into the airlessness of this place, into the rug and the curtains. It should have been bouncing off this floor, these bare walls and the plate glass windows. This place should be all echo but there was none, none at all.

She opened up her laptop as her phone wasn't fit for purpose and copied the URL into the browser. It was slow. The little circle circled then became a spiral before eventually loading the page. Before we go on, it said, you'll need to create an identity. She had to download a VPN.

Rachel heaved the sliding windows open. A breeze cool enough to feel cold came in, but it felt something like life. Sound, too—not much, the rustle of the trees, the low, slow breath of an occasional passing vehicle. She was too far up for footsteps, or even snippets of conversation and there didn't seem to be many birds, but it was something. She was glad the sound didn't bounce off the high ceiling.

She watched the final few bars of the download, thankful at least the internet signal had held, then her screen went black. The spiral appeared again, spiralling. Eventually a dialogue box appeared asking for a username and password. She wrote her own name, then tried her three email addresses before remembering the code she'd been sent on the WhatsApp.

It was good to be here, though. The coffee tasted good, even made in the shonky cafetière she'd rigged up. The milk was thicker here. She listened to it foaming.

A new screen greeted her in four languages. They wanted her to set up an identity.

Name:

Rachel. Rachel No/Yes. Rachel with the homophonically nominatively deterministic surname.

Tell us about you and your work. (Max 200 words.)

People find me difficult. However, they are wrong as I am a constant source of complete fucking joy.

The internet cut out again. She logged on again to find her words hadn't been saved. Perhaps for the best. She tried again.

Tell us about you and your work. (Max 200 words.)

I am an artist whose practice consists of writing applications for projects, residencies, and commissions.

True as this was, she should avoid any hint of the sharp, the smart, the difficult. She needed this one, even if only for the accommodation it'd provide for a bit.

Tell us about you and your work. (Max 200 words.)

I am not a sound artist; I am a silence artist.

She liked that. It was true, too: sound had made her, but silence had wrapped itself around her. Not only silence as a practice, but silence as a personality trait. Silence was who she was, or who she'd become. She could have been here with someone now, but she'd lost them to silence. Even if she had brought someone, she knew she'd probably have driven them away already. 'Silence artist' was too good a term to waste on this application—they wouldn't be looking for poetry. Try again.

Tell us about you and your work. (Max 200 words.)

They were tiny things at first, but significant: a rage for order, sequence. And from that, clarity, and from that—fairness. Justice, even. Everything in its place and everything part of everything else. Nothing better because bigger. Everything necessary, everything equal. I collected leaves and put them into groups (of colour, shape, suggestion). I loved order and form, tables and charts. Maps. I took a careers survey which told me I'd enjoy secretarial work, accounting perhaps if

I had the maths. A teacher suggested libraries, but books and words were not my habitat: symbols of things and not the things themselves. Later they gave me a camera but photographs weren't right either.

There it was, she hadn't even hit age 18 yet and was already halfway over the word count. Almost lunchtime and all she'd had was some coffee. She boiled an egg, made more coffee, and tried again. Rachel had done this hundreds of times before and never got it right.

Tell us about you and your work. (Max 200 words.)

I am a sound artist.

I am an artist who works with sound.

I am a sound recordist.

A recordist.

A soundist.

I want to know what things are.

Still not essential enough, not accurate enough. Still not her.

Tell us about you and your work. (Max 200 words.)

Rachel Noyes: structural vibrations, contact microphone recordings, ultrasonics, infrasonics, internal electronic signals.

Better.

Rachel Noyes: Sony M10 and a matched pair of Clippy EM172 mics; RØDE NTG2 shotgun with pistol grip and windcover; Tascam DR 10L and DR 07X with lav mic; Shure SM 58; Sennheiser HD 25s.

Best.

A shout in the street distracted her, but whatever had gone on had passed by the time she got to the window. She peered down through the branches but could see nothing. A delivery truck backed up, beeping its way into the space between two parked cars. A driver jumped out of the other side, doors slammed, then nothing. It was getting dark already. If this were a film she would have to descend into depravity or madness, but it wasn't, so she knew the far more likely outcome was that she would die of boredom.

Not an artist at all then, a listener, a recorder, nothing more. Perhaps she shouldn't be here after all, perhaps she was a fraud. 'Your trouble,' her tutor had told her when turning down her application for an MA, 'is that you can't really define a central research question. You need to know what you want,' he'd told her. She'd heard that question from others (What do you want?) and never known how to reply.

She wanted to go out, get some air, stretch her legs, that kind of thing. Find a corner shop, a supermarket, she was sure she'd passed a Netto or a Spar on her way here, get more of that cheese. A café even, a bar, have coffee, drink beer, meet people. This place was supposed to be a thriving artistic community, wasn't it? Or was that what she ought to do, rather than wanted to do? Maybe Kreuzberg was no longer the right part of town. Things must have moved on. Her hipster radar was admittedly outdated. Whatever. She'd definitely do that, once she'd sorted out this profile, identity thing. She had the day to do that, and then they would be in touch with her, and she'd know what her next step was. There'd been something about an interview on the email, but she couldn't find it now. Till then, everything felt like limbo. She should sit back and enjoy it, relax, but relaxing had never been her kind of thing.

She wanted to listen, that's what she wanted: it was only when she listened that the world opened to her. As a student she had stared at things for hours, trying to get them to reveal their immanence, their quiddity, their phenomenon. The thing as it was and resolutely, stubbornly nothing more. She drew objects in as much detail as she could (hence the Dürer fascination) but rapidly realised she was remaking them in another form, another form which would in turn have its problems. She did what her tutors told her and tried drawing the space between the things and not the things themselves, and that was better until she realised that the space between things was a thing as well, with all its thing problems. 'What are your objectives?' they'd asked her. 'What materials and processes interest you? How would you define your practice?' Posing such questions to then answer them seemed pointless. If she'd known what she'd wanted she wouldn't have wanted for anything.

She put her boots on without lacing them and stamped on the floor. The thick carpet, the plush sofa, the hermetic window, the walls themselves all sucked up the sound. She sat down again. She didn't go out.

Hiding in the college library, where she had spent more time than in the studios, she had come across an exhibition catalogue for Francesca Woodman. Leafing through the pictures she gained some sense of what she might want: these photographs, with their blurred figures and crumbling walls, their luminous windows like escape portals, their bare board floors—she could hear them.

Half-friends of half-friends knew squats in Leeds where she recorded herself walking through old houses and empty rooms. The thud and (yes!) echo of her footsteps, her hands stroking walls, plaster coming off in her hands. Running water when she could find it. For her degree show she recorded herself pissing in a bucket, then put a tape player playing the recording in the bucket. Recording things, she found, could hold them, and at the same time let them not be what they were.

She was hungry but didn't know what she wanted to eat. There it was again, that same question: What do you want? It followed her around like a lost dog. Someone she had carefully chosen to forget once whined it at her. She hadn't bothered replying, full-knowing that its very positing meant the relationship had reached its terminal phase.

Years in squats in Headingley then Hulme had followed. She was often invited to join bands but had little facility with instruments, couldn't abide the thought of singing and found herself better suited to cables, mics, amps and mixing desks whenever the sweaty men hunched over them would let her near. One lot had set up a rehearsal space and recording studio inside an old shipping container which had been dumped on some wasteland at the edge of the council estate. They'd decorated it with loads of trippy fractal designs and Möbius loops but the sound in there was terrible. Rachel was the only one who could make sense of it: she caught the natural reverb, the clang and rattle of it all. She recorded the space itself rather than the bands. She didn't like music much, she realised, but quite liked the sound it made.

Laziness begat laziness, her mum would have said, and Rachel knew her mum was right but still could not quite lift herself from the sofa, which despite its Ikea-ness, was disturbingly comfortable. The internet had gone off again and when she managed to log back in the words she had written had gone too. She cursed herself for being so bloody difficult, tied her shoelaces and made for the front door.

Field recordings had come next. This was what she'd always been doing, she thought, as she met enthusiasts, neither artists nor scientists but more like the technicians she thought she could be. Lots of talk about equipment and recording levels, good solid things, no theory, all practice. She wore a hard hat to get down into caves in Derbyshire, hauled kilos of equipment up fells in the Lakes. None of the results pleased her. 'What do you want?' they'd asked her, these men interested in winds and hillsides, bottling lightning and the breaths of ghosts. She'd already had enough of that stuff: she'd grown up there. The sound of her bedroom at night, amplified maybe, but still rain on slates and wind creaking between them. She moved back into the city, wanting urban field recordings—broadband cabinets, electricity substations, cable hum. She did a sound portrait of a rented house in Levenshulme, recording the fridge, the leaking taps, the creaking windows and the washing machine, and when her work had won praise for its feminine approach, its concentration on the domestic sphere, its attention to fine detail, she deleted it all. It had all seemed too much like the Marmite jars and the dead hare.

Only when she got to the front door did she realise she didn't have keys: there was a code to get in. She'd written it down but didn't know where. She checked the notes on her phone but couldn't find it. It was in an old email, or she'd written it on a scrap of paper, she was sure. She did not want to get locked out. Outside, the evening deepened. She returned to the sofa, rifled her pockets for the scrap of paper then scrolled through old messages looking for the door code, until she found it, but only the one for the main door of the building.

The webpage had timed her out. She logged back in. The last question:

What do you want from this opportunity?

As it grew darker the lights in the flat opposite reappeared, as though they'd been on all day and were only now revealing themselves. She slid the window back to listen, and there was sound, very quiet, though again no people were visible, as if a recording of party sound effects were playing. Perhaps there was a constant party happening over there, slowly building then decreasing, only to grow again as night arrived, and invisible to her. That was the vibe last time she'd visited, but that had been a decade ago, when she'd been younger, more visible.

A figure appeared in the window opposite. Silhouetted by the light, she thought it was a man but couldn't be sure. He stood there for a moment, looking out, then slowly turned and made his way back to what Rachel guessed must be the party happening in another room.

She scrounged through some earlier applications, successful and less so, copied and pasted a few of her best words, hit the 'submit' button. A message came back thanking her and telling her someone would be in touch with the next steps of the commissioning process. The computer screen glared against the growing dark of the room. Her eyes hurt.

Hang on, how had she got in here in the first place? If she'd got in she could get out. She went to the door, opened it, and looked for a keypad. There wasn't one. The keypad code she'd had was for the main door to the building. On this door there was only a normal key lock. She stepped back in and noticed a small hook by the side of the door: that's where a key should be, and there wasn't one. The door must have been open when she arrived.

The darkness thickened and the noise from across the street grew louder. The thought of the door being opened troubled her. She got up, locked it from inside, closed the window, got back into bed and held the pillow over her head until she fell asleep.

On the third day she woke with the sound of her dream still in her head. Rachel always dreamed in sound, not images. She'd been told several times that this was impossible, and that there had been images, but it was only the sound she was choosing to remember. She felt no inclination to argue with the men who told her such things, but also knew this was one of the reasons she was on her own. She was glad of the fact that she wasn't currently being bothered by one of the various Sams, Bens, or Jakes, Owen the asemic poet who lived in a caravan on Morecambe Bay, Josh who'd wanted her to be a witch, or Thom the chippy engineering student back up from Cambridge who claimed he'd spelled his name like that even before anyone had heard of Radiohead.

It had got too much, perhaps, her silence, her anger. She wondered if there'd been a turning point, a junction where she could have made a different choice and had things come out in another way but knew it had been more a slow refinement and concentration of who she had always been. That Conrad show she'd visited in London years back with its unexplainable rooms and illogical spaces, its strange hum. Maybe it had been that—the show hadn't illuminated anything for her, but once out she knew would no longer bother trying to be anything else. She hadn't been an easy person to be around, ever. But fuck them, fuck them all. I was right. I am right.

She pulled back the window on its plush tread and the party across the street sounded like it was still going, if only faintly, but Rachel could see no one. She wondered if that had affected her dreaming: usually she dreamed the sound of running water, but last night the sound had taken a different texture, an edge, a quality the haziness of her dream memory wouldn't quite let her define.

She'd slept through a WhatsApp bleep. 'Thanks for getting yourself set up. We'd like to take this to the next stage. We will be in touch shortly.'

Once, when she'd been stuck back at her parents, one of the frequent lulls in work, life, everything, Alysson from art school had got back in touch. She was making a film and wanted Rachel to do the sound. It was on an island in the Outer Hebrides. There was money enough to cover expenses and accom, with some left over. Rachel would have done it for nothing. The sound she had dreamed last night reminded her of South Uist.

The milk in the fridge was still fine. How long had it been here? The sell by was still a week off. She held the fridge door open a moment, listening to its hum and whirr. It could do with a clean: there was a trace of something growing around its seal. She could go out but was worried about the imminent contact. Would they knock at the door? Send a message? An email? Perhaps it would be a letter, a formal invitation.

On Uist she had recorded the days and spent the nights listening to them. The 'Great Piece of Turf' had something of the sounds of the island, minus the wind. There'd been a fuckup at the end of the filming and she thought she'd lost everything, but when she got home she found that while there was nothing for the film, there was enough for herself. She stretched the sound files, turning a moment into an age, then put the results, neither field recordings nor drones but with something of each, onto Soundcloud for no reason other than the fact that she could, then forgot all about them.

If the party across the road happened again tonight, she'd gatecrash. Walk in like she owned the place, pretend she'd been invited.

If she said she was an artist, doors opened. She never defined herself as an artist, but knew the label could be useful sometimes, especially when she wanted to be someone else for a while.

She set to recording the clicks of all the switches in the flat, then the plush swish of the window. She slammed some doors, but that didn't do much, nor did her footsteps: no echo, only that short sucking noise, as if the sound was trying to hide itself before it even registered. She hard-boiled an egg and rolled it across the floor and recorded that, too. She found the dicky router and tried to record its tiny hum. She lay on the bed and tried to record that, but it didn't even squeak. Whoever had put it together had done a good job.

She didn't have to decide about the party, not yet. The decision would make itself. Such was her process. Rachel no/yes, Rachel on/off, Rachel connect/disconnect. Everything was connected, she wanted to believe, but knew that nothing was. She certainly wasn't. Rachel could only observe. 'There's no empathy in this work,' she had been criticised. Of course there's no fucking empathy. All I wanted to do was see, listen, record. Not to transform one thing into another, nor to understand anything, but to hold it as carefully and as intimately as possible, to register its presence in the universe. 'It's not art, then,' her tutor had told her, and she had agreed, and failed.

It had been a few months before she'd gone back to look at the Soundcloud, and found she'd gained nearly a thousand followers and almost as many likes for her Uist drones. If only she'd sold them, she might have made a quid or two.

That evening, when dark settled and the party began again, she sat on the sofa and listened to the sounds of the day on her headphones. When a recording was really good she couldn't tell the difference between the inside and the outside of her head, like in her dream of sound, where her self dissipated, and her own sound could not be separated from that of the world, a tiny part of its endless flow. There was nothing of that in what she had recorded today. She'd hoped the lack of echo would reveal something, but there was little there: it was all magnificently bland, achingly polite, the sounds of boredom rather than discovery. She tried slowing it down to find a texture, a grain to it, and also: patterns, not melodies, god forbid, but connections. She listened back to discern two fields: the immanent sounds of the place, and the sounds of her existence within it. She could slow one and speed the other.

The figure she'd seen the previous evening appeared again. Rachel remembered her intention to go over and join the party and wondered if this was her invitation, but the man made no gesture, probably unable to see her as she was sitting in the darkness. Instead, he began to dance, very slowly and sinuously, his tall thin body undulating against the red-orange background light. There was no music she could hear tonight, as if the man were dancing to silence. She watched for a while, and decided not to go over for fear she should disturb him.

SHE WOKE UP ON THE fourth day to find another missed message even though she'd put the volume on her phone up to max. They wanted to do the interview via Zoom. Why the fuck had they brought her all the way here if they were doing the interview on Zoom? She'd packed her best top and everything. She should be glad she'd got to come here at least but god how she hated airports, the queuing, the expense, and so far Berlin had proved to be as drab as anywhere else. If they weren't bothering to actually meet her in person she must be pretty far down the list. They'd probably already discounted her and were only doing the interview out of politeness. It was tomorrow, too: another day hanging around. They'd be doing the A-list interviews today, she thought, face-to-face, and saving the dregs for after.

She had to get out, she needed some food. She couldn't survive on cheese any longer and that milk had probably gone off. She thought about taking a long walk, clearing her head, breathing some air that wasn't the stuff inside this apartment, but then worried about preparing for the interview. How could she prepare, anyway? They'd ask her to talk about her work, about what her plans for this residency would be. What she hoped to achieve. All the things she hated having to articulate. She'd have to deal with the familiar levels of mild anxiety, the knowing that she hated these people on whom she would depend, but at the same time be desperate to please them, whoever they were. She knew so little about them, about what she was doing here, about what she even wanted.

She pulled on her boots and was at the door before she remembered why she hadn't done this already. She went back into the open-plan living space and collapsed on the sofa. She refused to be a prisoner in here. Couldn't happen. She decided to ditch the long walk and just nip out to get some food and something to drink. She wouldn't be gone more than five minutes, ten tops. She could leave the apartment door on the latch. She had the code to the main building. It was safe here, surely.

She stood by the door and looked at the latch. What if it closed in the wrong way? What if she got locked out? She should take her passport with her, just in case. What if it didn't close and someone came in? There were too many risks. She was letting outside distract her. She needed to work out what she was going to say. There was enough food here. She needed to anticipate their questions and think of some good answers.

She went back and looked at the files for the sounds she had recorded yesterday; she'd planned to speed one track and slow the other. She didn't know why. To see what happened. To see what it sounded like. This was her method. That might be something she could use in the interview.

LATER, WHEN IT STARTED GROWING dark, she opened the window again and leaned out. The party noises had started up again, though again she couldn't actually see anyone in the place. She went back in and closed the window behind her, but could still hear the sounds. She checked the window: it was firmly shut, hermetic.

She walked around the apartment to see if there was anywhere else the sound could be coming from—upstairs, below, next door, the hallway. Nothing. And yet, there it was. She set up a mic, turned the levels all the way up, waited. She listened back to what she recorded: there was nothing. It hadn't registered at all.

She'd been sure it had been from the party happening across the road so stood at the window to see if anything was happening there. The light appeared again, and then the figure, dancing his strange dance, which Rachel then realised wasn't a dance at all. He was swimming, this man, very slowly, or not even that, he was being carried along in a current of water. He lifted his arm, part of the dance she'd thought, but now saw he was waving, or calling out for help.

THE NEXT MORNING SHE WOKE on the sofa where she'd fallen asleep. It was still dark. Without checking the time she trudged into the bedroom, pulled off her clothes and slunk under the covers. The interview wasn't until later, she should try to get a few more quality hours before then. Keep her mind sharp.

It was light when she woke up again. She checked her phone. 11. Not too bad. She had another hour. Coffee was needed. The patch of mould on the seal in the fridge had grown but the milk was still good. She took a shower in the dark and noticed that the mould in there had grown too. At least something was alive in here, she thought.

She left the bathroom door open to dry the room out. She should air this whole place, get some air for herself too. She went over to the big window but it had jammed. She pulled it harder, still nothing. Those plush hermetic runners had worked fine yesterday. How come they'd stuck now? She didn't have time to worry about it so went back into the bedroom, put her best top on and tried to make herself look reasonable in the tiny mirror in the dark bathroom with mould on the ceiling.

She opened up her laptop but the internet signal had gone again. For fuck's sake. An interview on Zoom when it could have been face-to-face and they'd put her in a place where the fucking internet didn't even work properly. That odd spiral again. She watched it unfurl then saw it slip and slide, rolling onto its side so it became a lazy figure-of-eight, lying on its side. It looked familiar but she couldn't remember from where. She switched the router off then back on again and got a few bars of signal.

Late, but only by a couple of minutes. She clicked the link.

There were three people there to interview her but their screens were blank. They didn't have names, only job titles: former resident; flow creator; director of management.

The internet cut out then came back on. She had to log in again.

There were faces this time, but none of them were moving.

'Hello! Sorry—my internet cut out.'

'You're on mute.'

'You're speaking but we can't hear you.'

Their voices emerged but she couldn't connect them to the three pale ovals in the frames on her screen. She unmuted herself.

'I can hear you. Can you hear me?'

The faces depixelated. One female with long straight black hair, the other two men, indistinguishable from so many other such interviews she had done.

'We can hear you. Can you hear us?'

'Yes, I can hear you.'

'That's great. Thank you for coming, Rachel.'

She could hear them but the voices were distorted. It was the poor signal.

'First up, we'd like you to'

The voices dropped out and came back on again.

'talk us through'

A strange whistle which became a rustle leaked from the tinny speaker on her laptop.

'Hang on, sorry, I'm having a few problems with my sound here!'

'That's OK Rachel. Take your'

The faces froze but the voices carried on speaking.

'time.'

Rachel smiled and pointed to her ears then realised that her picture had frozen, too, leaving her with her mouth half open and her finger raised. She looked demented.

'Sorry. Can you still hear me? Could you all try muting yourselves, perhaps?'

They carried on.

'Can you tell us a bit about'

'We were interested by your use of'

She unfroze and watched herself move forward through the past few seconds in rapid jerky movements. She tried answering but it was useless. The voices overlapped and caught in each other. There was a sound of rushing, twisting, skeining water which shifted and rose into a high-pitched metallic whistle. Their faces froze again.

'What would you bring?'

'What would you take?'

She logged off and logged back in again. They were still talking. The faces were moving but the voices had taken over, no longer connected to the faces.

'Are you there, Rachel?'

'What are you doing?'

'We can hear you but we can't see you.'

'We can see you but we can't hear you.'

'Are you there?'

'Are you having trouble?'

'What we really want to know is'

The sound of water hitting metal then metal hitting water, as though the voices were pouring from the taps.

'Who are you?'

'Are you difficult?'

'What do you want?'

Her own face had frozen again, passive, giving no sign of recognition. The connection dropped.

She got up, cursed, and tried the window again but the window was still jammed. In her anger she hit it but the thing was solid. She couldn't have broken it even if she'd wanted to. She sent an email apologising and asking if they could reschedule, but there was no reply.

She sat on the sofa, pulled her headphones on and tried listening to something. The sounds of the flat she'd recorded the other day. It sounded like chaos, all movement where in reality there was none. She looked for something else, something old. There it was—the sound of a hillside, she was sitting there alone, the grass and the insects, just enough wind. Maybe, in the distance, the sea.

A FEW HOURS LATER SHE came round. It was dark now. She hit the lights and checked her messages again. They'd written, but not a reply to her reschedule request.

'Dear Rachel Noyes,'

Full name. Not a good start. Probably an automated response. She rapidly scanned the message for the appearance of the word 'unfortunately.' There it was.

'Thanks for sharing your time with us. Unfortunately we won't be taking your application further at this point. We wish you all the best with your future projects.'

She went to the bathroom to be sick but then wasn't though the knot in her stomach stayed. As she knelt by the toilet she could see the mould growing.

It was airless in the flat, that was the problem, hermetic with a secret it wouldn't reveal. There was no damp but mould in the bathroom, in the fridge, on the windows. It was so quiet she could, finally, hear the sound of Dürer's 'Great Turf.' A hare would appear next, surely. Oh ffs. What if it shat everywhere? Please let it not start talking to me. She listened for the sounds of the party but it was early yet. She'd go over tonight, join in, find out what that man was doing, if he'd been waving or drowning. She'd forgotten what it was like to be outside, to be among people, could only conjure the memory through sound. She thought she heard the door opening, but remembered she'd locked it. Everything was too much, and not enough. She went to the window again and again pulled at it, then started banging her balled fists against it. Something clicked, the frame had buckled. Not so expensive after all. She pulled the handle again and the window heaved open, sticking slightly. She leaned out and breathed the deep sheer vertigo of possibility. It was only a few floors down, but think of that motion, that freedom. A man stood on the street looking up at her. She waved to him, he waved back, then turned and was hit by a cyclist coming full pelt in the other direction.

THE LAST MORNING SHE WAS woken by the sound of rain. The sound had been close enough to her dream to tangle with it, leaving her unsure if she were asleep and still dreaming or awake and listening. She lay there, and let herself stay for a while in that half-place.

By the time she got out of bed the rain had stopped. The sound of the rain on the windows. The window of sound on the rain. The rain of sound on the window. It would have been a good thing to record, but now it was too late.

She turned on all the taps, the sinks in the bathroom and kitchen, the shower. The twisted skeins of the sound of running water filled the place. She put the omnidirectional mic in the centre of the open-plan living space, timed it for three minutes, then played the recording back, as loud as she could, with all the water still running, then did the same thing again, and a third time, then opened the windows to let the mighty roar out onto the street. She opened the door too, and watched the sound pour out. She followed it, then joined it, floating, flying, madly swimming down the stairwell.

MANIFEST

On April 25th, 2022, the MV *Atlantic Echo* set out from Felixstowe en route for Rotterdam, after which it was to dock at Le Havre, Salalah, Colombo, Port Klang, and then Singapore before ending its six-week, 9000-nautical-mile journey in Laem Chabang, Thailand.

Records show the weather held an average temperature for that time of year, and although rain was forecast, it was not severe.

The *Echo* was an intermodal cargo ship, 300 metres long, with a 40-metre beam and a 16-metre draft. That is the length and breadth of three professional football pitches, and the height of three houses. It was built in Korea in 2004, and was all welded steel. It had no rivets. It had a Doosan-Wärtsilä engine which was the size of a house and was always working.

The ship carried a crew of twenty, and four officers. The crew were from Bangladesh, India, China and the Philippines. They were all men, apart from the cook, who was a Filipino woman everyone called Mary, though that was not her real name. They would say that race was not an issue, but others would notice that the officers were all white and the crew were all not.

The first leg of the journey was short and without incident. Felixstowe to Rotterdam is a well-worn route used by many large container ships. The captain spent this time doing admin. At Rotterdam more boxes were loaded, while the crew used the brief shore time to load up on the provisions they had not had a chance to get before.

Although we say their journey began at Felixstowe, for many of them the English port was merely another stop in an ongoing voyage.

The captain was called Andrea Lauro and he came from Naples, though his family were from nearby Amalfi. Amalfi, his family often reminded him, was one of the original four maritime republics of Italy, and they were proud he had chosen a great family tradition. Andrea had signed up for the Marina Militare for his national service and been posted to Trieste (one of the other original maritime republics) where he had then stayed on to study. He wrote a dissertation on the differences to navigation the maestrale, grecale, libeccio and scirocco winds could make. He had little use for this knowledge these days.

Nothing strange happened in Rotterdam, they would say later. Nothing untoward. They were all convinced of this. The captain was sure of it, too.

The ship had an open registry, more commonly known as a flag of convenience. The MV *Atlantic Echo* flew a Panamanian flag but was owned by a shipping agency in Malta. Brightwave Shipping Valetta, in turn, were owned by MarInt Management and Services, Livorno, and they chartered the ship to Marshall International, Nassau, who were legally represented by Fielding Crane, Lugano. Fielding Crane were majority owned by Hemcrest Investments, registered in Monrovia, Liberia. Tracing Hemcrest Investments later led investigators to a further twelve shell companies. No one on board really knew who owned the ship, not even the captain. It was quite possible not even the owner of the ship knew what they owned, either. This is normal in international shipping.

The captain had worked with the Dynamic Positioning Officer before. The DPO was called Callum McAllister and he came from

South Uist, an island in the Outer Hebrides. They joked about his name being none more Scottish. They said he looked like a film star, even though he didn't. Callum was far too aware of the continued tendency of his skin to break out in zits, even though he was 32. He had a stammer and never liked people much. The film star comments amused him but he was a deeply serious man. He played golf when ashore, even though he didn't like it much. The only thing that really interested him was the equipment in the wheelhouse: radar, ECDIS, AIS, VHF radio, gyrocompass, magnetic compass, echosounder, tachometer. A chart table housing drawers with 169 charts.

Sometimes, one of these massive ships could collide with a ship (most probably a fishing boat), and not even know it. The crew may see the boat, or what would be left of it, trailing after them. Nothing more. And maybe not even that.

The crew were not employed by the shipping line. They were all employed by a German-based maritime HR agency, Hansa Marine Crewing.

The other two officers were Greek and Latvian. The crew made fun of the fact that they were called Yannis Makris and Jānis Balodis, claiming they would be difficult to tell apart were it not for the fact that one was short, stocky and dark, and the other tall and fair with blue eyes. Greek Yannis was tall and fair; Latvian Jānis short and dark. Each officer, apart from the captain, took two four-hour watches. The 4–8 shift was for Callum, the 12–4 shift for Greek Yannis, and the 8–12 one for Latvian Jānis. The captain, officially, was always on watch.

As well as the crew and the officers, there was another person on board. A paying passenger on a cargo ship is called a supernumerary. No one knew much about the supernumerary, save for the fact that they were an artist who had booked passage on the ship as part of an ongoing art project. No one cared much, either, as long as they kept out of the way. It was the first time since the pandemic that a supernumerary had been permitted to travel. Though the supernumerary was seen walking the top deck, and occasionally appeared in the officers' canteen, few of the crew or officers had much interest in talking to them.

One day after leaving Rotterdam, the *Echo* docked at Le Havre. While the distance was short, the captain found this, as ever, one of the most difficult stretches of the ship's long voyage. The Channel is the busiest waterway in the world, and while rarely dangerous to life in a vessel the size of the *Echo*, collisions are frequent and the level of vigilance needed to navigate it is high. Later, some of the crew would have a memory of a minor disturbance, of almost hitting or narrowly missing something, they couldn't remember or had never known quite what, or of a small commotion on the deck, one which passed rapidly, swallowed by the night. Others, however, recalled nothing. Nothing happened, the captain assured them. The Channel was highly surveilled, they received no warning, and his record-keeping was punctilious. Nothing happened.

The stop at Le Havre was a short one but all stops are short for modern ships. The turnaround time is usually less than five hours. Five hours, however, is long enough to move several thousand containers.

ISO 6346 intermodal containers are 12-metre-long boxes made of CorTen steel. They have been described 'the greatest work of art of the 20th century,' though others have been less flattering. There are some thirty million of them currently travelling around the world. They can be stacked ten high and moved by any of their eight corners, and have an average lifespan of five to ten years, though once they are no longer good enough for shipping they are too difficult or too expensive to melt down, so they are usually repurposed. Over the last thirty years the quantity of goods moved by sea has increased tenfold. It has been estimated that 90 percent of everything (*everything*) has, at some point, been moved around the world in an ISO 6346 intermodal container.

Their departure from Le Havre was briefly delayed when a crew member was counted missing. The captain grew anxious as he knew that, while a brief delay could be made up in terms of time, the costs of being docked were astronomical. Even another hour would incur a penalty fine which would encroach on their narrow margin. It was Mary, the cook. They couldn't do without the cook, even though they all said the food was terrible. The captain was informed when Mary eventually showed up, bearing several bags of shopping. No one asked what she had bought, but they hoped it was fresh vegetables.

ISO 6346 intermodal containers blazoned with their logos and their crusts of grime can be seen everywhere, waiting by ports, being pulled by trains or towed by massive trucks along motorways. Many have passed them, stacked and ranged in huge depots by the sides of railtracks and highways, in expansive lots on the edges of maritime towns and cities, in reservations on semi-abandoned industrial estates in the midst of unimpressive countryside, rusting by canals. People eat in containers converted into restaurants or bars, visit them as parts of art or theatre experiences, or sleep in those repurposed as niche boutique hotels. ISO 6346 intermodal containers have been used as emergency housing, as mobile datacentres, as overflow prisons.

Andrea the captain slept soundly the night after departing Le Havre. Apart from the brief hiccup, the stop had gone smoothly.

Callum the DPO slept well, too, and dreamed of his home on the island off the west of Scotland. The supernumerary slept well, too, having got used to the noise by now.

The *Echo* was carrying twelve thousand containers, carefully stacked to ensure even balance. A distinctive company logo was inscribed on many of the containers, battered, rusted over and fading. No one knew what was in the boxes. The ship, like every other, carried a manifest, a careful catalogue of the contents of each box, but the manifest was so long that no one had really read it all. Moreover, it was known and accepted that clients may not provide all the information necessary, or that information may not be entirely accurate, and may, in some cases, be lacking altogether. Manifests, it is known, never tell the truth.

The noise, it should be said, is one of the most striking things about being on board a container ship of this kind. Even though we may see them, sometimes, perhaps from the shore, moving so slowly and so silently, any intermodal cargo ship, even at port, is a site of roars and clangs, of grinding and creaking, of throbs, hums, and drones. The sea is always working its way against the hull. The wind, even on calm days, pushes the boughs. The ropes and cables used to secure the containers, the immense chain used to dock, tense and strain and howl their resistance. If you board a ship of this kind, do not seek silence, for there is none. Below the water, these ships produce so much noise that whales can no longer hear each other sing.

The captain did know what was flammable: paint, lacquer, enamel, varnish and polish, certain chemicals. He also suspected there were car parts (there usually were). He could guess that there would be many other things in the boxes: flatpack wardrobes; plastic ducks;

ball bearings; machinery for grinding cogs; toothpaste; lightbulbs; dried noodles; sneakers; underwear. This, after all, is how everything gets everywhere. But neither he nor anyone on the crew knew exactly. They only knew that there were boxes on board, big metal ones, twelve thousand of them.

The *Echo* was not, as such, insured. Eight different companies insured separate aspects of the ship itself, and its cargo. Later, a long legal battle to establish quite who was responsible for what ensued.

The *Echo* made good time to Rotterdam where the berth was routine, and there was no repeat of the Le Havre incident. The weather was several degrees colder than typical for the time of year, but quiet. The sea was calm. Everything was normal. There was nothing, in particular, to cause concern.

While the others slept soundly, Jānis the Latvian dreamed of fire. Fire is the great dread of sailors.

In 2006, just south of the coast of Yemen, the MV *Fortune* burst into flames. Between 60 and 90 containers (no one seems to know exactly how many) were thrown into the sea and all of the accommodation quarters were destroyed. Undeclared on the manifest (possibly due to this incurring higher handling costs), seven containers held fireworks. They all exploded. The crew attempted to control the blaze but gave up when a twelve-metre crack appeared on the hull, then jumped ship to be rescued by a Dutch frigate on manoeuvres in the area. It took two days for firefighting tugs to arrive, but they then decided the best thing was to let it burn itself out. The ship was renamed *Fortunate* and towed to Liuhen Dao Island in China for repairs, whereafter it sailed for another ten years, before going to the final breakers' yard at Alang.

Strangely, though seafarers' superstitions are many, there are none that forbid the bringing of fire on board.

In 2002, 150 km south of the Sri Lankan coast, a fire began in the hold of the *Hanjin Pennsylvania*. Containers holding phosphorus and fireworks, wrongly stored below deck, had exploded. Two people died and the rest of the crew abandoned ship. The remaining hulk was completely rebuilt, and now sails as the *Norasia Bellatrix*.

In February 2022, only two months before the *Echo* set out, the Panama-registered, Japan-operated *Felicity Ace* carrying four thousand Porsches, Lamborghinis and Bentleys worth an estimated $400 million set out from Emden, Germany, en route to Davisville, Rhode Island. Two weeks into its journey, 250 miles south of the coast of Terceira in the Azores, it caught fire. The ship drifted guideless and burning on the Atlantic for a week. The fire, fuelled by lithium-ion batteries in the electric vehicles onboard, was still burning when it capsized and sank two weeks later. The Portuguese Navy said that oily residue and wreckage was visible at the surface, nothing else. The sea at that point is ten thousand feet deep.

Jānis the Latvian did not tell anyone of his dream, but wrote a description of it in the journal he kept.

In 2013 the MV *Rhosus* set sail from Georgia en route to Mozambique. The *Rhosus* was owned by a Panamanian company in turn owned by Russian magnate Igor Grechushkin. (It was later discovered, however, that Grechushkin had chartered the *Rhosus* from the Cypriot Charambolos Manoli, who was funded by the FBME Bank, based in Tanzania, and known to be the bankers of Hezbollah.) The *Rhosus* was carrying 2,750 tonnes of ammonium nitrate. Ammonium nitrate is primarily used as an agricultural fertiliser but can be combined with other substances to produce a powerful explosive. Two months after it had set out, it made port in Beirut, where it encountered difficulties. At this point, stories differ: some claim Grechushkin had gone bankrupt, and did not have enough to pay the crew or the substantial fees necessary for passage through the Suez Canal; others that the *Rhosus* had mechanical problems and needed to stop for urgent repairs. Whichever, the ship was inspected and it was found that heavy machinery had been stacked on top of the ammonium nitrate, causing safety doors to buckle, and the ship was declared unsafe for sail. All save four of the crew (mostly Ukrainian) were repatriated. The ship was left in the harbour where, five years later, it sank. The cargo meanwhile had been stored in a large warehouse at the port. Two years after the *Rhosus* had sunk, its cargo exploded, causing the largest non-nuclear explosion in history, killing 218 people, injuring thousands more, and devastating the city of Beirut.

The captain, generally a good man, had not read the manifest for the *Echo*.

Such events, though, are rare. Container ships are generally very safe ways to travel and to transport goods. Better tracking systems and better crews mean the great wrecks of history and legend are now almost unknown. The biggest problem, on a good run, is sheer normality.

After he had written it down, Jānis the Latvian realised his dream had not been about fire, as much as the sound that fire makes.

Normality is a friend and an enemy on a ship like the *Echo*. A friend because it means there are no problems; an enemy in that it can become boredom. No one mentioned boredom on the ship, they never spoke of it, because it had become the very texture of their lives.

It would have been like talking about breathing. The crew closed themselves in their cabins and watched the same DVDs for the sixth, seventh, eighth time. They were quietly thankful to be bored. They thought of their families back home, and of the paycheques they would send there. While the crew, if ever asked, would always say that there was no typical day, every day was typical.

The crew's days were busy and boring. The crew's days, they hoped, would be normal. No one on board knew much about how the supernumerary, the artist, spent their days. The supernumerary walked a circuit of the ship each morning and evening, and seemed to pass the rest of the day shut in their small cabin. They had been told that while taking photographs was not forbidden, it was discouraged. Security reasons. The supernumerary, as much as anyone noticed, did not take photographs. They merely walked, and looked out. It is easy to look pensive on a ship.

Much of what happened on board the *Echo* is not known. Much is lost in the sheer ordinariness, the sheer tedium of the everyday. Most of what happened on the *Echo* happens thousands of times every day, all across the seas which cover the planet. Much has to be speculated.

At this point, the ship now headed out onto its longest stretch. It was bound across the Mediterranean, through the Suez, then into the Red Sea and Gulf of Aden before reaching Salalah, then crossing the Arabian and Laccadive seas before reaching Sri Lanka, then Malaysia.

As the *Echo* moved south of Sicily and into the eastern Mediterranean the possibility of sighting migrant boats grew stronger. Though we may think of the Mediterranean as being a peaceful, calm sea, a place for sun-drenched holidays and cruises, the two and a half million square kilometres of its surface are the site of constant international tension and an untold number of tragedies. This is especially true of its southeastern corner. This is a wild place, out of sight. There is little reconnaissance here, and scant surveillance. There are miles and miles and miles of open water. Although some of the shipping lanes are heavily used, and some traffickers will follow these as they are often the shortest and fastest ones, others will try to stay out of sight and use the empty quarters, the vast lost spaces of the sea. Few know what has taken place there, and the true number of those lost who have never even been recognised. Here, though, for any passer-through, things supposed to be invisible may become visible.

It was in these waters, towards the middle of May, that Callum McAllister the DPO noticed something unusual. It had been a clear night, and on his shift Callum, though not a man given to such feelings, may even have been moved by the tangerine sky of the early dawn, and the stars still visible against it like so many tiny diamonds. This made it all the more unnerving when, not indicated by any of the forecasts, a number of heavy and unusually shaped clouds appeared, 'from nowhere,' according to Callum. 'It was like a whirlwind,' he said, 'only, there was no wind.' Then, as soon as the clouds had appeared, they went. Callum was far from being an old hand but equally far from being inexperienced, and had never seen anything like it. It may have been nothing, a rare freak weather event, an unusual conjuration of atmospheric forces, or perhaps pollution, a nasty engine discharge emitted by another craft somewhere not so far away. Callum, though, never questioned his perception. He had seen it. It happened.

One of the reasons he was so certain is that, for the few moments that the clouds appeared in the sky, all his equipment went out. Everything went blank, then flickered on again, seconds later, as if nothing had happened. Moreover, during those few seconds the noise on board stopped. All of it. Everything, just for a few seconds, fell silent.

'Calenture' is a sailors' legend, a fever or disorder once thought to affect those on long voyages across open sea. Suffering from calenture, a mariner would see the endless ocean as endless prairie, mile after mile of softly waving green grass. This kind of delirium sometimes made seafarers jump overboard, in the hope of finding their feet on solid, if soft, ground, and running through the fields. Calenture has no medical validity at all.

Two crew members, Mani and Vinod, also saw the clouds, and felt the brief silence. A third, Mo, was woken from his sleep by the sudden cessation of noise. It was possible others, too, including the supernumerary, saw something or woke up, but this cannot be certified. At the time no one told each other anything, apart from Callum who, after much consideration, decided that he ought to inform the captain.

Though the ship, generally speaking, is safe, seafaring itself is ten times more dangerous than land-based occupations. Some two thousand mariners disappear every year. The exact number can never really be known as many of these cases go unreported. Not infrequently, people fall overboard. At least, it is thought that they fall overboard; in practice what happens is that they simply go missing and no other explanation can be found. The crew had calculated this into their risk.

The captain was concerned but not worried and carried out a full systems check. They checked the engines; they checked the navigational devices; they checked the radios and signalling equipment.

Life for merchant seafarers is cut to the bone. There is nothing here but the minimum. Bare life. Cell phones don't work this far out at sea. The first mate would later deny that he was racist, but did admit that he hadn't taken the trouble to learn the crew's names, and that he found them indistinguishable one from another.

Nothing was found to be malfunctioning. Nothing was out of the ordinary. As there was no evidence of any damage, he made no record of the incident. Such things happen, at sea.

The MV *Echo* was 300 metres long, 60 metres high and 40 metres wide, with a Doosan-Wärtsilä engine the size of a house contentedly running at 80 rpm, the speed of a resting human heart. The *Echo*'s hull was all welded steel, and had no rivets.

'You look at the radar, nothing. The sea, nothing. The sky, nothing,' said the captain, when asked how life was far out at sea. He had meant this to be reassuring, but realised it could also sound bleak. The crew called the captain 'lolo,' a Filipino word to mean grandfather, or old man, generically. Andrea Lauro was 46 years old.

Nothing must go wrong on a ship, and absolutely nothing must go wrong in international waters. In international waters there is no police force, no agency, no military to assist. Container ships are floating micro-states, multilingual, multi-ethnic, and effectively under the rule of no jurisdiction other than that of the captain. The MV *Echo* was Panamanian, Maltese, Italian, Swiss, and at the same time, none of these.

In April 2020, when oil prices fell below zero, traders were paid to take as much as they could if they could store it. Old, rusting hulks were brought out of retirement. They just stuck around, mostly in the gulf of Singapore and off the US coast, not going far, storing. This was when great swathes of the land-based world were undergoing some form of lockdown. The captain, who was privately more troubled than he thought he should have been by Callum's report, wondered if this could have something to do with the anomaly, but dismissed the idea as there was nothing of that out here.

Though seafarers still run their risks, ships are safe and getting bigger: there is a promised 'Malacca Max,' named for the maximum size a ship can be and still get through the straits of Malacca. If any Malacca Max ship were to be built, and then to sink, or burn, it could take two billion dollars' worth of cargo with it. It would be so large many conventional ports could not harbour it. The idea of building offshore ports has been suggested, or using the great trash islands, such as those in the Pacific, as mooring stations. For a European harbour, Scapa Flow off Orkney has been mooted—it has deep water channels between its small islands, but there are currently too many wrecks there, too much history, for it to be viable. Along with some Norwegian islands, South Uist, where Callum McAllister was from, has been suggested as another possible port.

Mary noticed bits of food had gone missing.

The MV *Echo* used to be known as the MV *Atlas*, and before that it had been the MSC *Lorenz*. While it had officially always been used as a container ship, in 2014 it had spent two years in dry dock at Gunsan in South Korea, undergoing a refit. It had, in its time, been owned by companies from fifteen different nationalities, and had sailed under six different flags. The year following its refit, its whereabouts are difficult to trace before it was acquired by its new owners.

It was once said there were 'five keys to lock the world,' and these were the British-controlled waters around Singapore, the Cape of Good Hope, Alexandria, Gibraltar, and Dover. Now there are still five keys, but they are Malacca, Yokosuka, Hormuz, Suez, and Panama.

Though the *Echo* was a large ship (300 metres long, with a 40-metre beam and a 16-metre draft) it was but a tiny speck in the sea.

Mary didn't keep the kitchen or its cupboards locked. There was no alcohol on board. If crew members wanted, say, chocolate, or other snacks, they would supply their own. There was no reason to put locks on the kitchen door or its cupboards. Nobody much liked the food.

In October 2020 the *Nave Andromeda*, an oil tanker just off the coast of southern England, sent out a distress call. 'I need immediately, immediately agency assistance.' The Greek captain claimed that seven stowaways (who he believed had boarded in Lagos and then made themselves visible in Gran Canaria where the Spanish authorities had refused to let them ashore, and had since then been locked in a cabin) had escaped. The 22 crew members had locked themselves in the secure area of the ship called the Citadel. Within eight hours, commandos from the British Special Boat Service, supported by helicopters, stormed the ship. Within a few hours, the ship was being brought into port at Southampton, and the stowaways were arrested. The story, which had flared onto urgent breaking news stories across the world, quickly went to sleep. Within three months, all charges against the supposed stowaways (who, it turned out, had not escaped from the locked cabin) were dropped, and they were absorbed into the UK's asylum-seekers schemes. Quite what happened on board the *Andromeda* is still not known, but if a ship has stowaways on board, ports will refuse the ship permission to dock, effectively marooning it at sea.

It was nothing serious, Mary assured herself, as the amounts missing were very small and she knew they had more than enough provisions to carry them until the next stop. There were still 48 frozen chickens, and two hundred large cans of tomato soup, as well as everything else. Running out of food was a nightmare from olden times.

MANIFEST

Ships, even ones as big and as regulated as the MV *Echo*, are labyrinthine, and porous. They are filled with holes and gaps, spaces and nooks, crannies, runnels and storage tanks. Stowaways are a logistical and bureaucratic nightmare. The ship cannot house them; no port or country wants to accept them. They are impossible to insure, and the shipping company is liable for them. Delays to the ship's finely plotted course can cost millions. They can be shipped or flown back to where they came from or to anywhere else ready to accept them, if a party willing to meet the cost of it all is found. In some cases, it has been rumoured, they are summarily thrown over the side, no questions asked. The crew do not want any risks being taken with their pay. No one will miss them; it's easier this way. In other cases they are quietly tolerated, ignored—nothing seen, nothing said—then left to slip away quietly, at night, in port.

Channel 16 VHF is a radio channel which all maritime vessels should keep open, or at the very least, regularly check. It is a hailing channel for emergencies: any Mayday or PanPan calls are to be made through this channel. ('PanPan' is to signify an urgent situation that has not yet become an emergency.) The channel, however, is regularly abused. Crews have used it to mock or insult each other, with varying degrees of humour or ferocity. There are running jokes or themes (one about Filipino monkeys; another is a voice constantly asking if anyone has seen Mario). Pirates flood it with music when they are about to attack, as it is both unsettling and blocks the channel. Left open it should be almost silent, emitting nothing but a low, slow, gentle sine wave, interrupted only by an occasional crackle or hiss of static. Often, however, especially in busy areas, the channel is filled with voices, growls, whistles, songs, the polyphonic, multilingual, incomprehensible chatter of the sea.

Channel 16 is one of the many strands of sound onboard a ship, a sound which becomes complex, coming from many different sources with many different frequencies, and also constant. What is difficult is separating any signal from that noise.

Yannis the Greek thought he heard voices outside his cabin one night. He opened the door to see no one there. He thought it may have been the supernumerary, chatting with one of the crew, perhaps. He made up his mind to ask the supernumerary next time he saw them, but didn't get a chance over the next few days.

Mary heard voices too, or at least some sound that was different to the constant noise of the ship, and thought she might have found the reason for the missing food. When she entered the kitchen, though, there was nothing there.

Ships cannot dream, much less have nightmares, but were the MV *Echo* capable of involuntary oneiric vision or stress-induced parasomnia, it may have dreamed about Alang. Situated on the Gulf of Khambhat on the Kathiawar peninsula in the state of Gujarat, Alang is the world centre of shipbreaking. It is where ships go to die. Half of all ships, eventually, find their way to Alang, where there are heavy tides and a long sloping beach. If the ship is still capable of motion, it is sailed close to the port at high water; if not, it is towed there. The ship is then left until the tide goes out, leaving it to beach deliberately. Once out of water, the ships are unthinkable: against the long flat coastline and low buildings, they are impossibly huge, utterly out of scale, not of human origin. They become cities of rust. They look like iron cathedrals split in two.

Jānis sat down in the canteen one evening and the only other person there was the supernumerary. Jānis preferred to eat alone and didn't welcome company, but he had never seen the supernumerary in there before.

'May I ask you what the purpose of your journey is?' he said.

'Nothing,' said the supernumerary.

'Nothing? Aren't you painting pictures, or writing, or something?'

'No,' said the supernumerary. 'The journey itself is the work. That is all.'

Alang, though, is not a graveyard. Nothing stays in Alang for longer than a year; sometimes, the great hulks vanish within weeks. Even if the ship has been destroyed by fire or spent years lolling on an ocean floor, it still has value. Everything (everything) is stripped, taken, moved, melted down, recast, recomposed, recontextualised. First, fuel, then the empty fuel tanks, then engine parts. After that, anything that can still be found on board is salvaged: food, drink, personal effects, abandoned cargo. Then go wiring, electronics, panels, lightbulbs, flooring. Glass is lifted out of place, then metal: sheets of iron, rivets, screws, nails. Finally, the now-naked girders which look like oxidised dinosaur bones are axle-ground into saleable chunks, hauled onto the backs of trucks and driven away. The work is done by hand. The beach is divided into plots (parcels of land, conspiracies, stories) where a rough market is set up for smaller merchandise to be sold on to bigger traders in Bhaganvar, Vadodara, Surat, then Mumbai. Some elements will find themselves recycled to become parts of cargoes which will once again be stowed in containers and shipped around the globe. The ex-ships' microscopic toxic elements will seep into the ocean currents and circulate until there are no more tides, nor sea, nor dust. They will never go away, because there is no 'away.'

'I hear you're an artist,' said Callum when he sat down to eat with the supernumerary, having been unable to avoid them. The supernumerary nodded, but didn't say anything. 'There's some big artist has a studio—a whole warehouse, really, a hangar—near my home. My brother worked for her for a bit, I think. He's in the film business now, apparently.'

Other crew members sometimes thought they heard footsteps, or even a scuffle. Some wondered if there were rats on board, and that might be the reason for the missing food. 'At least rats might appreciate it,' they joked. Arguments broke out over accusations that some had been listening to their music or movies too loud. Most crewmembers had headphones, however.

The captain, who had neither heard nor seen anything, was wearied by all this. It was the boredom, he knew. The boredom had got too much for everyone. It happened, at sea. He had colleagues who had spoken darkly of outbreaks of mass hallucinations. Food poisoning was one possibility; poor crew management another.

The captain knew he had to take action swiftly, and organised a number of search parties who thoroughly explored the whole ship. They found nothing, not even any rats, and knowing they were soon to head into the Suez Canal, the captain relaxed again. There were twenty-five people on board the ship, none more. The sea lanes would become much busier, and so therefore would the crew. Suez was always a respite, the ability to see land at least, even if only for a day.

In 1976 the MV *Tananger* was built in Hommelvik, Norway. In 1990 it changed its name to the *Pomar Murman*, then three years after that, to the *Polar Trader*, then in 2000 to the *Avantis II* under which name it sailed for thirteen years before again changing its name to—confusingly—*Avantis I*, but only for two years, when it became the *Elias* for another two years, before settling on the MV *Alta*, which is still its official name, though it is perhaps now better known as the 'Ghost Ship of Ballycotton.'

In 2018, the *Alta*, under a Tanzanian flag, set sail from Piraeus in Greece en route to Port-au-Prince in Haiti. A voyage so long is unusual for a ship of the *Alta*'s size (a comparatively small 77 metres), and this may explain why instead of heading out into open water over the next ten months it docked at Kalamata, Paloukia and Salamina, all on the Greek coast. It then disappeared again before showing up ten months later in Ceuta, in North Africa, on the border of the Mediterranean and the Atlantic. Though fitted with an Automatic Identification System, its transponders appeared to go on and off before disappearing completely. It is not illegal to deactivate an AIS, but it is highly irregular. Smuggling (most probably of narcotics) or illegal fishing are the most common suspected reasons. The *Alta* was next located some three thousand kilometres away, in the deep Atlantic, far south of Bermuda, where a US Coast Guard cutter was forced to rescue the Honduran, Panamanian and Greek crew who claimed the ship's engines had failed. The ship itself was abandoned, left to float, and to drift.

There are a number of versions of what happened next. One story claims the ship was towed (by whom, it is not known) to Guyana, where it was repaired, then set sail again under a Panamanian flag before being hijacked (by whom, it is not known, nor why), and then abandoned again. It was definitively sighted by a Royal Navy icebreaker, the HMS *Protector*, in September 2019, this time lying northwest of the Azores. The *Protector* attempted to make contact, but received no reply, and for reasons still unclear departed, registering the *Alta*'s presence, but taking no further action.

The *Alta*'s AIS transponders came on again, but only sporadically, before eventually going off altogether. They registered that the ship was travelling at speeds of around 0.1 or 0.2 knots, which equates to around 0.2 to 0.3 kilometres per hour, that is, it was barely moving at all. It may have simply surrendered to the currents. However, its unusual looped movements, like a twisted figure-of-eight, suggest something may have been towing, or pushing, it for a while.

Then, on a cold clear morning in February 2020, a jogger in County Cork on the west coast of Ireland noticed something on the horizon between Skur and Ceann Capaill rock. Later the same day, the *Alta* ran aground on the rocky shore near the fishing village of Ballycotton. Though the area is comparatively remote, it is still not known how such a vessel, relatively small as it was, could have arrived so close to Europe without being spotted or registered at all.

Despite the remote wildness of the seas, ships cannot vanish. In some form or another, they reappear.

In 2018 officials in Myanmar found the 177-metre *Sam Ratulangi*, sailing under an Indonesian flag, drifting near Yangon. It had last been reported nine years earlier off the coast of Taiwan, some three thousand kilometres distant. The thirteen crew members left on board claimed they were being towed to a breaker's yard but that the tug had cut them adrift following a heavy storm. In Oga, Yurihonjo and Sado, on the western coast of northern Japan, small fishing boats often wash up on shore, occasionally containing human remains. They are thought to come from North Korea.

Suez came and went. The spectre of the helplessly blocked *Ever Given* still haunted all sea captains, but Lauro had done the passage many times and with the aid of his officers and crew, and a few small bribes, the navigation was smooth and confident. They were now into the Red Sea, from where they would pass through the Gulf of Aden and into the Arabian Sea.

The Red Sea always generated a certain amount of tension due to the once-high level of piracy there but the captain knew, as did the crew, that for various reasons such incidences had hit a low after the peaks of the mid- and late-1990s. Caution, as ever, was paramount, but there was no reason to worry. There were no stowaways. Things would go quiet again. Jokes would be made about the food. The same DVDs would be watched. Life on the ship would be boring again.

Mary knew there were no stowaways, but she did see people, at the ends of corridors or the edges of corners, figures disappearing just as she glimpsed them, slipping away almost before they were seen. Jānis the Latvian started writing a thriller about a ship which was boarded, but lost the thread after the first few pages. Mani told Vinod he was still hearing things during the night, and Vinod told him he was stupid, but then started a rumour among the crew. Most of the crew ignored the rumour. They were used to gossip and jokes running until they'd long exhausted themselves, but this was silly.

A number of them noticed strange smells, though, ones they couldn't place. They joked that it was Mary's cooking until Mary overheard them and cursed them out. The Indians said it was the Bangladeshis; the Bangladeshis said it was the Filipinos; the Filipinos said it was the Indians. They all knew it wasn't each other: the smell was something chemical, perhaps.

Third night out into the Arabian Sea and a number of the crew were woken by the sound of people running through the corridors. Some heard shouts. On getting up to see what was happening, there was no one there. Some of the crew had been playing football on the deck. 'It must have been us,' they said, and apologised.

Then it began to happen during daylight hours. Figures glimpsed out of the corners of eyes. Going around the ends of corridors. Out at dangerous points of the ship, where they could not be. Mary knew she hadn't been wrong.

Yannis claimed that the crew were all superstitious. 'We're all sailors, after all.' The captain did not agree and was concerned for morale. He ordered another routine inspection, and again found nothing.

Jānis started work on his book again, but it had become more of a classic crime story in which people on board a ship, one by one, began to disappear. The problem on the *Echo*, he felt, was a different one: people were appearing.

They asked the supernumerary if they had seen anything, and the supernumerary said they had spent most of their time alone in their cabin, and pointed out that since this was their first such voyage, they wouldn't know what was unusual and what wasn't.

'Are we carrying anything unusual?' Callum asked the captain.

'Define unusual,' said the captain.

'We need to know what's on board,' said Yannis. 'We can't risk a fire.'

The captain read the manifest but hadn't had a chance to tell anyone what he had found before another problem arose. It seemed the ship was lost.

'No, of course we're not lost,' said Callum. 'That's impossible.' And the captain knew that, and he agreed, but wanted to know what particular type of equipment malfunction they were experiencing. Callum tried to explain, but couldn't.

'I don't understand it,' said the captain.

'I don't either,' said Callum. 'I know where we are,' he said, 'I just don't know where anything else is.'

When the Scythian philosopher Anacharsis was asked if there were more people living or dead, he replied that he couldn't say, for he did not know how to categorise those at sea. In 1682 the Puritan minister John Flavel wrote *Navigation Spiritualized: Or, A New Compass for Seamen* in which he tells the story of Anacharsis and goes on to add 'that Seamen are, as it were, a third Sort of Persons, to be numbered neither with the Living nor the Dead; their Lives hanging continually in Suspense before them.'

Callum McAllister felt himself very much among the living as his skin broke out again. He had been told his acne was stress-related, but had never done much about it.

They assured each other that they were not lost, that it was impossible to be lost. They had a temporary navigation equipment malfunction which would soon be resolved.

The crew (and, privately, some of the officers) were beginning to believe that something was on board which shouldn't be on board.

The captain stood on the deck and wished for a maestrale, grecale, libeccio or scirocco, but there was no wind.

They kept on with the normality. The noise on board. The boredom. They ate the food that Mary cooked, and complained about it. They watched the same DVDs. The supernumerary walked out at night and looked at the stars. Jānis stopped writing his thriller.

Yannis suggested they should put out a PanPan signal, but the captain thought it was far too early for that. This was a brief glitch, nothing more. The captain was proved right when Callum told him the lights had come back on.

'I've established location, Sir, but there seems to be another problem.'

'What's that?'

'We've vanished.' Callum wasn't given to using dramatic language, but didn't know quite what else to say.

'Ships can't vanish. What on earth is going on?'

'I know where everything else is. I just don't know where we are.'

The MV *Echo* was failing to show up on its own radar systems. As if it had, effectively, vanished.

Mani thought he could smell smoke, or some kind of acrid gas. Vinod saw shadows coalescing into small clouds. Mary said a prayer, though she was not religious.

The only thing that could vanish, the captain knew, were certain kinds of military craft, not only submarines, but also surface vessels. Such blocking technologies were available. Things visible could be made invisible. But not to themselves.

Later, the captain would find that there had been a surveillance ship in the area, but it had detected nothing. He couldn't get much from his source as their ship was piloting equipment of national security.

The captain knew how to navigate using a sextant. Despite their situation he was pleased that this knowledge would come in useful. He realised that despite the engine the size of a house running steadily, the ship was moving in a spiral, its line of drift so faint it could hardly be traced, getting slowly wider and wider. This could be due, he knew, to some anomalous current in the area, though that would be almost unheard of.

A group of crew members came up to the bridge to ask what was happening. The captain told them he would address them all shortly.

They weren't happy, and wanted to know what was being carried on the ship. If there was anything they hadn't been told.

At this point, the captain told them that there was nothing on the manifest that there shouldn't be, and that there were no explosive compounds being carried. He knew, however, that manifests did not always tell the truth. Then there was the other concern raised by his reading of the manifest, one which he later conceded that he should have investigated earlier. The number of containers on board did not match the number on the manifest. There was one extra.

'What is it?' asked Yannis, seeing a chance to blame Jānis, who also should have known this, but Jānis, like the captain, did not know.

They had to go and find it, and open it.

The four officers followed by the group of crewmembers went down into the hold.

The noise on the ship, everyone including the supernumerary remembered, was growing louder. Yannis was thinking about his promotion and Jānis about his thriller. The noise was growing louder. It was hot. The crew thought about their paycheques and their families. It was loud, and it was loud and they all walked faster searching through the identical yet different containers. All different all identical. One extra. None vanishing. The noise on the ship and the wind and the *Echo* the clouds the captain the engine the officers the stranger the pirates the migrants the stars the noise on the ship the five keys the flags the owners the fire the keys the compass the charts the crew the watch the night the stars the food the terrible food the noise the dark the boredom the noise the boxes the smoke the fire the shadows the heat the *Fortune* the *Ace* the *Rhosus* the *Alta* the *Atlas* Alang Alang Alang Alang the keys the lock the lost the found the

Echo the silence the noise the radio the sea the noise the sea the noise on the ship the noise the signal the noise

Captain Andrea Lauro stepped forward and pulled the bar on the extra container.

LATER, MANI CLAIMED THAT HE had seen shadows escape; Vinod saw black mechanical shapes, some kind of machinery which he couldn't describe; Mary had seen darkness, a deep black nothing where there should have been at least something; Yannis had seen the same but saw there were some kind of boxes or containers in there; Jānis remembered only how cold it had been in there, colder than it ever could have been; Callum saw nothing but empty space. The supernumerary wasn't there. The captain thought he had seen his own face, staring back at him, but he never told anyone this. The crew, fearing for future employment, all signed a pact swearing each other to secrecy. Many of them respected it.

But all this happened on the ocean, so far from our eyes, as if it didn't really happen at all.

DEATH #47

Oreste Lauro stepped out of the pub and onto the street and the moment his foot hit the pavement the knowledge was there: it always happened this way, the mute throb in the temples, a sinking in the gut, the light starting to fracture and spangle. He struck a straight line with speed and commitment (this, previous experience had taught him, helped) but the pressure spread to the back of his neck then up to the base of his skull, poking its way into his amygdala, reaching toward the frontal lobes. He spat out his frustration in a hot glob of phlegm which spluttered onto a paving stone and was rapidly dispersed by the trudging feet of the masses entering and exiting the station opposite. A wave of anxiety skulked in the offing, welling, ready to break sometime soon. Not now, not today, he thought, but knew his thoughts would serve nothing. As soon as Oreste Lauro had stepped out of that pub he knew he was about to die, again.

A bus clipped the curb, a wanker on a scooter wove through the crowd, a chugger accosted him, but Oreste ploughed on. Not today would he be crushed beneath the gargantuan tyre of public transport, floored by a lazy office worker on a wobbly two-wheeler or subtly stilettoed by Animal Concern. He continued, keeping his path direct, linear, a vector of escape. If he had intent, he told himself (and Oreste narrated himself in the present, making and unmaking his story with each step), nothing could touch him. People (and, he hoped, other things) avoided a man who showed intent, and today Oreste very much wanted to be avoided.

Today would be difficult enough without death being involved, his own above all. Today was the day Oreste's debts were being called in, the day his time had run out; today was payback day. Trouble being what trouble was, Oreste still didn't have a penny and feared his impending demise may be the only acceptable cash substitute. Today was a complicated one indeed, and, fuck, it was his birthday, too.

Oreste noted something off about the weather (and Oreste was nothing less than barometrically sensitive, able to detect dips and surges in atmospheric pressure as others could tell the time), something inert, something lacking, as if it almost weren't there at all. The sky was white. The air was neither cold nor hot. There was no breeze of any kind. Whatever this portended, it wouldn't be good. It was the weather as much as the premonitions of his own demise that was fucking with his brain.

Oreste kept walking, it was the best he could do, a straight line up the gentle slope of a hill heading somewhere less crowded. He ignored the temptations of bars on either side of the city centre street. Too dangerous. He balanced the merits of keeping his head down (a sign of determination, an aid to avoiding recognition) with those of keeping it up and looking around carefully (a sign of confidence, an aid to recognising danger) and went for the former with the addition of quick glances up, ahead, side to side. Problem being he didn't know who he was looking for: it could have been anyone. He'd have preferred a glamourous woman in shades (a wig too, a trench coat, the full noir) though a man in a mackintosh with a poison-tipped umbrella would do. It'd be great if it came from the non-human: a hooded figure, the proper full-on *Seventh Seal* shit, or (better) some kind of pale horseman, or (better still) a hand forming from one of those greyish clouds that were now appearing against the white sky, its finger reaching down from above to indicate him, and him only, as though (finally!) he had been chosen.

More likely it'd be a standard-issue thug, shaved head, nasty cheap suit or a Kappa trackie top.

He saw a homeless woman crouched in a doorway, two men in chefs' scrubs sharing a cig next to the bins in the alley, a white van bleeping as it slowly reversed towards him, its driver's face concentrated in the wing mirror. Any of them, it could have been. Perhaps they'd just send a drone to do him, or hit him with a bullet from a clinical sniper posted up in any one of these anonymous office blocks. Head down, Ore, you've done this before, he told himself, while full knowing that among the various ways he had died, he had never yet been murdered.

Though Oreste had not formally drawn up a catalogue of his deaths, his own thanatologue (believing the act of listing, numbering and referencing his various deaths would bring finitude, completion, death itself), he knew it intimately: drug overdoses (Class A, Class B, opiates, alcohol); car accidents (driver, passenger, pedestrian); heart attack (obesity, fear); accident (falling from ladder, chainsaw); drowning (canal, sea); shipwreck (*vedi* drowning: sea); poisoning (food, various kinds, several times; unknown toxins, twice); things falling on him (cast iron abstract sculpture); illnesses (many); viruses (MERS, SARS, Covid). He was currently missing only lightning strike and murder. The chances of the former he knew (having researched them thoroughly) were anything between ten million to one and three thousand to one and he could discount this as today, he feared, the latter was much, much closer.

Oreste's various deaths, obviously, were not final. Others would merely mark them down as nasty accidents or misfortunes, and note both how accident-prone he was, and how resilient. But Oreste felt different: each one of these grave mishaps he was determined to register as a death.

But it was OK, because he had a plan. Act not react, someone had once told him and act he would: all he had to do was keep walking, even if it was mere superstition—death could not take a moving target. Motion = Life. Something to do with energy. Wasn't energy always moving? What about static, then? What was that—static electricity? Oreste tried to slow his brain. He did not want to think about invisible forces. There was nothing virtual, delayed, suspended, or aethereal about getting coshed.

Today's death would be at human hand. He had to avoid someone. Problem being: he didn't know who.

Oreste had (in some minor sense) got away with it once today. He'd been certain that there was something off about that random who'd somehow found his number and called him up wanting to talk about Sigi Conrad. (Sigi! How long had it been since he'd even thought about her?) Flight was his impulse but by this point, having met death head-on 46 times, Oreste had acted against character and decided to rise to the occasion and meet the interlocutor. (Two decisive factors in this decision: firstly, his mortal experience had taught him that the foreseen deaths tended to be slightly less traumatic than the unforeseen ones; secondly, he had wondered if he might request a fee for his time and knowledge, any cash at all being welcome.) His

DEATH #47

disappointment on finding this oddly named potential iteration of death (who in good fuck's name is called 'Che'?) looking like a scraggly arts journalist, a failed writer, stinking of cigarette smoke with a whiskery beard (in short: not unlike himself), was matched only by his relief.

Sometimes the vibes didn't tell it straight. They'd been wrong before. This could have been a mere migraine. That said, Oreste was full aware (Deaths #13 and #21) that poison took its time to act. That third pint had tasted a bit funny.

He rubbed his stomach and perched on a low wall by a little park at the top of the hill, took out his phone and scrolled through his contacts. The phone had been dropped and spilled upon many times, and though its screen was cracked it was still viable and, most importantly, its memory was intact. There it was—a number for Sigi. He ought to tell her that someone was asking after her. He hit the button, held the phone to his ear and waited through the brief silence until there was a click then some kind of engaged tone, a hurried bleeping, as if it were frantically trying to tell him something he didn't understand. Nerves now even closer to the edge, he shoved the phone back in his pocket and headed off again.

Oreste Lauro was from Naples, and thus had intimate familiarity with the Smorfia, the book which transposed everything one might dream about into numbers (numbers which were, in turn, to be played on the Lotto). Oreste knew that in this book the number 47 equated with death. Non e' vero, ma ci credo. Though it wasn't true, Oreste believed it. Today was not only Oreste's birthday, but his 47th one.

He leaned into his superstition, let the anxiety flow through him, stared the paranoia in its beady eye, and kept walking. 'Bring it!' he shouted, noting the people looking at him as he moved into a scrubby park, benches for vapists and pigeons.

Though he loathed the idea of ever being pinned down, defined, owned or owning, of stasis, Oreste was a man who liked to catalogue, to classify, to define, to pin down. He loved lists, top tens, best evers. Charts, catalogues, rankings and encyclopaedias placed form on chaos, shaped the void, gave order and sequence to the randomness and complexity of existence. His job, as far as he had one, was to make connections, to find things, to put people in touch with each other, to set up or perpetuate a flow. Oreste s'arrangia as they said back home, but that was not how Oreste saw himself: Oreste wanted to find order, to index, to classify, to find containers for things. How was everything held? What gave matter form?

He needed another drink. It was his birthday, after all. Everywhere round here looked like some kind of chain pub, though: all trying to be different, all the same. He moved to the other side of the park, hoping the vista and potential for a decent bar would improve. It didn't. He sat himself down on another low wall and noticed weird markings on the pavement and road surface, lines, letters and numbers like some kind of Cabbalistic graffiti done in pink and blue. Today, everything was a sign.

It was probably for the best there was no pub, pubs always meant trouble of various kinds, one being the kind that had led him to today's predicament. Seven years ago (was it to the day? Quite possibly—that would explain why he had been drinking more than strictly necessary with a group of random strangers) Oreste had been in a bar where the talk (as it often tended to be when hanging out with the art crowd) concerned where the new Berlin might be: it was Krakow, they said,

DEATH #47

it was Dresden, no—Sarajevo! It was Chemnitz, it was Leipzig, it was Brno. It could be anywhere—it was Lviv, Malmö, Reykjavik, Tartu. It was Plovdiv, it was Cluj.

Oreste, though not usually given to music, had decided the babble sounded like a song, and let his (admittedly limited) skill for spontaneous improvisation take over, and burst into song.

> *When you're still living in that hovel*
> *unable to complete your novel,*
> *When you're anxious about payday,*
> *not finishing your screenplay,*
> *When all you want to talk of is hegemony, praxis, the*
> >   *liminal*
> *And you prefer your techno minimal . . .*

AT THIS POINT, ORESTE, A man usually noted for his reserve, must have been on drink number six, if not seven, and began to envision himself in full slap at some Weimar Cabaret, singing this little-known Brecht/Weill number, backed by wheezing accordion and skinny violins, interrupted by delightful androgynes shouting geil! and fantastich! at the end of each line.

> *Komm, komm, komm! It's the new, it's the new, it's the*
> >   *new Berlin!*

HE KNEW HE SHOULD COME up with a snappy chorus here, but the rhymes were still spilling from him.

When you're feeling like you're shafted
and you prefer your coffee hand-crafted,
When you're really quite annoyed
that you live in a cultural void,
When you believe everything is dialectical
And prefer your feminism intersectional
Komm! Komm! Komm!

AT THIS POINT, HE DIDN'T like to remember, he may actually have been dancing on the bar.

Let the speculators sing,
'The artist is king!'
Hear the cash tills ring,
and the card readers ping
And come, come, come—to the new Berlin!

HE THOUGHT HE'D ENDED WITH some kind of a flourish, one which had probably looked more like an accident, but it had mattered little, he'd run out of rhymes and felt he could legitimately expect some applause by that point, and (convinced of himself in a way that sometimes happened when he hit a certain level of alcohol in his bloodstream) began to demand that someone arrange, record and produce his song immediately.

He'd foreseen royalties from the streaming, ad revenue on the YouTube or TikTok clicks, maybe even a limited-edition coloured vinyl 7-inch, get someone to do a good cover for it. It would have been part of his (as yet still non-existent) portfolio. Oreste had a long list (which existed solely in his head, though he had thought many times of writing it out) titled 'Things I Should Have Done' and now, still perched on the wall, Oreste finally added this missed oppo to the mental catalogue. The money could now have been used to bail him out in some kind of perfect circle payback.

When a guy in hi-vis appeared, Oreste buckled and tensed, adopting a brace position he hoped would protect him, but there was no need, not this time. The man was joined by another, then by a flatback truck from which they pulled some metal fencing which they started to throw up, circling the multicoloured glyphs on the street area with alarming speed. Power tools appeared and the men set to. Drills squealed, saws ground, hammers hammered. Sparks flew and the noise was torturous. Someone could have easily got injured in a situation like that. Oreste shuffled away from the scene.

Oreste's bar-stool singing debut hadn't been the end of that story, though Oreste now wished it had been. Turned out one of the men in that bar had indeed been in music: ordinary looking, shortish, regulation black suit/grey shirt buttoned up to the neck combo. A manager or promoter, a mover or shaker of some kind. Oreste couldn't remember now, remembered only badgering him to record the certain smash hit. The man had demurred, muttering something about passing the idea on to one of his artists, maybe, though he wasn't really sure it was his thing.

'It's not that, though,' he'd said.

'What is it then?' asked Oreste.

'You know it exists, right?'

'What exists?'

'The New Berlin.'

Oreste knew he drank too much, and blamed much on this fact. The drinking was his slow death, the one which (in darker moments) he feared would be the final one. It was a strange vice for an Italian, especially a Southern one, and one he'd found easier to hide in Northern Europe, while in Eastern Europe it'd seemed practically obligatory. Oreste had imagined himself as a social drinker, a glass or two with a meal, something fizzy for a celebration, and a pre-dinner aperitif was only polite, after all, but then (perhaps to overcome the shock of Death #1—trapped in the door of a departing train) he'd instituted the pre-drinks drink (the drink you'd have to set you up before going out drinking) and then (post Death #7—head injury, sustained after falling down stairs) the after-drinks drink, the wind-down one, and from that followed the drink to bring you down from the wind-down drink, then the one after that, the one that would take you into sleep, or beyond it. It was all a process, carefully calibrated. He had, in honesty, started to worry when he found himself drinking alone, though knew that drinking was a way to feel like he wasn't alone: when he was drinking, there was always a party going on. Before long, however, he realised that he preferred drinking alone, as there was no one there to bother him, or disturb his train of thought, or—worst of all—to try and stop him from drinking. Drinking alone he could get absolutely legless falling over drunk, and no one need ever know about it.

Oreste knew well (and had thought of cataloguing) the qualities of the different kinds of drunkenness (which included: the light and sparkling drunk, when he'd be all wit and charm; the heavy and slow drunk, torpid, usually occasioned by strong ale; the gently languid drunk, allegro, a good one for a summer afternoon; the woozy drunk; the drunk when you don't realise quite how drunk you are; the drunk when you're drinking on a hangover, its long start then eventual layering of qualities of different drunkenesses; the interior explorer, a good one when drinking alone, asking some big questions; the explosion drunk, usually from drinking a lot on an empty stomach, and characterised by complete amnesia the following morning), and also those of hangovers (which include: the Lurker, the Slammer, the Grudge, the Dread, the Sweater, the Hysteric) each of which could shade over or into one another, or arrive two at once (a Sweater and a Dread, say), or one could horribly morph into another over the course of an entire day.

If Oreste right now were undergoing a Dread, for example, the sound occurring some two hundred metres behind him would turn it sharply into a Hysteric. The sound was a scream, brief but intense, and one that Oreste unfortunately recognised as that of a human being injured by improper use of a power tool (Death #32).

It may have been the drunkenness (a light and sparkling one, giddy) which had led Oreste, suspicious by nature, to listen to the music guy, a man who was clearly hiding something, or, if not hiding exactly, definitely had something, somewhere in his past or present, that he wasn't going to be keen on talking about (Oreste now wondered if, maybe, he was about to find out quite what that was, or if it would remain one of the many mysteries which lurked in the corners of his various lives). The man was very pleased, however, to talk about the New Berlin, not as a mere shit-talking in the bar thing, nor as the content for a cleverly satirical song, but as a real, actual, true, tangible and currently ongoing project. Not some kind of neo-colonial appropriation, though, no gentrification-max, occupying some entire underperforming Central or East European provincial town or former Hauptstadt with the sole aim of lining a few incomers' pockets with capital both literal and cultural, no no no. It was something far more interesting than that.

An ambulance came hurtling down the street towards Oreste and, for once, soared past him. Oreste wondered if he had narrowly missed his next appointment, if the Reaper had swung too wide and missed, or if harm was merely particularly busy today. He breathed relief and reminded himself that he was, after all, a man who had died many times, and each time he had come back. Death, he told himself as he eyed a potentially quiet corner pub, one with a gloomy back room where he could sit in silence, was not an event in life, we do not live to experience death: Wittgenstein's dictum was a perfect excuse for a drink.

The New Berlin, it turned out, was a concept more than a place, one unlimited by strict notions of geography or time. It wasn't a residency, nor a commune ('definitely not a commune'), not a workshop as such, and not quite a school either. 'It's not easy to explain,' the man had said, the man who had a name so slightly odd that Oreste (usually adept with languages) could not pronounce it, 'a kind of academy, perhaps, not a club. A movement, more than a thing. A process, not an event. It's all about flow.'

Oreste had spent much of his adult life around artists and was highly aware of the bullshit that was often spoken around them, yet this awareness had no effect on his immunity to it; on the contrary, Oreste loved it. He didn't even understand what New Berlin was yet, but knew he was in.

The corner pub was almost empty, which was good, and indeed

had a small corner room, the kind of room which would once have been a snug, which was also good: Oreste could sit with his back to the wall and his eyes on the door, ready for anyone or anything. He ventured to the bar, went for a lager, something cooling and fizzy, kegged, no surprises.

Plans were still at the ideas stage at the moment, the man had told him, they were looking at the possibilities of physical location, somewhere east, but not too far east (nor south nor north), somewhere property was still cheap (relatively speaking), one which could be a place to build, 'build' of course, in one of the word's many senses, if not construct, make it happen, bring it into being. There were a number of variables. (Oreste, being Oreste, liked how loose the idea was, seeing vagueness as flexibility, potential, fluidity.) They'd identified a decommissioned military site, a black village. Some big shot architect was on it. By now Oreste was practically waving his imaginary chequebook at them, whoever they were. The guy, who seemed to know a lot about the project while insisting he didn't have much to do with it, said he'd be happy to put Oreste in touch with people, who could put him in touch with other people.

Oreste downed half the pint and it almost came up again. Wicked heartburn. That would be a new one. Could you die of heartburn? He downed the second half of the pint. Motion would help. He got up to go for a piss, he'd have a cheeky vape while he was in there, much safer than standing outside and smoking an actual cig.

The New Berliners were soon in touch. A WhatsApp directed Oreste to an encrypted website where he could find out more. It showed AI-generated pictures of beautiful people doing beautiful things, CGId montages of sunsets over waterside cafés. It wasn't a 'hub,' it was the whole wheel. They told him the plan was fluid, liquid, flexible. They told him they were speculators, predicting futures, then bringing them into being. It was all about flow, they said again, and Oreste loved it again. It was a new form of investment, they told him, deracinated, folds and rhizomes, not hierarchies. Anti-capital capital. 'We're building a cultural capital, using cultural capital.' There was no ownership, stakes weren't held but endlessly deferred, and never present. 'Value isn't inherent. It passes through the chain.' Oreste didn't know what they were talking about but loved it nevertheless. 'We're all companies, multitudes—shells hosting shells,' they told him. 'We could call them shares, but they're not exactly shares, they're tokens, signs, symbols of commitment to the main company from which revenue will generate—the assets fund themselves.' Oreste didn't exactly understand this, but was happy to let himself be persuaded.

The urinals were busy so he went into the stall. The stink in there was vile—not the usual piss/shit odour, but something worse, something far more corporeal and rotting. There was some kind of matter in the bowl. He didn't look too carefully, but knew he couldn't stay there so went back to the urinals hoping no one had entered in the meantime who would suspect him of depositing whatever that was in the toilet. He thought about rolling a real cigarette to smoke so it would at least cover up that stench but didn't want trouble with anyone, so reached for his vape. The urine flow took its time to come (everything was knotted up in there) so meantime he took a deep drag, holding the vape in his left hand. The door slammed and there were voices. He tensed and his stream (now steady) swerved, soaking his shoes. The voices passed so he re-aimed at the bowl and noticed the urine level was already above the P-wave mat, and frothing danger-

DEATH #47

ously. There was a hair in there (pubic?) twitching furiously as the jet of pee taunted it. The hair began to move. Oh god, it wasn't a hair—it was a spider, drowning. The spider made a break for it. Oreste, wondering what kind of spider could live its life semi-submerged in piss in pub urinals while also remembering Death #28 (the bite of an orb-weaver), felt the vape slip from his fingers and saw it splosh into the bowl where his flow was now pouring majestically. Fuck. He didn't have an emergency one and he was down to his last few scraps of tobacco. It had to be saved. He jutted his hand out and grabbed it as quickly as possible, zipped up, then rinsed the vape under the stuttering tap. When he pressed the button it merely fizzled. Fucked.

Oreste had never owned much in his entire life (and what he had owned he had managed to lose or break—vedi the vape he had just drowned). Ownership scared him. Ownership meant anchors, weights, balls and chains, not being able to move from city to city and country to country following the latest job, project, whim, flight, or need of money. This opportunity was perfect: he would trust the New Berliners in the way that two untrustworthy people often trust each other. Oreste visioned the pure rush of liquidity, capital registered as zeros and ones flowing right through him. He wouldn't be an owner but a permanent speculator (a term he liked despite its strange ring from the Italian POV where speculation wasn't about predicting the future, but about looking into mirrors, which—he now realised—should have been an alarm). He would be free of all responsibility while raking in the cash. Well, not cash exactly. The value, the credit, the future. He would be a link in the chain, a man in the middle, passing things on. It's what I do, he'd told himself. There was a minimal stake, they told him. He was in.

He crept out of the toilet and felt the heartburn surge then pass, but now his heart skipped a beat, perhaps two, then started up again at twice the pace, not relenting until it was hammering away like a late-90s drill 'n' bass tune. That was one Oreste hadn't been expecting, a surprise after all—were we repeating already? (Death #16: a collapse at the airport in Miami—fortunately the staff at MIA were well prepared, it was common enough there, and he was soon defibrillated and back on his way.) Today Oreste had drunk four espressos and five pints. He had eaten nothing. He did not blame his diet.

Oreste's desire to be in, however, depended on his own potential contribution, that minimal stake: if not dank greasy cash, then at least some form of capital. Being a man who never cared much for stability, possessions, or—indeed—money itself, mistrusting it as he mistrusted much in this world, Oreste, with 50 on the horizon and without a lira, work ever stuttering and uneven, knew that each death could be the final one. This was his chance to dodge, or—at least—glide through it: there would be money (or if not the cold hard stuff, then at least some form of liquidity) on the other side.

He would have to call in some debts, or favours, trouble being he probably owed people more than they owed him. He'd missed the chance to get in early and buy a Conrad or a Hirst or an Emin while it was cheap, something which could now be safely stashed in a vault, emanating money without doing anything. A bank wouldn't go anywhere near him. There was nothing coming from the family: Oreste's dad had been a bank clerk which meant the stuff passed through his hands but never stayed, and while papà claimed connection to the branch of the family with interests in shipping and politics, the other, richer, mightier Lauros had never popped round for dinner.

DEATH #47

A few deep breaths (inhale, count, exhale) then a brief deliberation about having a second beer to calm that raging heart but prudence won out: he should get out of this pub, he'd been stable too long. Once back pounding the pavement he took a left turn for no better reason than it felt unexpected to him. The clouds up ahead where the street opened out were welling and there was a strange buzz in the air, a literal one, more of a hum, more of a drone. He paused to listen but there was no clarity; he couldn't place it. This was all part of the familiar migraine-like announcement/augury, but it seemed even more intense today. Could a sound kill you? That would be a new one at least. Oreste liked to keep himself informed and had heard about ultrasonic weapons, the Havana Syndrome, ultra-low frequencies, but wasn't the point that they were inaudible? He briefly imagined himself blasted into pieces by sound but realised that would mean having to kill half the street too.

It didn't have to be money that he invested, though. What is your value? they'd asked. What can you offer? Little, thought Oreste. He wondered what he did. What his use value really was. Though he was known as a fixer, and thought of himself as a lister, he knew that in reality he was a disappearer. Oreste had disappeared many times, usually (though not always) following one of his deaths. It was an art; he did it exceptionally well. Here he was now, trying to do it again. E' scomparso they'd say at home: 'has disappeared' euphemised 'has died.' Each time Oreste Lauro died he left and started again until he died again. Each time, after each iteration of the blue light appearing from the void, the hand reaching out to him (always the same; always different), he'd find himself delivered back to the mortal world as ever in need of cash and a place to stay, picking up threads, connecting again, until today, when (due to that 47) he started to fear that this would be the last one.

While he'd been weighing up his potential investment quota there'd been more communications, changes of plan and the direction of the flow. They'd moved on to talk of seasteading, building a floating community, freed from territorial responsibilities. 'We want you in, Oreste,' they'd said. 'Sign a contract. All we need, for now, is your name.'

His name.

His name was Oreste Lauro and he hated it as it had belonged to his mother's brother, a man who had died before Oreste had even been born. He hated it because it was an old man's name, a dead man's name. Names were a curse not a heritage, or an honour, or a tradition. Names were there to get you from the start. By naming something, you killed it. Occasionally, through the course of his many lives he'd thought of changing his names, and had several times done so. (He'd spent a few days at the Venice Biennale as conceptual artist Olmo Nund, a couple of weeks in Vienna as philosopher Franco di Franco, and nearly a month posing as Maurizio Bentivoglio, a louche antiques dealer in Nice, but none had stuck and somehow he'd always slunk back to being Oreste.) His name was his destiny. He was named for a dead man, and he'd died many times.

(Others, more rational, reasonable and perhaps just downright kind than Oreste himself, would again remind him that he hadn't died at all, that he was merely being melodramatic, and that he had merely had one more lucky escape/bizarre accident/brave comeback. In his more lucid times, Oreste had to admit to himself that although he had seen the light and the end of the tunnel, the shadowy figure, the welcoming hand reaching out to him, he had never—as yet—reached out for it or gone into the light. Oreste told himself he was happier in the dark.)

DEATH #47

He took another left, again for no other reason than sheer momentum, noticing the temperature dropping by a degree, two maybe, and noticing himself speeding up wondered if he were in a kind of fugue state, a trance, and that none of this was happening, but no, there was too much physical awareness, his feet hurt, he needed another drink, he could hear (almost feel) that weird noise getting louder. He was most certainly real and (for now) alive.

There was, of course, the logical get out: Why kill a man who owes you money? The dead can't meet their debts. There would be no payback from the other side. The event of his death would register as nothing more than a missing link. Oreste, hoping his pursuer was a logical entity, one with whom he could reason, bargain, negotiate, thought about making a deal when or if they caught up with him. Would they be deal people? Or a deal person? Negotiating was something he could do well. Negotiating was part of his skill set.

Keep walking, keep walking, keep walking. Endless motion, speed, velocity. What was the difference between speed and velocity again? Someone had once told him. Something to do with mass. One or the other had mass. Which one? And which one did he have now, barrelling along the street as though his life depended on it (which it may well have done)? Would it make any difference?

Oreste didn't even know where he was now and slowed to look around. He was now, he thought, on a dérive, being guided by forces greater to and other than his own will. His whole life had been a dérive. That was one of his good thoughts, he should write it down, make a list of all the ways in which his life was like a dérive, and number them. He could call himself an artist and claim his whole life was his work.

The message had come two days ago. 'New circumstances,' they said. 'Your position has changed,' they said. 'Think of it as a fork in the blockchain,' they told him. 'There will be collectors.'

The clouds had moved overhead now. Strange ones. Strato cumulo nimbo something. Not those. Didn't they try to get a new one added recently? What was that?

Oreste wondered if it was the clouds that were making that sound.

Oreste wondered if it was that sound that was producing the clouds.

A chunk of falling masonry narrowly missed his head, hitting the pavement with a sound that was both a crack and a thump, and Oreste scarcely acknowledged it. He might as well let them take him. His existence on this planet was insignificant and meaningless and the place would not miss him were he to depart. He was tired of trying to outrun all these deaths, tired of his body aching and his mind driving him to distraction.

Each death had taken a little more life from him. Not that each death left him diminished exactly, but neither had any of them been learning experiences (not even Death #17, the time when he'd passed over after consuming God-envisioning quantities of LSD).

Oreste slowed until he was scarcely moving. He realised, all at one stroke, that he was nothing but a grubby little schemer, a petty thief, a drunk, a man who never was anything and would amount to even less. The only thing he had learned in his 46 years and counting was that good bars were downstairs and not upstairs, and that one should never drink in a pub with a flat roof, and he had not always acted on possession of that wisdom.

No one even remembered him, most of the time. That Dutch guy with the funny name? (Oreste had been mis-nationed as Dutch many times, and had no idea why and when he asked people they didn't know either.) People didn't believe who he said he was, and perhaps they were right. At least with Sweeney—that odd guy who'd hung around the Sigi Conrad group—people remembered something about him, even if only his name; with Oreste, it was more often a total blank. This was not mere self-pity, nor a Regret hangover, this was not anxiety, this was a bolt of truth as solid as that mass of brick and plaster that had just finely dodged him.

Any point (looked at carefully enough) was only a series of smaller points, all themselves turning: Oreste Lauro's life was an endless spiral array. He had tried to see each death as a turning point, but knew there was no 'point,' only one more node in an ongoing cycle. Oreste thought his deaths may be one long chain, a vast loop or volute ever reaching for its vortex, the definitive status change.

And it was at this epiphanic moment when a black Nissan Offender rounded the corner way too fast for this narrow street and Oreste (even through the tinted windscreen) could only glimpse the coked-up face of the driver and think, no, not this one again, how banal, I've already had this one (Death #4, Rome, 1982) before feeling the wing mirror batter his head and hearing the driver scream (approximately) outofthewayyoufuckingcunt then screech off leaving Oreste foetal on the ground but not dead and not even bleeding (much) and only slightly concussed and (most significantly, and for the second time in only a few minutes) illuminated: his endless attempts to connect had led him to catastrophise the whole fucking thing. This whole thing was nothing more than a self-wrought McGuffin. There was no way anyone wanted to kill him. There was no one coming for him. The universe was supremely indifferent to insignificant Oreste Lauro, and this entire day (birthday or not) was one more much like any other.

He rolled over, sat up, aware of the road grit pressing into his backside and pain in his head and let the air into his lungs. He breathed deeply and (almost) started laughing. He reached for the piss-rusted vape, sucked on it and realised he almost liked its taste of glycerol, burning and toilet water.

And then they appeared. They appeared on the massive LED displays outside the station. They were on the CCTV monitor he could see in the security guard's cabin. They were on the telly in a pub whose window he could see right through. They were on the cracked screen of his phone which had fallen from his pocket.

There were three of them, maybe more. Though he could hardly focus, Oreste knew who they were, and that they knew who he was. They did not become corporeal, nor produce weapons, nor load him into the back of a van.

And this was where it started getting weird for Ore, Ore who was more than used to weird, who positively attracted it, and (usually) felt perfectly at home with weird. This was something very real in a day which had felt decidedly unreal.

'Hello again, Ore,' they said.

He'd seen them before, these strange characters, with their too-perfect faces, their strange hands. He'd heard them speaking, in their flawless English with accents impossible to place. The videos for the New Berlin project, the ones he'd watched and let himself be seduced by. Here they were again.

'What do you want?' he shouted.

'Hello again, Ore,' they said. There was a momentary glitch, like they were buffering.

'What do you want? I've got a piss-soaked vape and enough tobacco to make two crumpled cigarettes. Any use?'

They laughed.

'I've got about six quid in loose change. And a few euros, maybe.' He panicked. 'But I can call in some debts, just give me time.'

'Oh, Ore,' they said. 'We don't want money.' Their voices didn't match their mouths. They were out of sync. Oreste couldn't tell where the sound was coming from.

'You could have my soul, if you wanted it, but I'm not sure it'd be worth much.'

'Don't worry, Ore.'

'We don't want your soul, Ore.'

'We already have everything we need.'

'The only thing we want is this.'

'We want you to think about these faces that you see, this world around you, that pavement on which you are so inelegantly slumped, all those screens around you. They are nothing but your interpretation of them. You can stretch the boundaries of your interpretation, but not in an unlimited fashion, after all, it must be bound by physics. The face must have eyes, nose and a mouth, skin. The pavement has mass, heat, form. The people passing you so pitifully have trajectory, velocity. The question is, how do you interpret these faces, those screens, this very street?'

'Simply, Ore, what is real, and what isn't?'

'That's all, Oreste.'

'Go on, get up. Live again.'

And with that, they were gone.

Oreste's phone started ringing. He picked it up and looked at the screen which (despite being ever more cracked) told him it was Sigi Conrad returning his call. He hit the green button but all he could hear was some kind of static or white noise.

He picked himself up (again) and realised where he was—the train station, that pub, and though it all looked different seen from this angle, this was exactly where he had started, only an hour or two ago, trying to outwalk the inevitable. He'd come in a massive circle. Everything seemed to be going simultaneously faster and slower. The noise which had dogged him all day was roaring. Through the noise, he heard someone call his name and as he turned to find who it was, he looked up and saw how heavy, how low the clouds were, and then (at a probability of somewhere between ten million or three thousand to one) he was hit by a bolt of lightning.

COMMISSION

Ryan Vaunt built tiny models of rooms, or sometimes entire buildings, to scale, out of cardboard, then painted them, then photographed the models he'd made, and then painted over the photographs he'd taken of the models.

'It seems like you're taking the long way round.'

'I don't know any other way to get there.'

'Couldn't you just, like, paint the thing in the first place?'

'No. I couldn't.'

Jen was patient with him. 'It's all about process,' he told her. 'The exchange between one form of representation and another.' And she nodded, but he was never sure she actually got it.

Ryan woke early in the mornings to make the best of his time before the world kicked in. On good days he'd be untroubled and find his concentration accentuated by the thick peace of the as yet unbroken promise of morning; bad ones would see him stymied before he'd even started. He told himself this was the best time for working but spent most of it looking at the internet, reading the news, checking social media, practically inviting the world to do its worst. Around 8 he'd make coffee for Jen and take it through to her. Jen always slept badly, so it was the least he could do. If she was working from home then he'd get on his bike and head off to the studio space he rented. If she was out at the office then he'd tell her that was what he was going to do, and sometimes actually do it.

He had a semi-regular gig taking pictures of imported food products (tinned Portuguese sardines, jars of Gordal olives, Korean black noodles) for the website of an upscale online deli, but he hadn't heard from them for a while. There was still some money from the last job but it was dwindling.

'I make enough to support us both,' Jen said, but she didn't, and they both knew it.

Some days Ryan would shell out the four quid for a flat white and spend the morning in a café where he'd at least see people, if not actually speak to any of them. He'd lost all his friends. It had been the pandemic, he thought. They'd drifted, got lost in their own lives and never really got back on track. Him and Jen moving out of town hadn't helped. But sitting there, trying to inhale the last bit of cold foam at the bottom of the cup, he knew the great dwindling had started long before that. There'd been that thing with Sigi Conrad, and nothing had been quite right since then. Thing was, his friends had also formed his professional network, and without them there were no contacts either. Everything was falling away.

So, empty cup in hand, feeling guilty about not working when he could have been, a DM from Kasha Hocket-Baily, someone he'd known years ago and never much liked, cheered him far more than it ought to have done.

'Hey Ryan! You still there? It's been a while!'

He didn't get back to her immediately, thinking he should take his time and compose something witty and smart but which would start a conversation, at least. He googled her to see what she was up to these days. He wondered where 'there' was, and indeed if he was still 'there.'

'Good to hear from you! It *has* been a whole! How are you doing?'

It had taken him nearly an hour to come up with that, and there was a typo, too.

'Sorry—'while'! Though it's been a whole long time, too!'

God that made him look like an idiot. His other gambit, to question the deictic or referential meaning of the word 'there' would have been better, though he well knew that was the kind of thing that made people think he was odd. She was some kind of consultant now, too.

'Lol! Are you still doing portraits?'

He wasn't, not after everything that had happened. Portraits had been Ryan's thing, what he'd specialised in, what he'd presented for his degree show (where, he thought, he'd first met Kasha), then managed to sell a few of, and in turn ended up being commissioned to do. Inspired (perhaps a little too much, some had noted) by Gerhard Richter, he'd worked with photographs, not necessarily posed ones, any he could find in the public domain, then painted over them. He called them 'erasure portraits' and tried to brand his practice as 'aporetic painting,' but when the commissions had started to come in he often found himself being gently asked to ease up a bit on the erasure and aporia. Wealthy clients liked to see themselves, not their likenesses being blotted out by swathes of grey paint. He'd obeyed the market then fallen foul to it after 2008 when the commissions had dried up. After that he'd had the call from Sigi Conrad and ended up part of her underpaid, overworked and ill-credited team, until everything that happened there and it all going south, too. Then the pandemic hit and Ryan had decided he never wanted anything to do with the human again, and turned to architecture, and space, and pure form. Which was what he wanted, but had led him to where he was today, avoiding painting pictures of photos of models that he himself had made, taking photos of cans of over-priced Lebanese baked beans for money, sponging off his long-suffering wife.

'Yes,' he wrote back. 'I am. Portraits. That's what I do.'

A week later he was sitting in the bar of a hotel that was far too expensive for him. He was never at ease in a place like this, always waiting for some shiny-shoed flunkey to come up to him and say, 'Excuse me Sir, I think there's been a mistake—I'm afraid you're northern and working class, so I'll have to ask you to leave.' But he was damned if he wasn't going to take them for a proper martini before they turfed him out.

'Thanks for giving up your time with us, Tyrone.' There were three of them; they all had the same haircut. One had a Filofax (a Filofax! How long was it since he'd seen one of those?), the others improbably thin phones. They wore dark-grey suits, well cut and well fitting, and lanyards dangled around their necks.

'It's a pleasure,' he said. 'Thanks for considering me, but I'm Ryan, not Tyrone.'

'Ryan,' said the woman, pausing over the first syllable. 'Sure. Glad we sorted that.'

'We spoke to your agent.'

'My agent?' Ryan didn't have an agent.

'Kasha?'

'Oh, of course. Sure, she's not really my'

'She sent us over some of your work. We liked it.'

'That's great.' Ryan hoped he wasn't going to have to give Kasha 20 percent or whatever the rate was now. 'Anything in particular?'

One of the men checked his phone.

'I've got something from the Kunstkeller in Berlin.' The other man nodded.

'And Spazio Otto in Turin.'

'I liked the Tobacco Factory ones, New York.'

Ryan had never shown in any of those places, but he was past caring.

'OK, great.'

'Great.'

'So, Bryan, I'm not sure how far up to scratch you are with where we're at.'

Ryan knew she'd said 'Bryan' with a y. He could just tell.

'Ryan. Ryan.'

'Ha! Sure—sorry! I obviously need more coffee!'

'Too much coffee, more like!' said one of the men. They all laughed, apart from Ryan who looked down at the martini he'd ordered.

'Ryan!'

'Yep. That's me.'

'Ryan Ryan Ryan.'

'Sure.'

'We like what you do, Ryan.'

'We do.'

'We really do.'

Ryan realised they didn't have a clue who he was, but that had been pretty standard in his experience.

'You've worked with a number of HNWIs before, right? You'll know they can be demanding sometimes.' Luckily, he had, and didn't even have to ask about the initialism. 'Can you tell us about a difficult situation you've faced in your professional career, and how you approached it?' Ryan felt like he'd walked into a job interview, which, of course, this was.

'Well, uh . . . I had one client who had very little time, so we made the step to working from photographs, rather than sittings.'

'Photographs?'

'Yeah.'

'Like you didn't paint him, you took a photograph of him?' They all looked concerned.

'No, I made a painting based on the photographs. It worked well.'

'Oh.'

'OK.'

'Anders is great, though.'

'Oh yeah.'

'He's a pussycat, really.'

'Once he likes you, sure.'

'A pussycat.'

'He'll like you, I'm sure.'

'Next up—can you tell us about your process, Ryan?'

'I like to work from photographs.'

'Hm.'

'Time scale, what are we looking at? I mean, does he have to sit still for hours and hours?'

'Might be tricky.'

'Very.'

'He's a busy man.'

'Well,' said Ryan, 'as I said, I like to work from photographs.'

'That's interesting.'

'Very.'

'Trouble is, Anders doesn't like having his picture taken.'

'I work from photographs,' said Ryan.

'Interesting.'

'Can we find a work round here? Is there one?'
'We could get Zinnia on board?'
'Oh, she's in.'
'She is?'
'Totally.'
'Phew!' The woman mimed wiping her forehead with noted exaggeration. 'Zinny's the daughter,' she explained. 'She's'
'Demanding.'
'Ha! Sure. Demanding. Right.'
'She'll be fine.'
'Sure.'
'It's art. She's all about art!'
'She loves it.'
'Zinnia Laerp? You'll know her.'
'She's big on Insta.'
'TikTok.'
'Podcasts. She has a podcast. Have you heard her podcast?'
'I'm afraid I haven't, no,' said Ryan.
'You should check out her podcast.'
'I'll try,' said Ryan.
'Sooooo . . . do we want to talk numbers? Is it too soon?'
'Or is that best left to your agent?'
'That's fine,' said Ryan, not wanting Kasha to have anything to do with it. 'Let's talk numbers.'
'You're OK to talk numbers?'
'I'm OK to talk numbers.'
'That's great.'
'Great.'

'An artist who talks numbers!'

'Great.'

'Anders'll like that!'

'We have a ballpark figure,' said the woman, and nodded to the man with the Filofax who tore a sheet from the notebook, folded it and handed it to Ryan.

'Ballpark,' he said.

Ryan unfolded it, looked at the number and said yes, and they looked surprised but wanted to arrange a preliminary sitting right away.

'Have you got a window?'

'Can we contract you?'

On the way out, Ryan knew he should have asked for more.

TWO MONTHS LATER HE WAS back in a different hotel, this time in the top-floor suite rather than the bar. At least, Ryan thought it was a hotel: it was one of those places that was so discreet it didn't have a sign, not even the smallest brass plaque by the door. He wasn't sure it was the top floor, either—it was some secret floor above the top floor that he'd had to take a special lift to reach. Nor was he even sure which part of the city he'd come to: somewhere in Mayfair or Belgravia, that strange hinterland of central London, one skirted by most mortals, a place that had always sounded like a different country to him—Mayfair and Belgravia, a hermit kingdom hiding in the city, untouched by time or financial regulation.

Having spent the last five years in jogging bottoms and shapeless jumpers, Ryan had forgotten how to behave in such circumstances. He'd decided on the black rollneck sweater rather than the denim workshirt, which, paired with black jeans, he'd thought would still pass as the standard artist's uniform and while it had seen him waved in promptly enough, ushered into the magic elevator, then shown a chair in the corner of the suite which seemed to cover the whole floor, it now seemed to be rendering him invisible.

He sat there for ages.

The lift door opened and Ryan looked over and a small huddle of people, all dressed in black, came out and didn't look at him before disappearing. He could hear a low hum of conversation, the occasional laugh, but nothing more.

'Can I get you anything, Mr Vaunt?' asked a sharp young man in a sharper black suit, and Ryan said, 'Yes, tea please, milk no sugar,' and the man nodded with a vague air of disappointment, and didn't come back. At least they'd got his name right this time.

Three times, maybe four, the lift arrived, disgorged another black suit, then left.

Ages, he sat there.

No one took any notice.

After an hour, maybe two, maybe three, without warning, the suits all appeared again, congregating around the lift door like a flurry of jackdaws. Ryan almost expected flashbulbs when the door opened, but there were none, only a more intense hum, the sound of people who had a task determinedly doing it. It was like watching a clockwork mechanism spring into action. They fell into groups, then a line, as coffee appeared, phones were checked, iPads were prodded and messages passed back and forth. Ryan couldn't actually see who was at the centre of this mechanism, but knew it had to be his man.

He stood up, cleared his throat and tried to pick someone he could approach, but before he'd settled on anyone they swarmed into a large room and sliding doors pulled shut. As rapidly as they'd arrived, they disappeared. Ryan sat down again. He knew what it was that was making him anxious: that feeling of simultaneously loathing these people, utterly despising them, mixed with his urgent desire to impress them.

The sharp man passed by again and said, 'Tea! I'll be right with you,' and then vanished.

More time.

Eventually the doors slid back and the flurry re-emerged, each component heading with intent in a different direction. A small knot persisted at its centre, grouped around a table. One of them looked round at him, turned back, head lowered. There was some muttering. Two heads popped up, turned to him, returned, muttered.

Five minutes later one of them moved and came over to him, leaving the others undisturbed.

'You're the artist guy, right?'

'Yes, that's right. Ryan Vaunt.'

'Can you give us five?'

'Sure. No problem.'

Jesus, Ryan was bored. Not anything else, just bored. He'd been here hours now and not one of these fucks had taken the slightest bit of notice of him. Actually, no, not just bored, frustrated, too, and fucking angry. He'd done enough of these things back in the day to know not to expect an open-arms welcome, but this was the worst, this kind of petty power-gaming, letting him know they knew he was there then making him wait. He needed to get up and say something, or—better yet—just go, leave.

'Sorry Ryan. Can you give us another five?'

'Oh, sure. No problem.'

It was inescapable, this double bind. He'd felt it so often, and always gave in. Ten minutes later, maybe more, the lift door opened again and this time someone not wearing black walked out. She was so not wearing black that she was wearing yellow, entirely, a jumpsuit, shiny lace-up boots, huge woollen scarf all in a shade of yellow so yellow it dazzled. Ryan wondered if there could be any colour less black than yellow. White was pretty much counter-black, another version of it, but yellow? Yellow had to be a statement, but Ryan had no idea what it was stating.

The woman sat down next to him and gave him a look. It was a look Ryan knew, one he'd been given before but always from the kind of men who would describe themselves as 'alphas,' not the quick up-and-down measuring he occasionally got from highly assured women, but a proper male eye-to-eye challenge, a bit of a smile, a hint of threat to put him in his place, a suggestion that if-you-play-your-cards-right-I-might-even-let-you-be-my-bitch. He'd never had that from a woman before.

'Where's your stuff?' she asked. At least someone knew who he was. He picked up his bag and took out the Nikon D850. It was the flashiest thing he had.

'That it? He won't like that.'

'To be honest, I was going to use my phone.'

'You'll need more.'

'I only need a few pictures. I can work from those. I thought he'd be pressed for time.'

She paused and looked as if she had something more important to be doing, then shouted, 'Pappy! Pappy!'

Ryan looked around for the small dog that she was, surely, summoning, but instead the tight circle of bodies around the table parted, offering Ryan and the woman a perfect view of what lay at its centre.

A man with a thick head of floppy silver-grey hair and a slightly over-pronounced jawline. Very pale skin, thin lips and a long nose. Expensive glasses behind which tiny blue eyes flicked. The clothes were discreetly well-cut, a burgundy quarter zip with the collar of a crisp white shirt protruding, a dark-blue jacket thrown over the back of his chair. While Ryan hadn't thought much about who he would be painting, he had vaguely expected one of the usuals—a titan of industry playing the part, cigar-chomping jaws and a jokey baseball cap, or an ostentatious tie with a suit that was too shiny, usually a fair amount of physical heft, whether bulked-up muscle or fat. This man looked like the deputy head teacher of a pricy independent school, the person responsible for keeping the accounts and raising funds, or the paterfamilias in a stock photo of a white family having a festive brunch.

'Pappy!' she said again, and stood up. And then, with a grand gesture, 'This is my father, Anders Laerp.'

Ryan was trying to catch the right pronunciation of that surname but was distracted by the dart of the blue eyes which checked Ryan with what he perceived as the tiniest note of panic before they rapidly swivelled back to the daughter.

'This is Ryan Vaunt,' she said. 'He's an important artist. He's come to paint your picture.' The eyes fell again and the man, having been reminded of something he'd been trying to forget, sighed then immediately recomposed himself, stood up and extended his hand. The process was more like unfolding, as Ryan realised that Laerp was at least six feet four with arms nearly as long.

'I hope we haven't kept him waiting,' he said, his voice reedy, an emission of air from deep down passing through his mouth which scarcely moved. 'I could hardly see him there.'

'Don't be rude, Pappy,' said Zinnia.

'I'm never rude, darling. Where are all his artist things?'

'Artist things?'

'Paint. Brushes. Artist things.'

'He's just going to take some pictures today, Pappy.'

'No. No pictures. You know about the pictures. I don't like pictures.'

'Are you worried he'll steal your soul, Pappy? Not much chance of that, is there? You don't have one.'

'No pictures.'

'It doesn't hurt. And it'll take up less of your time.'

'I'm very busy right now,' he said, twitching as he spoke, glaring at Ryan's camera as though it were a weapon. Ryan felt like a dentist with a phobic patient.

'Would you be able to move a little toward the window, Mr Laerp?'

'Laerp,' he replied, with a diphthong so slightly different from the one Ryan had essayed.

'Sorry, yes,' said Ryan, 'Mr Laerp,' still not convincing himself. 'By the window? The light is better there.' Laerp responded by fluttering a long hand at the end of his long arm and almost whispering.

'No, no, no. I'm quite comfortable here.' It didn't really matter. Using the big Nikon the available light was enough, though Ryan knew he'd get more of what he really wanted from his phone. He moved around the room to get Laerp from a few different angles and the man winced throughout. A scarce five minutes passed before he said, 'Enough now,' and they were done.

'Is that it? Is that all?' he heard him ask his daughter as the doors closed behind Ryan and the flock reappeared and regrouped around him, briefly, asking him to sign a flurry of papers—waivers, NDAs, other stuff he didn't know but hoped guaranteed him some money—then Zinnia was ushering him back to the lift.

'You weren't the one we wanted, you know.'

'Thanks,' said Ryan.

'I've seen some of your stuff. I didn't like it. But I think we can work together.'

The lift doors closed. It wasn't the clothes that made her stand out, thought Ryan. It was her face. It looked like it was already a photograph.

LATER THAT EVENING, RYAN WAS looking through the pictures he'd taken. He shifted the filters, contrasts, settings, but nothing worked. That man, all that height, the centre of gravity for all those people, and there was no presence at all. Ryan couldn't understand it, there was light, and lines and shades which defined the light, but it was as if the man wasn't there.

'How do you mean "not there"?' asked Jen.

'I don't know really. Come and have a look.' Jen leaned over his shoulder and squinted at the screen.

'I see what you mean,' she said.

'He's both immense, and utterly negligible.'

'What was his name again?'

'Laerp. Anders Laerp.'

'What?'

'Laerp. I think. I'm still not sure how to pronounce it.'

'Never heard of him. Is that Dutch or something? Finnish?'
'I don't know. They sounded English. The daughter did, at least. Or, a bit American. Transatlantic. Difficult to place. He didn't speak much.'
'I can't believe you haven't googled him.'
'You know how it is. I want the person. Not their reputation.'
'Is that "ea" or "ae"?'
'Ae, I think.'
'Hmm. You maybe should've done some research. Turns out he's one of the richest men in the world.'
'You're shitting me.'
'Well,' said Jen, hunched over her laptop, 'it's always difficult to calculate these things. But he's probably up there.'
'I knew I should have asked for more.'
'CEO of the biggest global corporation you've never heard of,' she said. 'Only, it's not one corporation, it seems to be loads of them. I'm not quite sure I get exactly what it is that they do.'
'Do I need to know this?' Ryan asked.
'Don't be disingenuous. You know what they want. They want you to paint the business, not the man.'
'A bit of both, maybe.'
'It's a corporate commission, right? Corporate. The body. The man. The embodiment of the company.'
'Are there any pictures of him?'
'No. None that I can find, anyway.'
'So who is he?'
'That I can't tell you. But there is some stuff on what he does.'
'Go on then.'

'They're Norwegian. Or they were, at least. That goes back a while. They started out making rope, for ships. And string. They were big in string.'

'He's a string billionaire?'

'Is that possible? I think it was the rope that might have made them more, but who knows? Rigging, for ships. All kinds.'

'Not so much call for that now, is there?'

'Pretty niche, I'd think. But that's not it—seems they diversified a long time back. From rope, on to cables—electric cables, around the end of the 19th century, boom time. Power cables. Then telegraph ones. They were going up everywhere then.'

'Cables. Is that it? Is that where I've seen the name? I never look, really.' Something about the name came back to him, though—a logo perhaps, the a and the e coiling around each other.

'Mining too. Copper.'

'I suppose they needed something to make those cables out of. Own everything, from the bowels of the earth to everything above it.'

'They owned a clothing manufacturer, too.'

'String vests?'

'No, rainproof, weatherproof stuff. Galvanised clothing. Rubber-coated. Then found the clothes they made strong enough for Norwegian winters made perfect covers for the miles of undersea cables they were laying. It all came together.' She scrolled down the page a little more, clicked on a link, then another. 'Goes a bit quiet during the Second World War, mind. Not sure what went on then. But they soon reappear after, with some nice fat military contracts, it seems. Then on from there, they seemed to slowly devour everything. Shipping.'

'Shipping?'

'They needed specially fitted ships to transport the massive reels of cable they were sending all over the world, and decided that it was better to build their own rather than have some other company have to refit. They own a shipping line, too, now.'

'Maybe we'll get a cruise out of it.'

'Not sure they do those, mind. Seems to be mostly commercial freight.'

'Do we still need cables? Isn't everything virtual now?'

'I'm not sure about that, but I see what you mean, and that's where it gets baffling. I'm looking at what they do now, and like I say, I'm not really sure I understand it all.'

'Let me have a look.'

Jen passed Ryan her laptop.

'"Our dynamic teams of engineers, technologists, scientists and creatives,"' he read out, '"collaborate across disciplines to design flexible solutions to meet customer needs; delivering agility, creativity and protectivity where others can't.

'"We are now complementing core products,"' he read, '"with robust, high-performance links to the AI-powered Internet of Things, driving tracking and connectivity with tags and devices that enable business-critical processes. '"We establish reliable, connected environments,"' he read, '"where end-to-end asset management, in-process visibility and real-time control, right down to the individual level, is now a cost-effective reality."'

'I'm not sure I understand that one,' said Jen.

'"Drone logistics and image automation across multiple platforms, infrastructures, and networks. We change perceptions. We arrange relations. As fragile realities are continually exposed to risk environments, we work with the limits of what can be mapped and measured, the seen, the unseen, and the unforeseen."'

'That is, actually, beautiful,' said Jen.

'"Durable. Versatile. Reliable,"' he went on. '"Asset lifecycle,"' he read. '"Operational efficiency across the supply chain. AI-powered deployable system-agnostic T&E capabilities. Force generation. Rapidly evolving threat landscape. A unique blend of operational ethos, technical capability and a collaborative mindset."'Fuck,' he said. 'They're arms dealers, aren't they?'

'Not dealers,' said Jen. 'Manufacturers?'

'Is that better?'

'I don't know. Maybe?'

Ryan's phone pinged. Zinnia.

'Sorry about how it went today. There's a story. I'll tell you.' They agreed to set up another meeting. 'Somewhere less formal,' she wrote. 'We'll send a car. Bring artist stuff.'

A WEEK LATER RYAN WAS sitting in the back of a BMW Intimidator as large and as black as he'd expected it, though he hadn't expected to find Zinnia Laerp, this time wearing an ankle-length purple dress as though some kind of pre-Raphaelite goth milkmaid, already there.

'So what's the story?' he asked her.

'Story?'

'You said there was a story?'

'Oh no. No story. That's just how he is.'

'There's a story as to why someone "just is."'

'Is there? I'm not sure. He doesn't like having his picture taken, that's all.'

'No traumatic incident involving a camera?'

'Not as far as I know. Pappy was born like that.'

'Like what?'

'Like he is.'

'Will he be better today?'

'I doubt it.'

'Will he be busy?'

'Pappy's always busy. We make sure of that. I mean, he doesn't actually do very much these days. We invent little tasks and projects and problems to make him think that he's still in charge.'

'Who's really in charge?'

'To tell the truth, I have absolutely no idea.'

They drove for ages. Ryan didn't know where he was.

'I brought artist stuff.' Ryan had managed to borrow an easel from someone at the studios. He thought that would qualify.

'So I see.' He planned on setting it up then ignoring it. He'd actually considered bringing a smock and a fucking beret. Zinnia would probably have appreciated that.

'Where's the picture going, anyway? I mean, once I've finished it.'

'The plan was for the new HQ. But then we ditched that.'

'The plan?'

'No, the HQ. We don't need buildings anymore.' The car pulled up into the driveway of a large house. 'Apart from this one, perhaps.'

'Where are we?'

'Home. One of them, anyway.'

GROUND FLOOR, TOWARD THE BACK of the house, a room the size of a school gym, huge windows giving out onto an endless garden. Mostly empty apart from a utilitarian sofa and a small desk in the corner. This wasn't the rich-chic Ryan had expected, Empire furniture and every possible surface gilded, but looked more like it was inhabited by a student who couldn't afford it, or as though it was waiting for someone to move in. Apart from the walls—the walls were covered in maps, every available inch, ceiling-to-floor: sea charts, star charts, A–Z streetfinders and geological maps. Some were standard OS, others looked like they'd been rescued from a fake English pub, others still seemed genuinely ancient and would be better housed in a dusty corner of the Bodleian or the British Library. It took Ryan, engaged in admiring this cartographical wallpaper, some time to notice Anders Laerp, already in the room, sitting in the corner, his back to the light. His height was all still there but he seemed reduced, hunched over a desk too small for his frame.

Someone asked Ryan where he wanted the easel; Zinnia told them where to put it. Ryan was, at least, grateful he'd been acknowledged this time.

'What's with all the maps?'

'They're so ugly, aren't they? But it's a family thing. Ask him.' She gestured towards the angled shadow in the corner, her father. 'It'll give you something to talk about.'

Ryan worried about how he was to pass the morning. He normally took a few photographs, or made a model, and then spent any time with canvas deeply alone, inconsiderate of time. He'd have to take pictures very discreetly while pretending to be painting, and wasn't sure he knew how to do that.

'OK boys, I'll leave you to it. Play nicely.'

'Has he learned how to pronounce our name yet?' asked Anders but Zinnia had already left. Ryan was sure he felt the temperature fall. The room seemed vastly empty, and dark despite the light through the windows.

'My daughter,' said Laerp, his voice an echo with no source. 'Do you know what she told me? She told me that I have no soul.'

Ryan looked at him intently. Laerp flinched. A man who was used to being listened to but did not like being observed.

'And is she right, Mr Laerp?' Once he'd spoken, Laerp still held the room's focus, the same as he had the last time they'd met in the hotel, but this time he wasn't the centre of gravity, the still point around which everything turned, but a tiny leak in space. You'd have to look to find it, but there it was, the point through which everything escaped.

'I don't know. Who am I to say? What is a soul, anyway? I'm a businessman, not an intellectual, not an artist.' The last comment felt like a barb, which only served to embolden Ryan.

'So if I were to paint your soul, Mr Laerp, what would it look like?'

'That's your job. Not mine. Will this take long?'

Ryan busied himself making marks on the paper, having decided to do some large-scale drawings from which he could work. He knew that Laerp would have preferred a canvas, paints, but there was only so far Ryan could pretend. Painting, for Ryan, had to be done alone, unobserved.

Apart from the sound of his pencils on the paper and Laerp's breathing (heavy, reedy, a dry wheeze), the room was silent. The silence curled around them both, spread itself over the walls and blocked any escape routes. Ryan wondered if the room was soundproofed. Silence, he thought, was a luxury for the rich. Most people went through their days blocking sound out or covering it up in some way or another. This silence, unexpected, uneasy, made him feel ill.

'So, could you tell me about a typical working day, Mr Laerp?'

'What?'

'Your typical day. I'd like to get a sense of you and your work.'

'I can't reveal any confidential information.'

'No, of course not. I just mean...' Ryan trailed off. He didn't really know what he meant, but Laerp had a speech ready.

'I direct strategic development and practice management. I work towards high-quality design which brings added value,' he said. 'We harness passion, knowledge and expertise to evolve powerful and pragmatic solutions and I inform and direct the ambition and quality of our work.' He went on, scarcely pausing. 'I develop strategy, overseeing legacy, ensuring quality and continuation, while always searching for new possibilities. We are building, developing and ensuring sustainable resilience.'

'I see,' said Ryan, and in his way, he did. Laerp had nothing more to say and the silence fell again.

'You like maps?' asked Ryan. Laerp didn't know what he was talking about. Ryan gestured to the walls. 'Aren't these yours?'

'Oh no. My father's. He wasn't interested in much, my father, apart from his mines, and his businesses, and his beard. He had a big beard, I remember. But he collected maps. I don't know why. He wanted to see how much he owned, I think. But they wouldn't show him—so he bought more. But they don't, they don't show everything. I can't see anything in them.'

'You don't think they're beautiful in themselves?'

'Beautiful? No. Just lines. And some colours.'

'What do you think is beautiful?' Laerp's eyes turned to meet Ryan's for the first time. The man was nonplussed. He'd never been asked a question like that before.

'Beautiful? I don't know.' He moved in his chair, the lengthy mass of him, with difficulty. 'Numbers,' he said. 'I like numbers. They move around on screens. They never get angry with you.'

'And are they beautiful?'

'I don't know. I let my daughter worry about such things. It's not important.' Ryan knew other portrait painters who had a patter, like a hairdresser or a shrink, some way of getting the sitter to relax and open up. It was something he had never perfected, and regretted it deeply now. A silence fell again, broken when Laerp said, 'Cables.'

'Cables?' asked Ryan.

'Yes. They are beautiful things,' he said. 'That's what I do. I make cables. I think they are beautiful. You should see them sometime. Ask my daughter.'

'Aren't they vanishing, cables? Isn't everything in the aether now, all virtual? Wireless signals and all that?'

'Of course not. You can't see them, but they're there. We have the world linked, connected, tied together. Nothing is virtual that is not also real.' He kicked the table in front of him. 'See that. Not virtual. It's a table. You can't have a virtual table. We need cables like we need tables.' Ryan wasn't quite sure what he meant, but didn't want to ask for fear of upsetting him. 'That would be a good map,' he went on. 'A map showing all the cables across the world. That would be something. That's the kind of thing you artists do now, isn't it? That's something you should do. Though we'd never tell you, of course. Wouldn't tell you where they all are.' He coughed a dry heave which Ryan thought must have been a laugh, or the closest to it this man would ever get.

Silence resettled, the light was going already and it wasn't even lunchtime yet.

Ryan stood back and looked at what he had so far. There was nothing: just lines. There was the simple caricature of the man: the chin, the nose, the glasses, the hair, the height, but it didn't amount to anything looking human. Marks on paper, nothing more.

Laerp pulled a phone out of his pocket. Light from its screen threw him into relief, as if he were materialising, finally, this contradiction between matter and nothingness. He moved, his long thin finger jabbing at the screen. Ryan thought he'd be looking at his money, both real and virtual, migrating across the screen, doing whatever money did. It was this, nothing more, which animated him. Here, Ryan thought, sat a man whose only happiness had been found hunched at a desk late into the night, poring over Excel spreadsheets, sacking workers and fiddling his taxes.

Ryan pulled up a new sheet, began again, but this time the lines and shades made even less sense. He was doodling to pass the time until he could reasonably quit, nothing more. Ryan began to feel almost giddy, as if slowly falling. The thick silence seemed to have been switched off and a sound, some kind of white noise, as if the room's natural ambient hum had been turned up to maximum volume, buzzed in his ears. He could feel himself disappearing. The magnificent nullity of Laerp's questionable soul started taking him over. This wouldn't be one of his erasure pictures. This would be him having to put something where there was nothing.

He breathed deeply, poured himself a glass of water, breathed again, then took out his own phone and texted Jen.

'I thought I knew what the void was. But then I met Anders Laerp.'

'Don't stare at him for too long,' she wrote back.

An hour later, as he walked out, he stole a glimpse at Laerp's phone screen. Laerp was playing Candy Crush.

'YOU SHOULD HAVE ASKED HIM more questions,' said Jen, later. 'It sounded like he was almost opening up there.'

'The maps thing, you mean? The cables?'

'Yeah. Or his dad's beard.'

'I don't know how to talk to people like that. What can you ask them?'

'What did you have for breakfast? Which is your favourite pair of socks? Tea or coffee? Cats or dogs? Did you get on better with your mum or your dad? Do you know any jokes? Were you ever happy, I mean really, really happy? Who do you love? Why cables? Why anything? Just why? What's it all about, Mr Laerp? Do you fear the void, Mr Laerp? Do we have a soul? What does your soul look like?'

'I actually did ask him that one.'

'What did he say?'

'He didn't reply.'

'You should have insisted.'

'You can't insist with people like that.'

'Were you afraid of him?'

'Terrified.'

'Really?'

'No, I suppose not. Just bored. Terrifyingly bored. I had some kind of a funny turn.'

'How do you mean?'

'I felt like I was vanishing.'

'Weird.'

'Eerie.'

'So what are you going to do now?'

'I don't know.'

They were supposed to have another sitting the next week, but no one had mentioned it on the way out nor on the drive back into the city (where, mercifully, Zinnia hadn't accompanied him) and Ryan half-hoped it would be quietly forgotten.

The money, though.

The next morning Ryan sat at their breakfast table looking at the best-before date on the carton of milk, realising it was long past, and remembered the figure scribbled on the piece of paper and knew it would be enough to change his and Jen's lives, if not forever, then at least for a good while. His phone rang. He hoped it would be one of the flunkeys but it was Zinnia.

'What went wrong?' Ryan knew, somehow, that she was dressed from head to toe in something cerise, or mauve, or indigo, one of those colours he'd always thought awkward, if not plain wrong.

'Nothing.'

'Pappy said you walked out.'

'Only when I'd finished.'

'Finished? So have you got something for us?'

'Not yet, no.'

'Then you haven't finished, have you?'

'Well, I suppose not, no. I mean, I was finished with him. I got enough. Probably.'

'Probably? For fuck's sake Ryan, we picked you because you're supposed to have experience working with people like Pappy. He can't adjust his schedule according to your whims. He's a very busy man.'

'Is he, though?'

'Busier than you, evidently.'

'I'm working on it,' Ryan lied, and again somehow knew that Zinnia knew he was lying.

'You weren't our first choice, you know.'

'You told me that.'

'But after they dropped out, and a couple of others, we figured you'd be capable, at least.'

'Thanks.'

'So, I'll ask again: What is the problem? God knows we're paying you enough for it to be solved.'

'There isn't a problem.'

'What is it?'

'He doesn't really photograph well.'

'We told you that.'

'I mean, almost literally, he just doesn't appear.'

'Are you telling me my father is a vampire?'

'And the drawings I made—they're just lines.'

'That's what drawings are, Ryan. Listen, I have one of the most successful podcasts on the contemporary scene. Nearly half a million subscribers. I know art. And, I'm sorry, but I thought I was talking to an artist here.'

'You are.'

'Then get arting or whatever it is that you do. And learn how to pronounce the name properly!'

Ryan spent the next few hours arting, trying to pull something together from the few pictures he'd taken and the sketches he'd made. He knew they wouldn't like it whatever he managed to produce.

Some time that afternoon Zinnia was in touch again. 'Sorry about this morning,' she wrote. 'I was having a bad one.' Ryan thought she might have changed her outfit. 'I think the problem is that you don't have him in motion,' she went on. 'We're all about motion. You need to see him actually working, moving. Get some of his energy.' Ryan was actually afraid of Laerp's energy. 'I'll fix it for you to come to an event next week. There's some security stuff to sort out, but I'll get that cleared. How does that sound?'

'That sounds great,' Ryan replied, hoping she wouldn't be able to detect him lying via text message.

THE CAR CAME FOR HIM, a Mercedes Threatener this time, as large and black as always but thankfully not containing Zinnia, and took him to some huge hangar on the edge of the city. There were security cordons, police, hi-vis jackets and walkie talkies. They gave him a lanyard bearing his picture and a QR code. He wondered where they'd got the picture from—it was one he hadn't even seen before. He had to go through an x-ray machine and have a pat down. They took his phone and put it in a baggy and then put the baggy in a locker. Where the fuck was he? He shouldn't be so blithe about stuff like this, he knew. He should've asked Jen to check it out. She probably had. He thought about texting her then realised he didn't have his phone.

Zinnia, inevitably, stood in the entrance hall, wearing a parachute silk emerald dress, which looked more like a parachute than a dress, with the most hideous pair of white moonboot trainers Ryan had ever seen. They made her about six feet tall and even more terrifying than usual despite the fact she didn't seem to be able to walk in them.

'Pappy's already in. I'll take you to him. He won't have much time to talk, but that's OK with you, isn't it?' Ryan nodded.

In his time, Ryan had been to Documenta, Frieze, Frieze Masters, Art Basel, Art Basel Miami, TEFAF, ARCO, FIAC, the lot. At first, he thought this was one of those: the same spacious hangar, striplights obscured by impressively large booths with bouffant sofas, the same suits, frocks, shiny shoes and high heels, their wearers all looking over their interlocutors' shoulders in case anyone more useful were to walk by. Brittle tension. The smell, sound and taste of money.

And yet. The sumptuous unease here was broken by the copious booze being passed around. There was always plenty of it at any art fair, sure, but not this much, and not at 11 in the morning. The suits and gowns were Loro Piana and Bottega Veneta, not Vampire's Wife and Agnès B. More than that, they were broken up by a disturbing number of military dress uniforms, little wizened old men or sagging beefcakes weighed down by gold braiding and epaulettes. The male staff at the display stands, so discreet as to be almost invisible, were flanked by what Ryan could only describe as dolly birds—the phrase, like the women, seemed to belong to another age: shiny blondes and brunettes, few older than 20, pneumatic boobs held back by near-vertical necklines.

Zinnia ushered him through the hall, moving quickly and talking incessantly, not letting him pause until she deposited him by the side of a military truck. On its flatbed, a string quartet were playing a piece Ryan vaguely recognised. It was something modern, not what he'd have expected, but he couldn't place it. The incongruence made him think that, perhaps, this was an art fair after all. He was sure he'd seen something like it at the Armory Show, the one time he'd been.

One of the exhibitors, polished, earnest and grey-suited, was giving his spiel to two men who Ryan just knew were junior defence ministers from a minor European state. Ryan leaned in. 'Challenge is not now in the kinetic or even virtual worlds, but in the cognitive ones,' he was saying. 'Traditional distinctions are no longer applicable,' he went on, a speech so carefully rehearsed it seemed a presentation delivered by an avatar. 'We have a grey zone.' The junior defence ministers nodded. 'And that grey zone is filled with state, non-state and malign actors.'

The avatar looked up and noticed Ryan, so Ryan rapidly turned away to find Anders Laerp and his entourage right behind him. Laerp wasn't listening, though, and didn't seem to register Ryan at all. He drifted away, but without apparent movement, as if on invisible wheels. The group formed and reformed around him like a cloud. Ryan followed them. How was it possible to be in motion yet be motionless? Laerp continued his movement, not stopping anywhere, not acknowledging anyone, not even looking, and everywhere he went more people joined the throng around him until he vanished in their midst. Ryan looked around for Zinnia, but she'd gone.

He stopped at a booth and looked at the pictures on its walls. A dolly bird smiled at him.

'What are the pictures?' he asked.

'We work with mapping technologies,' she said. 'Non-static ones.

Maps with disruptive capabilities.' She was joined by her colleague, indistinguishable.

'We create environments,' said the second one. 'Environments to harness conflict-trigger events.'

'We partner with thought leaders to develop narratives,' said the first. 'Narratives to influence or secure objectives.'

'You look worried,' said the other.

'Are you worried?' asked the first.

'Try this!' said the second and handed him a rubber ball which Ryan realised was in the shape of a bomb, a good, old-fashioned bomb. A Tom and Jerry, Bugs Bunny bomb, the kind of bomb that moustachioed anarchists would have thrown in late 19th-century pulps, black and spherical with a long red fuse protruding. 'It's a stress ball!' she laughed.

Ryan moved on. He was sure those pictures had been early Conrads.

Laerp moved back into view. Ryan caught only a glimpse of the man, towering, static, centripetal, before the crowd reformed. Zinnia appeared, pinging back and forth, around, amid, then through the flock, apparently having learned to walk in those shoes, a kinetic force to counter her father's strange inertia, or feeding off it.

'Have you got what you need?' she asked Ryan.

'I'm not sure,' he said.

'Be sure, Ryan. Let me see something soon.' And with that, she was gone.

'HOW WAS IT?' ASKED JEN when Ryan got in.

'I'm not sure,' he said. He took the rubber bomb out of his pocket and put it on the table.

'Is that for real?' asked Jen.

'I'm not sure,' said Ryan.

'Jeeezus,' said Jen. 'What are you going to do now?'

'The usual.'

RYAN SPENT THE NEXT TWO months making tiny models of Laerp's study and the trade fair. He had to work from memory, and his memory would have to do. He photographed them, then superimposed the images, printed them off and began to paint over them. He wanted pure surface. He thought about a story Jen had told him about a place she used to work. He took the bomb and melted it until it stank and blackened everything, then covered his paintings with the sticky residue. It looked good, when he'd finished. They'd hate it, he thought, but they'd probably accept it.

SIX VERSIONS OF THOMAS VYRE

Thomas Vyre looked out of the window of his large room on the 47th floor of a mid-range hotel on the edge of a Tier 3 city in southern China. A crane driver sat hunched in his cabin, as high up as Thomas, and as equally alone. Beyond him, nothing but sky. Below, Thomas knew, cars were flowing into the city, crossing a wide bridge which would deliver them into the cluster of towers at its centre. In theory, and Thomas liked theory so much better than practice, a view from this height could have been infinite but the vanishing point of his sightline was radically foreshortened by the confusion of pale orange light and thick grey cloud. Thomas did not like such confusion. The windows needed cleaning. The air closer to the city's lower surfaces was less dense so rose until it cooled then fell again, creating a turbulence, refracting the light in patterns which, studied carefully enough, were not irregular but could reveal the exact temperature of the many objects in the field, among other things, but Thomas didn't need to look that closely: the weather was hot; this room was hot. He put the air conditioning on and within minutes it was freezing.

Of the three rooms in his suite Thomas Vyre liked only the bathroom, where he could sit on the pot and look out of the floor-length window while he did his business. When he had first come here four months ago, he passed his time in the bathroom looking down at the remains of a field and its bright-red earth being dug up. Now he looked out at the apartment building (or, perhaps, another hotel) which had risen opposite. He had never seen anybody in there looking out at him, and did not care if they did. He was sure they wouldn't be able to see in, anyhow: the shifting direction of the optical wavefield—reflection and glare. The new building, almost as tall as the one he inhabited, seemed to be entirely empty. The crane, terrifyingly high with its tiny cabin perched on top, worked away, endlessly lifting something from the depths below, turning so slowly it was hardly perceptible.

The new buildings had the making of a perfect Kármán vortex street. The design was shoddy: those towers should be tapered on top, built to different heights, or have a helical structure at their apex. If not the laminar flow of air, even the slightest wind, would stream through the gorge the buildings had created and make everything judder with a pattern it was, Thomas knew, near impossible to predict. The flow here was all wrong.

He could have stayed in his club, one which was supposed to have places all over the world, but there wasn't one in this city, it seemed. It didn't matter: the anonymity was useful.

Every morning someone came to clean his room and if he was awake he would send them away and if he was asleep they did not disturb him, but in either case they left something which looked like an apple but did not taste like one. Sometimes it was something which looked like a pear but was the colour of a lemon and almost the size of his head. If he saw the person who came in he would nod his head and say, 'Zhee zhee,' the word for 'thank you' being one of the few he had learned in his time there, despite never really knowing how to pronounce it. Something about the consonant sound bothered him. Thomas wasn't great with languages though he often tried to cover up this fact. The fact that he couldn't learn languages other than his own bothered him immoderately. At the beginning he had tried the fruit but found it rarely tasted of anything. Of slightly stale white bread, perhaps, little more.

Other than this daily interruption, the room was completely silent. Sometimes, the only thing he could hear was the ringing of his own nervous system. Today, he noticed, he couldn't even hear that.

He sat down and looked at the six Word docs and fifteen browser tabs open on his laptop. He couldn't remember why most of the browser tabs were open, what it was precisely that had taken him to an essay on the dialectics of bridge construction, a review of an architecture biennial in Shanghai, or a research paper on ballistics and the Kuznets curve, but he did not close any of them. He turned instead to his writing and reread the opening paragraphs of the unfinished essays on system agnostic technologies, the evolving threat landscape, and force generation and operational realism. The others were articles he'd been asked to peer review: none had any validity. He didn't know why he'd been asked, but should, he thought, at least be grateful that someone was bothering to contact him at all, though he may not have been the Thomas Vyre they had meant to contact.

Thomas Vyre's identity had been stolen. Some might have found this troubling; Vyre was happy about it. It hadn't suited him anymore. He had long since grown weary of the man he had been, or, at least, the man that others had thought him. Anyone who wanted his identity was welcome to it. (His bank account less so; fortunately no one had tried a hit on that yet.)

It wasn't worth ploughing on with the essays. No one would publish them. He could repurpose them as conference papers, but no one was inviting him to conferences any more. At least, not him, not the

Thomas Vyre currently sitting in a large room on the 47th floor of a mid-range hotel on the edge of a Tier 3 city in southern China, a city whose name he couldn't even remember, let alone pronounce, were he ever asked.

One of the other Vyres, the first one Thomas had become aware of, had appeared at a conference at a tech institute way below his standard somewhere in the US, delivering a paper which Thomas at first thought was plagiarised but then realised was actually a half-finished draft of something he had been working on. (He had been hacked, he knew; he was careless about such things, and—besides—felt that all information wanted to be free.) When they'd had the gall to put the footage up on YouTube, he was almost charmed. The man didn't look much like him, other than being around the same age, tall, skinny, and white, but he supposed that an English accent and a fake email address was all it took to fool the Americans.

Everyone thought they knew who Thomas Vyre was. He had read articles explaining his own work back to him. None of them understood it, not really, nor what he was trying to do.

And what he was trying to do currently lay in disordered manuscript form next to his laptop. No one would be allowed to casually hack and rip this one off. Whatever it was. Though he had no shortage of ideas, form was eluding Thomas. Decisive moments. Turning points. Corporate technocracy. Everything working to natural laws, with human intervention kept to a minimum. Systems alignment. AI-aided, of course, but not reliant. No A would ever match his own I. The use of tracing and mapping technologies. The algorithmic sublime. The Leap. His magnum opus, the one he'd been working towards, no, working on all this time, really. The sum of all he had done.

The problem was, it simply didn't flow, even though its essence was flow. The work kept on breaking into pieces, it was too much for its constituent parts. It had to be a book, even though books were, surely, dead by now. It wouldn't work as a series of technical papers or conference presentations. He'd thought back to his novel-writing days and considered a work of fiction, but no fiction could hold what he wanted to say. Something theoretical-critical-philosophical, perhaps, like that Lukas Lemnis guy everyone swooned over, only more comprehensible. Better still, a series of aphorisms, Wittgenstein-style: 'Nothing is true,' Thomas had written, 'but anything can become so.'

There was a knock at the door. The room looked a mess but he didn't want anyone in there: everything in the room was perfectly ordered according to his own system.

'No thank you. Not today.' Two women lingered on the threshold and looked at the fruit on the table by the doorway. It hadn't been touched. Without asking, one of them stepped in and took it away while the other took an identical piece of the unknown fruit from her trolley in the hallway and placed it in exactly the same position.

'Thank you,' he said. 'Zhee zhee.' They nodded, and left.

Voiceless alveolo-palatal fricative. That's what it was. He should be able to do it. That's what his work was all about: sound, flow, pressure, resistance, the movement of things unseen.

That's what he'd started with, anyway. Cambridge (Trinity, Materials Science), straight on to doctorate at MIT, research fellowships at CalTech, Zurich, then back to Cambridge. From fluids to light to sound. All different, all the same. He'd worked out how to use the pattern of light flashing off any reflective surface to reconstruct the room that surface was in. The tiniest video clip could accurately model a location. From a glimpse of the light reflected in someone's glasses he could build their office, or conference suite, or hotel room. And then the same with sound: Thomas knew that every echo was a leak, a clue, a map of space. He could reconstruct an audio signal by analysing the minute vibrations of any objects in the visual field.

Although he'd moved on since then, audio signals still fascinated him, which was why, one night when he was awoken by a buzzing which had no apparent source, he had got out of bed and searched for insects. There were none in the room, large or small, he was certain. The sound was coming from outside. It must have been a drone. He'd moved to the window, still in the darkness, but the city below was orange and the night above was black and revealed nothing to him. He'd done enough work on making sure those things were stabilised and silent, though. If anyone had set a drone after him, they should have known to use one of his own designs. Perhaps he credited his antagonists too generously. He'd make sure to close the curtains at night, though.

Drone technology would have to form part of the work. Perhaps an entire chapter or essay. He had to keep on with the essays. The book—or whatever it turned out to be—would find its form eventually. Even though he hadn't published for a while now, he could find some of his old contacts. He wondered if he should put some of the articles up on a Substack but knew it beneath him. He deserved better.

People had liked his work, at first. They'd offered him money, travel, the chance to stay in nice hotel rooms, prestige, recognition. There had been the inevitable resentments and backlashes, the jealousies, the gossip, the snark, the backstabbing, but he'd got past that by writing a paper for *Science* on 'Uropygial gland excrescence and its effect on beading in the Anatidae family'—water off a duck's back (a joke which had also netted him an impressive amount of cash from a manufacturer of top-end raincoats). He'd started to get a reputation.

The second not-Thomas Vyre had written a piece for a British art magazine, applying his (that is, the real Thomas Vyre's) work to some artist or other. His nephew had forwarded the link to him, back in the days when they were still speaking. Thomas quite liked this Vyre, and would have liked to meet them, whoever they were, but when he contacted the magazine pointing out that their correspondent was not *the* Thomas Vyre, they never replied to him, though he noted the piece had rapidly disappeared from their website. Art was one of the many things that Thomas took an interest in, even though—he knew—he could never really quite see the point of it. It was great to have something to decorate a wall, of course, but most often it was the wall that was more interesting to him. There was that lad who'd painted his portrait but then rubbed the face out. Thomas had appreciated the concept but found the idea of hanging a picture of his own obliterated head on the wall more than a little disconcerting. He'd liked Hito Steyerl and Trevor Paglen, and thought they could learn one or two things from him, but it had been Sigi Conrad who had interested him the most. Her work had an intangibility which intrigued him, an interest in flow and materiality. Thomas, for once, almost felt that he understood it. Conrad made art that clearly wasn't decoration, though he couldn't quite understand what it was instead. They'd fallen out, of course, as Thomas fell out with everyone sooner or later, after he'd told her she should be clearer in her intent. 'You can't just juxtapose a few objects and let people make their minds up,' he'd told her, and she told him that while he might know everything, he understood nothing, and he'd gone back to thinking that artists should be decorators or entertainers after all. AI would soon do for most of them, thank god.

He went into the bathroom, sat on the pot and tried balancing his laptop on his knees, but it didn't work. Too wobbly to write. He could have dictated but had disabled the voice recognition feature. He should have a secretary. Thomas Vyre was definitely the kind of man who should have a secretary. Maybe one of his alter egos did have a secretary. Even artists had secretaries these days, or PAs, or whatever. He could ask one of those Chinese women if they'd be interested. He looked out of the window again and wondered how his name had generated all these alter egos while he had ended up here.

The crane was still there. It had rotated almost 180 degrees since he'd last looked, and now vibrated, almost rocked, buffeted by the wind currents that must be there. The figure inside didn't appear to be moving, rapt in concentration, or boredom, perhaps.

Vyre's reputation had grown when his work on the Kármán vortex, the winds whipping around radio antennae or overhead power lines, work he'd thought minor, was used to stabilise landing planes, ships in storms and rockets in flight. Cloud formation followed: what to do with apocalypse weather.

Thomas Vyre was the man who could see form in chaos. It said so in a *Sunday Times* feature, and he had started to believe it. People began to ask him to appear on podcasts and panel shows, to write think pieces, to hang out around swimming pools with tech billionaires in Silicon Valley, to consult with governments. He was a visionary. It said so in *Wired*.

A third Thomas Vyre was on all of the social media platforms and

Thomas had a real problem with this one, as he was no visionary but a mere shill for various cryptocurrencies. Thomas didn't necessarily have a problem with crypto, in practice. It was the theory that bothered him.

While theory was, in theory, so much more elegant, so much more artful than practice, the problem with it, unlike his acknowledged problem with languages, was that others seemed permanently ready to wilfully misunderstand it. The fact, for example, that all his theoretical work could be used in a reverse sense had been obvious to him: it was only when people actually started to use it that a certain kind of problem emerged. If a landing plane could be stabilised, it could be de-stabilised. If environments could be reconstructed from the sound of a mere breath, then environments could be constructed that would make people breathe, or speak, in certain ways. All material was materiel. Vyre became known as the man who could make submarines fall apart, the man who could make people hear voices, the man who could work the weather.

He found himself being invited to speculate on deepfaking, what had really happened in the Dyatlov Pass, about the Tunguska incident, the Hum, Malaysia Airlines 370, the mystery of Ettore Majorana, the Ghost Ship of Ballycotton, the Havana Syndrome, Hollow Earth theory, Hollow Moon theory, and had before long found himself feted by conspiracists, accelerationists, dietrologists and ufologists, and he had an opinion on everything, and he had loved it all. He'd been invited to hang out with handsome t-shirted and tousle-haired young men in the US who'd started apps and had more money than their confidence, which had been boundless to begin with. They thought everything was about gambling. Thomas didn't, but after fluid dynamics probability and statistics were a cinch and their week in Las Vegas had been impressively profitable. What those boys didn't seem to understand, though, was that however good they were at it, someone else would be better. The house would always win.

A fourth Thomas Vyre wrote horror stories. This one had his own website where you could buy his books which he published himself. They didn't look bad. Technology was, Thomas had always insisted, an occult power. He'd had his own Lovecraftian phase, back when he was seventeen, and had also tried his hand at epic verse. It hadn't been very successful, even by his own reckoning. Perhaps this Vyre was an accidental one, someone who'd had the fortune to be actually born with the same name as him. Apart from his brother and his brother's offspring, though, Thomas didn't know of any other Vyres. A thankfully rare name.

He had on occasion speculated about who some of the Thomas Vyres might be. There were those few disgruntled, the ones who felt they hadn't been adequately credited, paid or honoured. There had been gossip, scurrilous, that not all of his work was entirely original. Were some of these pseudo-Vyres people he'd known, now out for revenge? It would have been a strange way to go about it.

Not a novel then, no, he thought as he circuited the room again, half-avoiding the pile of papers and notebooks on the desk. Aphorisms neither: they'd be widely open to misinterpretation. A film, perhaps. But that would mean having to deal with a whole raft of other people to risk ending up on YouTube. Visual art was too abstract or merely decorative, he thought, but he could try getting back in touch with Conrad. That would mean attempting some kind of rapprochement, which was quite definitely not in his skill set, but she would be the kind of person who would know what to do. She'd been interested in maps, hadn't she? Maps were to be the thing around which his work turned. An understanding of space, and time, but not maps which indicated the nearest liquor store or subway station, or had little icons showing historic churches and B&Bs, certainly not cumbersome fold outs or easily viewed on a phone screen. Such an error to perceive space as a flat plane: space was a dynamic, relational force-field in which objects and actions had to be seen in constant and contingent relation with other objects, events and actions. It was when opposing networks overlapped spatially that conflict occurred. Thomas mapped flow patterns, echoes, turbulence and distortions of all kinds.

Lines, thought Thomas, were one of humankind's greatest lies and limitations. Nothing was linear—everything worked as matrices, networks, intersecting vectors, spirals and vortices, curves which could at least be plotted on a graph at their simplest, though 3D modelling was nearly always necessary. Events could not be predicted, as some simpletons thought he had claimed, but they were nodes on a vector, a range of likely outcomes, albeit aleatory, a range which—when calculated accurately enough—could be predicated on a single event. And from that, people, too, were not fixed entities but a range of likely outcomes. Thomas had always had more difficulty with people than with events. So much more complex. Or perhaps they were too simple and he was crediting them with more complexity than they actually had.

There were now, to the best of his knowledge, five Thomas Vyres on the circuit. None of them were the real Thomas Vyre. At least, none of them were him, sitting now on the edge of his bed in this hotel room.

But who would know? Perhaps they were Thomas Vyre, and he himself was the impostor. He chided himself for the banality of the thought. He had to believe his senses and his intellect were telling him the truth.

Thomas found himself looking out of the window in the bathroom again. The building opposite had grown in the last thirty minutes. The crane had rotated another 90 degrees. The figure in the cabin sat there, and for one second, less, Thomas thought that he had waved. Motion interference. Persistence of vision. Lens refraction. The dirty windows. Thomas should get his eyes checked. Then again, clearer this time. Yes, the man was clearly waving, and waving at Thomas. How was that possible? That wasn't possible. The man wouldn't be able to see from where he was.

A gentle tintinnabulation floated across the room, very quietly at first, getting slowly louder. Its top end had a marked squeak which irritated Thomas. He looked around to see what it might be and realised it was the little phone by the bed. It had never rung before. Not in all this time. He picked up.

'Hello.'
'Hello?'
'Hello.'
'Hello, yes?'
'Who is this?' said the voice.
'That's what I ask, not you.'
'Mr Thomas?'
'Professor Vyre.'
'Not Mr Thomas?'
'Professor Thomas Vyre, yes. Who is this?'
'Reception calling.'
'Hello Reception.'

'A man here, Professor.'

'What?'

'A man here to see you.'

Thomas hadn't been expecting anyone. No one came to see him here. No one knew he was here. No one had been allowed.

'Are you sure?'

'Professor Thomas Vyre?'

'Yes, that's me.'

'Man here to see you.'

'Who is it?' There was some muttering in the background.

'Thomas Vyre.'

'What?'

'Man to see you. Thomas Vyre.'

'No, I'm Thomas Vyre. Who is here to see me?'

'Sorry, yes. One minute.' More muttering. 'Reporter.'

'Reporter?'

'Yes. From newspaper.'

'Which newspaper?' Mutter.

'Times.'

'Which *Times*?'

'Can I send him up, Professor Thomas?'

'Can I speak to him?'

'Man coming up, Mr Thomas.'

Thomas Vyre was not unhappy with his life, though nor was he happy with it. He had no care for such concerns. He had left them behind long ago, or with the other Vyres. Any reputation he may have had he had sold, deliberately, intentionally, happily. Happiness was fleeting, not a thing to be pursued. Equilibrium, perhaps, homeostasis, was something to be sought, a still point in the flow. He was neither happy nor unhappy and this was where he wanted to be. On the 47th floor of a dull mid-range hotel on the edge of a Tier 3 city in China. It didn't matter: every territory was a border territory. He'd written that, somewhere.

China was certainly better than Russia. He'd ended up hating Russia. At first he'd loved it more than the Russians themselves: during the Soviet period they'd produced the best mathematicians and engineers in the world and Thomas wanted to find them, if any were still alive. Kolmogorov, Kutateladze, Alexandrov, Urysohn. He'd started off in Petersburg where he fancied himself some kind of exile, but then went out to some other place, one which hadn't even appeared on maps for a long time. (He'd realised why: it wasn't for secrecy, it was simply that there was little to map—in the traditional sense, at least.) One of Thomas's only good memories of the place now was watching some kids out there climbing up to the tops of massive radio masts, crazily. They reminded him of himself as a kid, climbing up the antennae his father had worked on in South Uist. He understood Russia better than the natives did, but they'd neither got over their past nor made the best of it. He wrote a piece saying exactly that, that Russia was essentially Tsarist and that it was great that way and should continue to be Tsarist. That had landed him in hot water. It was a misfire, he admitted (and Thomas Vyre rarely admitted such things to himself): his grip of history wasn't as good as his grip of fluid engineering, very low frequencies and fractal dynamics. Once they got what they needed from him, he'd been asked to leave.

Not asked, really. Told.

Not told really, unless 'told' meant being bundled into a Lada

Brutal at five in the morning and taken to the airport. The guy had been really friendly, though, as he threatened him with death, or something death-adjacent. (Thomas's Russian wasn't too good.)

This was but one of the reasons Thomas didn't take kindly to unannounced visitors.

A knock at the door. Thomas trusted his senses and—somewhat less—his intellect and got up to open it. A man stood there, about 5' 10", white, thin, indeterminate age and hair colour, grey suit, no tie but shirt buttoned up to the top. Perfectly bland. Shirt aside, not dissimilar to himself.

'Hello,' he said, and held out his hand. 'I'm Thomas Vyre.'

'No you're not,' said Thomas.

'Well,' the man laughed. 'Who's to say?' Thomas was about to reply I am, but realised that he wasn't, not at all.

'You're not a journalist, are you?'

'Of course not.'

'How did you know I'd agree to meet a reporter?'

'Everything can be predicted Thomas. You predicted that.'

'I said that everything can be predicted, but not necessarily correctly.'

'There is no such thing as a blind spot—you wrote that. There are only errors in calculation.'

'It's true.'

'It is true. We predicted that you would be vain enough to respond to a request for an interview. Was there an error in our calculation?'

'Vanity is pointless. I am confident. I am not vain.'

'Of course. Can I ask you some questions, then?'

'Who are you?'

'No, Thomas, who are you? That was my first question, actually.'

'This is ridiculous. I'm going to have you removed.' Thomas picked the phone up.

'How are you going to do that, Thomas? Are you going to call the police? Would that be a good idea?' Thomas put the phone down.

'At least, something. Some credentials. Some ID.'

'Ha! Do you want me to show you a passport? A piece of paper? I can if you want.' The man opened up his wallet, threw a credit card on the table. Thomas Vyre it said. 'I've got several.' He found another, a Chinese permanent residency card. Vyre, Thomas. 'Told you.'

'But that's not how this works. You have to approach me first. Make an appointment.'

'Do you have a secretary, Thomas? An agent? A PR?' Thomas said nothing. 'You're a difficult man to get hold of.' Thomas found the thought comforting.

'If you've managed to find me here, you could have contacted me.'

'You don't answer your emails, Thomas. It's a bad habit.'

'Most of them aren't for me.'

'But people love you, Thomas!'

'They do?'

'You have legions of fans. All the Thom Vyres do. Besides which, I can predict that you would have refused, and that would have made everything much more difficult.' Thomas knew the man wasn't wrong.

'What do you want?'

'It's not the what, it's the who.'

'If it's my name you want, it seems you already have it.'

'I'm here to give you a friendly warning, Thomas.'

'About what?'

'You're about to be arrested.'

'That's ridiculous. By whom?'

'Well, I've got a list . . . seems there are a few people out there who would like to talk to you in detail . . . '

'What for?'

'Fraud. It's fraud they're going for.'

'I can't be a fraud. I'm the one who's being defrauded.'

'I know, right? They've taken your name!'

'Precisely!'

'What were you expecting?'

'Tax evasion, probably,' said Thomas with a sigh.

'That would have been a good one,' said the man, 'but too . . . obvious maybe?'

'Yes. They could have gone for national security, at least.'

'That would have been a good one, wouldn't it? Trouble being . . . '

' . . . they'd have to say exactly what it was . . . '

' . . . and reveal a ton of their own grubby little secrets in the process.'

Thomas hadn't been entirely true to himself: he'd always known there were people after him. It was a professional hazard, it came with the territory. The impersonators he hadn't reckoned on; the lawyers he had. A hit equalled a writ. He hadn't, perhaps, always credited other people in the teams he'd worked with for their share, but they'd done OK out of it, hadn't they? Though he'd always enjoyed the acclaim, the attention, the prestige, he may not have always been responsible for all of the things attributed to him, but—and this was where it got really annoying—there were some things he had done that he had not been recognised for. What about those? There was always some blather about state secrets, military sensitivity, commercial IP, but still.

'So why fraud?' he asked.

'I don't know, really. I haven't seen the charge sheet yet.'

'What about all the other Thomases? Do they know? We could pin it on one of them, couldn't we?'

'We?'

'I thought you were here to help.'

'Did I say that, Thomas?'

'If they're after Thomas Vyre, why are you using my name?'

'Don't worry. I have several.'

Thomas Vyre had always known that, inevitably, one day, sooner or later, he would be hauled up onto a tribune, dressed in ill-fitting pyjamas, arraigned by the Jacobins, Bolsheviks, Roundheads or Khmer Rouge of the day, confessing to something that he now believed to be a genuine crime. He could make a fitting speech, a long epitaph, something for history to judge. He could play different versions of himself—why let others have all the fun? He was merely the eccentric, absent-minded, essentially good-hearted but naïve scientist who had, admittedly, been somewhat myopic about the purposes his work had been put to. If it hadn't been him, someone else would have done it: a well-worn line of defence, but still a valid one. He could, on the other hand, be a scientist-philosopher, above the worldly fray, or a postmodern Cassandra, ready to spit truth to those who wouldn't listen, or a jumped-up foul-mouthed tech-bro telling everyone he was the only solution. He could lean back, steeple his fingers, smile enigmatically and tell people why they were fools. But no, he would tell the truth, such as it was.

The man checked his phone then got up and turned the TV on. He flicked through a few channels until it landed on CNN.

Thomas Vyre: The Facts said the chyron. They were showing the video of Imposter #1 at that conference.

'It's out there Thomas,' said the man without turning away from the screen. 'How does it feel to be wanted again?'

'That's not even me,' said Thomas.

'I think they know that.' He turned the sound up.

'The rogue inventor has been sending out impersonators in order to throw investigators off the trail,' said the anchor.

'The facts?' said Thomas, and he kicked the table, partly out of anger, and partly because he knew that it was not a table, but an agglomeration of complex polymeric materials and organic extractives, cellulose and lignin, mostly carbon.

'Don't facts exist, Thomas?'

'There are constructions of events, and their interpretations.'

'Very good, very good.'

'And I'm not an "inventor," for god's sake. This is why I stopped watching the news ages ago. There's no news. Only speculation, prediction, forecast.'

'Have you googled yourself recently, Thomas?'

'I can't get google here.'

'Other search engines are available.'

'I can't even get a VPN.'

'Oh dear, Thomas. Are the times changing too quickly for you?' He checked his phone again. 'Here, let me tell you. Five accounts under the name of Thomas Vyre—all now deleted. One's written a confessional—it was just a stunt. You're doing the opposite of breaking the internet, Thomas. You're disappearing.'

'Will it have to be the Paraguayan embassy, then?'

'Not even them, Thomas. No one wants to upset China.'

Thomas Vyre knew he had been content enough here, in his large room on the 47th floor of a mid-range hotel on the edge of a Tier 3 city in southern China. He had reached a point of stasis while maintaining flow. The big work had, slowly, been finding its form. He had not been happy, but nor had he been unhappy. But now the equilibrium had destabilised, the system had been disrupted, the flow disturbed. Why had this visitor thrown him so? It wasn't the first time he'd had to flit. There was something he had missed, or failed to understand, or miscalculated, but he could not see what it was.

He went back into the bathroom. Though anxiety visited Thomas rarely, he knew it always went for his bowels first. The crane hadn't moved at all, and the man in its cabin was still there. Again, he turned slowly, and again, his arm stretched upward, he began to move his hand from side to side. Thomas felt safe, just about: behind the reflective glass of the hotel windows, he knew he was effectively invisible. Was the man waving to someone else? Or just stretching his arm? No, there, he did it again, slowly, deliberately, not as if saluting Thomas, but more warning him.

There was a curtain, he remembered, he had never bothered using it until now, so drew it across the window, then began to take his clothes off. The fluctuating pink noise of falling water always helped the pace of thought. He'd take a shower. His visitor could wait, or leave, or whatever. He caught a glimpse of himself in the mirror. He used to admire his body when this happened; now he saw only his pale sagging skin, like some kind of creature that had lost its carapace.

He turned the water on full and stood there watching it, in and outside himself. He was not present. He was elsewhere. The feeling was unfamiliar and Thomas did not like it. Perhaps his identity hadn't been stolen, but merely escaped, and multiplied, and now they were out there in the world, a host of Thom Vyres, appearing and vanishing, making the provocations and carrying out the thought experiments which, he had once claimed, were his only intent. He had become a range of possible outcomes, and they had brought this unwelcome visitor and his troubling news here. He felt the soul in which he did not believe lurch inside his body.

He stepped into the shower and the water and its noise did its work: the doubt evaporated. He was the original, unique and authentic Thom Vyre. He had never won the Nobel he'd deserved, no, other over-rated supply-chain engineers, smart-assed self-promoting middle managers, grant-winning administrators and clever-clever bean-counting gamblers had always pipped him to that, but he had always known exactly what he was doing and had no apologies to make nor shame to carry. This was who he was. Any prick of conscience was merely rational scepticism, and once acknowledged could be safely ignored. He would turn himself in and make his speech. They might be waiting outside for him; he'd need concentration and focus. Flow, it would be about. Flow, echo and refraction. Natural, scientifically verifiable, material forces would make everything happen, and everything would be for the best. We have no agency. There was no controlling hand. Nothing was him, but everything passed through him. He was but a conductor, a focaliser, a clarifier. He could prove it all with an equation, but they never went down well, especially with the larger public he would be reaching.

By the time he was out of the shower and had put on a clean shirt, he almost had the speech written.

'OK,' he said. 'I'm ready. I'll come with you now.'

'Come with me? No, Thomas, I'm sorry. This wasn't an invitation. I'll be leaving on my own, thank you very much.'

'Are they outside already?'

'Not as far as I know.'

'Then who's coming for me?'

'No one, if you're lucky.'

'I don't understand.'

'I never thought I'd hear you say that.'

'I'm on the news!'

'You were. You'll probably have dropped off the cycle already.'

'But you said I'd been charged.'

'With fraud they can freeze your assets. They want you disappeared, Thomas, but they don't actually have to bother doing it.'

'But I have a speech.'

'Put it out on Telegram or Yandex or Weibo. No one really cares anymore. It's all noise, no signal. They would have left you alone. You could have spent years here. But what is possible has become necessary. They will find you not because they want to, but because they can. If you invent the car, you also invent the car crash.'

'Did I write that?'

'No, Thom, I don't think you did.'

'It's the maps they want, isn't it? The current work.' Thomas gestured to the pile of notes on the desk. 'My work on them is nowhere near finished. I hope they know that.'

'It's not the maps, Thomas. They can work that out. They have worked it out. They're way beyond that. Thing is, your work is no longer of interest, not in its practical aspects. You've been decommissioned. They don't need the scientists anymore. Too much physics, too many equations, not enough grasp of theory. They're more interested in artists at the moment.'

'Artists?'

'They, unlike you, are not replaceable.'

'AI?'

'Come on now Thomas. Let's be serious.'

'Why did you come here?'

'I told you. I'm Thomas Vyre.'

'How did you know where I was?'

'Oh Thomas,' he said. 'You should have worked that out.' He looked at the fruit on the table.

Of course it was. The fucking fruit. Not bugged, that wouldn't have been necessary, but to anyone who had learned from Thomas's work, the curious glossy sheen of its skin would have been enough to volunteer all the necessary information. He picked one up and threw it against the window where it didn't splatter, or even bruise, but merely bounced back onto the floor, rocking until it expended its potential energy.

He circled the room as if looking for a way out, but there was none. His visitor had gone. The windows wouldn't open. He went into the bathroom and heaved the curtain back.

Though it was dusk now, and the sky had turned a deep orange, he could still see the crane driver. He waved again, then lowered his arm, stood up and opened the door to his cabin. That wasn't possible, surely. There must be some kind of mechanism to stop that. What kind of safety measures were in place? He couldn't do that. But he had. The door was open, and then the man stepped out.

Out.

Out into the nothing of the sky.

He fell, of course, just for a moment, then remained hanging on a cord, or a belt, or something, a safety rope. There was some safety mechanism. Thomas breathed. He'd be OK. They'd bring down the crane, or send someone up to him, or something. The crane driver swung at the end of the cable, a metre down from his cabin. Swung in the wind. For minutes.

Then he looked over to Thomas again, and again he waved. And with this wave, Thomas didn't know how it was possible, but he smiled. Thomas was sure he saw the man smile.

And then the cord gave way. It didn't break. It just, sort of, unhitched. Like a safety belt. It flapped frantically in the wind as the man plummeted.

Plummeted.

From the Latin. Plumbum. Like lead. That was how he fell. Directly, like a lead weight, like a stone. Thomas knew his body would have both met and generated intense currents on the journey down, but none seemed to touch him. The centripetal forces and air density would be strong enough to give him a heart attack, if he was lucky. He'd be dead by the time he hit the ground. Hit. The impact trauma would be tremendous. What would be left of him? Thomas looked down, but could see nothing. The man had vanished into the haze.

He ran back into the main room and picked up the phone but the line was dead. He turned to the window but from here it was dark and he could see nothing other than his own reflection. He well knew it wasn't himself he stared at but only the specular impression of the changing direction of an optical wavefield interfaced by two different media, but that didn't matter. Everything was perception, and everything was real. Everything could have been predicted, apart from the future. Time was still the unknown, the x at the centre of it all. Thomas Vyre could see the movement of everything apart from himself. He was his own blind spot, undone by what he had done. His own homeostatic system had been unstable, and its gradual perturbation had led to its catastrophic restoration as a new and complexified equilibrium.

There was another knock at the door. Thomas opened it wearily. The two housemaids stood there.

'Good evening,' they said. 'We're Thomas Vyre.'

ICH VERSTEHE NUR BAHNHOF

Were Sweeney ever asked, which he never was, how long he had spent on the train, he would not be able to answer with exactitude, but would say that he had passed his entire life there.

Sometimes he changed trains, but never at a station where he was required to go above ground. His favourite places to change were those where he merely had to cross one platform, without having to use steps, an escalator or a lift.

Sweeney would say he had spent his entire life on the train despite the fact that he could not remember a childhood on the train, nor any adolescence, nor the experience of being a young man there.

In his pocket Sweeney carried a map of the subway system which told him everything he needed to know, and would ever need to know. He carried nothing else with him.

When he tried to remember the past, which he sometimes did, Sweeney believed only that he had been there forever, and would forever be there.

One day, a man came to him and handed him a message written on a folded piece of paper. Sweeney did not read it but knew he had to hold on to it until he was asked for it. After that day, Sweeney carried a map of the subway system, and the message.

Sometimes memories of another life, not before this one but alongside it, showed through his memories of being on the train, like an old poster on the wall appearing from beneath a newer one which had begun to peel, or individual threads becoming visible on a worn coat. Such memories, though, were often interrupted by his dreams.

Were Sweeney ever asked who had given him the message which he had to hold on to, which, up until now at least, he hadn't been, he would have trouble remembering who this man was, or if indeed it were even a man at all and not a woman. Were he ever asked, he would not know if this had happened this morning, or some days ago, or some time before that. He had been on this train for such a long time. All his life, perhaps.

Memories of doors, or windows, or voices, or people's faces, were not always the doors of the train, its hermetically sealed windows, the voices of the station announcer or the faces of those who got on and off the train, but of the doors of a house where he had once lived, or perhaps still did, the windows of a museum where he had once worked, the voices of those he had worked with, and the faces of those who had known him.

It may have been, he thought, that it happened every day. That someone, a man or a woman, came and handed him a message every day.

He was never quite sure which were dreams, and which memories.

Like all trains, Sweeney's carried him through space and time but also through tunnels which linked everything that could ever be known. All places, all secrets, all beginnings and all endings. The tunnels the train passed through connected them all.

Some dreams, he knew, were projections: the things he hoped, or knew, would one day take place.

Sweeney knew that history emerged from geography, and believed that the planet's primary geography was that of the rails. The rails spread obeying their own necessity, the obscure logic of interconnections, places chosen or bypassed, gradients possible and impossible, depths which could be tunnelled and those which couldn't, rivers which could be spanned by bridges and those which ran too wide. The rails were capital made material, a map of power flows, a matrix of meaningful points, each a coefficient in the world's unwritten equation. Sweeney also knew that the age of the rails was dead and gone.

Sweeney counted the number of stops people stayed on the train. Six was the average. It was rare that other passengers would notice him, though he did see some who glanced at him then turned away. This pleased him as he knew then that he had not fallen into invisibility; a brief glance was enough for him to know that he had not disappeared. He wondered, though, if he had in fact vanished, and it was only when people looked at him that he shimmered into being. Perhaps he did not exist until he was perceived.

Sweeney often fell asleep and dreamed and knew that he was dreaming. He dreamed he was on a ship which was starting to leak, he dreamed he was sitting on a hilltop looking out at the ocean, he dreamed he was building a model of a house in which he was to live, he dreamed he had been tasked with carrying a heavy crate from one place to another but did not know where or why. He surfaced from sleep and brought pieces of the dreams back with him but could never connect them, never form them into some whole, so kept them, as if in his pockets, thinking they would come in useful at some later date, and worried about losing them.

And yet, if he did not exist until he was perceived, how could it be that he was aware of his own existence, there, then, on that seat in the train, his back hurting or his eyes tired, the very fact that he was asking himself this question.

Sometimes, on emerging from dream-ridden sleep, Sweeney awoke in a bland hotel room. It was snowing outside. He walked out of the hotel to the park, his feet crunching the light snowfall against the cinder-black path, and sat on a bench and waited, as he did every day. He knew that someone was coming for him, though he could not think who it was. Then he woke again to find himself still on the train.

Once, Sweeney had seen faces in everything—fire extinguishers, door handles, the discarded lids of coffee cups. Now he did not see faces, nor the forms and shapes of things themselves, but the patterns those things made: he saw spirals, arrays, circuits. These belonged, he knew, to a system that was obscure to him and which he could not explain. He studied them intently, as if meditating upon them would eventually reveal their significance. If ever above ground, which he sometimes, rarely, was, he saw letters, then words, then whole sentences being spelled out by flocks of birds, litter in the street, queues of cars. When on the train, the letters, words and sentences came from the number of people in his carriage, the colours of the clothes they wore, whether or not they carried luggage. Everything was a sign which led to another, then another, then another, like the never-ending linked carriages of the train itself. In overheard fragments of speech he heard entire conversations. From these connections, he thought, he would be able to predict the future, to know what was coming next, but something was always missing, one word or one item always lacked from the chain to make it whole, complete, to allow him to see clearly, and from that, to foresee. Some of the spirals, arrays and circuits he saw had no possible explanation. They could not exist, he knew, in the physical world.

He wondered if he were visible and waved his hand at someone getting on, and they looked at him, then immediately turned away. He did not know if that was an acknowledgement, however slight, of his wave, or if perhaps the motion of his hand had caused some ripple in the air, and if it was this ripple that the person had acknowledged. This, he thought, was how he existed in the world, as a ripple or movement of air, a slight disturbance of the fabric of the everyday.

Once, he had gone in search of the end of the train, or its beginning (he was not sure which was which) but could not find it. The train, he realised, was of course without end or beginning. Sweeney also knew, however, that his attempt to find the end of the train may have been a dream.

The network of trains, Sweeney knew, marked an alternative map of the city. It extended further than anyone suspected. Sweeney had travelled across continents without ever rising above ground. There, places may have had names which loosely corresponded with their overground other, but they had thrown off the fetters of such geographical space. The trains annihilated space through time.

Sometimes Sweeney got off the train while it was still under the ground, but he did not do this often. This was not a good thing to do. There were places where he had no wish to return, and some of these were down there in the dark, warm tunnels. Anyone could get to these places, he knew, anyone could find them, and many had at some point in their lives. They were easy to reach if one looked carefully then practiced not-looking, because they'd come to you from the side of your eye, in the half-light, when not thinking, or searching. A service elevator, the back stairs, the rarely-if-ever-trodden passage between buildings where nothing lives but garbage and vermin and decay. Sometimes, a quiet suburban street never traversed simply because too bland, too ordinary, too boring. Other times, the entrance could be found in that office block passed so many times, the house with boarded-up windows, the doorway leading nowhere, the shop no one ever frequents, the pavement that rolls out before it. Nothing spectacular, nothing intriguing, places simply not noticed. These would be an entry level, a starting point, a gateway to the Un, the Ex, the Outer, the Under, the Anti, the Non. The Other Place. The Not. If you find yourself here, you are in a bad place. If you want to go further, you should disobey your feelings and turn away immediately. But if you are here, if you have been invited, or drawn, or pushed, you cannot leave, because it is already—as far as time has any sense at all now—too late.

You have, almost certainly, been here before. This is the place you have been to end relationships or have them ended, to argue fruitlessly and brutally, or later, to cry silently. This is merely the place where you hit that realisation, the place where you took the phone call or first heard the news. Again, there is nothing special about this place: it is the forgotten end of a grotty street, a building site that will never be redeveloped, that odd parcel of land too small to be built on, the small untended patch of thin, weary grass where dogs go to shit. It is the corner of the car park, the hard shoulder of a cold and windy road, the back end of the building used for storing rubbish, though there is no rubbish here now. There is only you, standing by the long-out-of-service phone box that does not work and is due to be removed, the lot with planning permission pending and never to be granted, the tree not quite dead but certainly never to leaf again, by your feet a lump of plastic and vegetable matter which has rotted so far but will decompose no more and will never be shifted. It's the place you wanted to move out of, needed to move out of, had to move out of, but could never afford to, where the skirting boards failed to meet the floors, where the wind howled in and the smothering heat never left, where the dust piled and could never be moved, the dark back of the cupboard, that part of the dead garden or the damp shed where . . . let us not think of what happened there. Easy the way that leads into Avernus. Look carefully, always from the corner of your eye, and figures may emerge: Papa Legba, Hecate, Hermes, Diana Trivia, St Peter, Shen-shu and Yu-lei, Munshin, Yama, Charon, Amokye, keepers of doorways and crossroads. They will watch but not address you, for they will come no further. There are no psychopomps here, no Norns or Moirai to carry you, no Virgil to guide you. You are alone. This place is not a place of honour. No highly esteemed deed is commemorated here. Nothing valued is here. This place is best shunned and left uninhabited. Lasciate ogne speranza. There is no spirit here, only matter. Voi ch'intrate. You can see nothing but it matters little as where you are going you will not need eyes. There, further on, in the lightning-scored, whistle-resounding darkness there are only misshapen sewer gods, catacomb grotesques, katabatic creatures with no consciousness.

And yet, you are called, drawn, summoned to a second level where there is another door, perhaps, no handle, after which there may be a staircase or ladder of chipped cement, rotting wood or rickety iron, and light too, a cold white strip high above, flickering and buzzing, dead flies in its casing. This is a plateau, a bardo, a limbo, an antechamber for the lost. There may be a lift daubed with glyphs and stinking of piss with only one button, no letters or numbers, no arrow to indicate direction of travel, for up and down are to lose meaning here. There is a strange warmth, that of rot and fug, and the hum of machinery you will not see. There are, perhaps, piles of empty plastic bottles, battered out of shape, a heap of soiled and discarded clothing, clots of hair and dust. Move on again for you cannot stay here, through a low, narrow corridor which opens into a huge space with a ceiling black or distant or non-existent, a concrete floor pooled with slicks of oil or black water or chemical gunk that no boots will protect you from, where the hum and buzz turns to a roar, still distant but a roar no less, with sparks and grinds and flashes, where there is light of a kind but you do not know where it comes from because there is little possibility of light here, there are no windows, and even if there were windows (smashed, filthy, cracked, boarded) they would open onto nothing, there is no day nor night, there is only noise and a smell that thickens at each turn, an invisible cloud, now mineral (toluene, ethanol or Lysol), now vegetable (rotting onions), now animal (groin sweat, blood, burnt hair). Everything human is alien; everything alien is human. There is no backward, no forward, no up, no down, no in, no out, but there is always that smell and that noise, the hum, the drone, engulfing you in a breathless, panicky, claustrophobic tunnel, spelunking you into a pothole black as pitch and filled with warm murky water. Now you are being pushed through pipes thick with fuzz, mould, coffee grounds, oil, constituents of rotting fatbergs. Something, you think, may be alive in there, something which will not let you breathe, but out you come again and breathe you will and breathe you must because death itself would be scared to come here, for this place allows no death, no non-being. Nothing here is animated with meaning. Nothing connects with nothing. There is no association. There is nothing behind this. There is no meaning to this. The most unfortunate of us, in visions and nightmares that we may be lucky enough not to remember, have known this: the world as it really is, its naked power and greed laid bare, all pretence gone, a raptor with its skin scraped back, strong jaws, sharp beak, claws, teeth and blank dead eyes coming for us, though it has no interest in us, for we are mere carrion, expendable, nothing, we do not matter here, nothing matters here, here where there is nothing but matter, and none of which matters.

Then it is gone, leaving you in a place where there is only the clicking of insects' legs and the flap of their leathery wings, the rustle of furred bodies of huge moths, the snapping of spiders' tiny teeth, the cawing of crows, grackles and vultures whose eyes have been pecked out and whose feathers are covered in dust and shit. There are whispers and breaths and voices and you will hear them, their gibber and squeak and chatter, and understand nothing, for this place has no speech, and no understanding, and it is good that you do not understand, and that you will never be able to speak of this again. This is not Hades, nor Gehenna, nor any other hell, inferno or purgatory. This is not the kingdom of the shadows because there are no shadows here, nothing to cast light and nothing to obscure, everything is tangible physical matter and there are no projections, and moreover this cannot be a kingdom because there is no monarch here, no toothed but eyeless rat king, no twitching spider queen, no diseased trash prince nor crazed junk princess, no greed-addled frog lord, no squamous pseudo-god, nor rapacious goblin potentate. They could have no throne of bones here where there is neither centre nor periphery, neither heart nor limb, neither head nor body, they will make you no offering of even ashes to eat or bitter water to drink. But make no mistake, they are here, and they are everywhere, eternal and omnipresent, here where time has annihilated space and space has annihilated time.

And though neither space nor time have meaning, you will pass through them, or they through you, for you know that they must exist, and the place will always change and always be the same. You will pass through a low narrow tunnel alongside a dank canal whose tow-path becomes a bridge over a murdered river, pesticide-choked, a blood-coloured nitric dribble, which becomes the end of a motorway hard shoulder, covered in shattered glass, which leads you onto a slip road to a factory floor which becomes an abandoned office block then a basement car park where all the cars have been robbed and shattered and covered in cement dust. You will pass through the vestiges of the world, its detritus, its spolia, through things recognised but no longer remembered, their forms familiar yet strange. All the things you have ever lost are here though you will never find them again because what is lost is lost and will never return, not from here. Things inconsequential, hardly noticed at the time (sock, paperclip, loose change) and things which it destroyed you to lose (a passport shortly before leaving on a long journey; a wedding ring; a treasured book with its inscribed flyleaf reminding you it was a gift from a precious friend, that friend now also lost), all here, amid the junk which passeth understanding, the deepreal, the sheer too-fucking-much-ness of irreducible matter itself which can be changed into something else (dust, ashes, gas) but not into nothing, for nothing ceases to mean. There is nothing, and it is everything. The absence of presence and the presence of absence. Here there is everything but none of it has any meaning. There is no art, for art cannot exist here. Nothing can be created here. No form, shape, colour. Neither map nor territory, neither figure nor ground. We cannot tell stories about this place, about those who have passed through and those who have remained, about those who have eaten of the darkness, because there is no time here, no cause and no effect. Time is senseless: no now, no long ago, nor anything to come. Space, endless, ceases to mean: nothing above or below, closer or more distant.

And yet, it moves. The drone shifts pitch to a gentle E flat, the dissonance subsides and the darkness shrinks into corners, casts shadow where shadow should be and no further. Form divides and space makes sense: there is an up and a down, a backwards and forwards. Time thickens. There may now be an after. Light appears, as if a tentative morning. Though it will take time, and may be faint, there is a path out of here. Walk now, and there will be a ticket booth, and a platform, and a train waiting for you. You will need to buy a ticket, but you will have no money, so look in your pockets, and offer the clerk what you have, a button, a till receipt, a coin from a country you once visited but have forgotten, a shopping list, a photograph showing the face of someone you once loved, the visiting card of a vegetarian restaurant, a safety pin. If it is your turn, they will take this and exchange it for a ticket. And you will take the ticket and hold it carefully between your thumb and forefinger, and you will get on the train, which is about to depart.

Sometimes Sweeney had the feeling that he was running away from something, but was never sure what; other times, Sweeney felt that he was chasing after something, but was never sure what.

Though Sweeney obsessed about patterns and connections and spent his life on the train, he knew too that he had failed to make connections so many times. There were times he had missed planes or arrived late to appointments. There were times that he hadn't recognised people or mistaken who they were. There were times that he had failed to understand the situation he was in. He had always been in the wrong place at the wrong time, days, months or years too early or too late. He had been in one room while something important was happening in the room next door.

There was one point on the train, or one of the trains, or a platform, where he could see the screen showing CCTV images of the people getting on or off the train. He looked at it carefully, observing the place where he knew himself to be standing, but his presence did not register on the screen. Where he should have been there was an empty space. It troubled him, this evidence of his own disappearance, or his inability to show up on electronic digital media, but then he realised he was not standing where he thought he was, but on a different platform or in a different carriage observing people on a different train. When he crossed the platform or moved along the carriage the camera showed him, his long hair, his unkempt beard, his old coat.

Sweeney loved to listen to the announcements. He could enunciate every station on each line in every underground or metro system in the entire world, and mouthed the words along with the announcer. He knew the announcer was an electronically generated voice but also knew that were he ever to meet them, they would fall in love.

Sweeney rode the metro because it was the city's unconscious, its other-map, its bi-located sense of itself.

Sweeney knew that everything was connected and that nothing meant anything. Sweeney knew that the spaces between the signs, the gaps and the lapses, were as important as the signs themselves.

Sweeney rode the U-Bahn, the Tube, the Métro, the BART, the DART, the MTA and the TTC, and whether Moscow or Shanghai, Seoul or São Paulo, he knew they were all the same, and all different. Echo and drone; drone and echo.

Sometimes, Sweeney heard his own voice coming through the old Tannoy or sleek, discreet speakers announcing the name of the next stop, and whether the exit was on the right or the left.

If anybody should have asked what Sweeney was doing on the train, or where he was travelling to, or why he had spent his whole life there, he would have avoided answering, then, if pushed, would have said merely that he was waiting. No one ever asked him what he was doing, or where he was going, or how long he had been there. I'm waiting, is what he would have said.

Sometimes, Sweeney consulted the map he kept safely in his pocket. He traced his route on the map. The route was not purely circular, even though he often wished it to be so. He could not travel a purely circular route on this train, on this subway network. Perhaps, were he ever to be in another city that would be possible, but it was not so here. The route he followed was neither loop nor drift but somewhere between the two, like the impossible spirals, arrays and circuits he saw in the patterns the world suggested to him. His route was a fugue, but that of Bach, not a fugitive.

Were he ever asked anything at all, or were he ever engaged in conversation of any kind, which he very rarely was, Sweeney knew that, once the questioning or conversing was over, his interlocutor would leave and by the end of that day scarcely remember him, or any conversation that had taken place. The interlocutor would wake the next day, or the next week, or month, and have a vague memory, perhaps, of having spoken to a man who was English, or Irish perhaps, or Dutch or Finnish or American or Russian. They might remember a slightly odd conversation, about trains, or birds, or windows, or ships, or boxes. Some would remember a friendly man, if eccentric, others a tediously garrulous one, others still an awkward, difficult, shifty man, a man who clearly had something to hide.

Sweeney was both magnet and magnetised, the current and the drift, the motor and its output.

Sometimes Sweeney refused to sit down, or even to stay still. He never held on to a safety strap or doorhandle. If it were possible he would not even have touched the ground. At such times, his preferred place on the train was in the space between the carriages. At other times he sat still, fixed to the seat, and did not move for hours.

As he travelled, Sweeney listened, and he heard the music of the train, its drone and its echo, non-identical twins.

Sweeney knew that everything he had ever done, or written, or said, had left a trace, though he never knew how scarce or strong this may have been. He knew that in every place he had ever been he had left an image of himself, his negative, and that this had become another person, who was out there in the world, now, doing the opposite to what he was doing.

Sometimes, Sweeney barely thought himself alive. He felt not full-human, but a collection of ciphers and tropes, of tics and twitches all held together by his old coat. He needed that coat. He felt that he had been assembled for a job, a job he did not know how to do, or what it was, or was still waiting for someone to tell him his mission, his purpose, and meantime had been pushed into an elliptical orbit around some unknown object and continued to spin, some life force, some kind of energy driving him on, until eventually that too would slow, and he would stop, somewhere.

Other times, Sweeney was acutely aware of himself as a living being, as a composite of skin and bone and blood and breath. His physicality disturbed him. He wanted to be aether, to scarcely exist, to signify but mean nothing.

And when he felt of aether, scarcely existing, he wanted nothing more than to be blood and bone and sheer human heft.

And when he felt that heft, his smell, his hair and the ache in his back, he wanted nothing more than to be aether.

Sweeney thought about the forces which simultaneously held the universe together and forced it apart. Was the force which kept him there, on the train, centrifugal or centripetal? Was he being pulled away, or towards? Was the train circling, or was he? Were the two not the same thing? It was a question of frame of reference, of point of view. When he saw himself from the outside, he was being held by the centripetal, keeping him there, ever-revolving. Once inside himself, he felt pushed away from whatever centre may also be pulling him. Sweeney existed in a stasis of motion, a perfect paradox.

One day, Sweeney was sure, someone would ask him how long he had been on the train, and if he would like to leave.

Sweeney watched those leaving, those waiting by the door then pressing the button and the doors opening and them stepping out onto the platform after which the doors would close and they would disappear, forever, or perhaps to return the next day, or the next, or the one after that, at the same platform but on the other side, or at a different station, sometimes, even, returning, not quite the same, aged now by a few hours or days even. They would come back, he told himself, those who left. They would always come back.

CRAZY RUSSIAN KIDS CLIMB OLD SOVIET TOWER

'Good news,' Kristian texted, 'they want one of your tunes for a film soundtrack.' Ton asked which one and Kris replied, 'Fluss/Strom,' and Ton thought, fuck, of course it would be that one, but why not? He texted Kris back and asked if there was money in it. 'Not much,' replied Kris. 'WTF,' wrote Ton, letting the letters autocomplete. Film was where the big money was these days, that and video games. Everyone knew that. He'd once done the music for some engineering company promo which had kept him going for a year even though it was only on the web.

'It's a low-budget thing, independent,' said Kris when Ton called because he wanted to talk this thing through, not spend all day waiting for Kris to reply to his messages. 'It's got prestige.'

'Prestige doesn't...'

'... pay the rent, I know.' In truth Ton's rent wasn't too bad but he lived in dread of it going up. In Neukölln of all places. He'd always said Neukölln would never become fashionable and now it had. Where next? Marzahn ffs?

'There's this other thing, too, some kind of commission. I was going to pass on that though. Wasn't sure it was your kind of thing.'

'Why are you turning down work for me? You're supposed to be my fucking manager.'

'And you know what that means, Ton—I have to choose the best things for you.'

'Like that Rave Fest?'

'That again? How many times do you want me to apologise for that? Why are you always so hostile nowadays? Is this about something else?' The One True North Festival had seen Ton stranded for a week on some island in the middle of the Baltic or the North Sea, or somewhere, he couldn't actually remember if it had been Scotland, or Sweden, or Norway or even on the edge of the Arctic fucking Circle, whatever, maybe he'd never even actually known, all he knew was that it had pissed down with rain for five days straight, he'd had to sleep in a converted shipping container and he'd managed to get bitten to death by midges. His hearing had never been the same since, either.

'OK. So-reee!' Kris was right and Ton knew it: he had been going on about it too long, and there was something else wrong. Keeping a business partnership flying in the teeth of romantic estrangement was not easy. 'But what about this commission thing? What do they want?'

'I'm not sure. It's all a bit vague.'

'Shall we have a talk about it, at least.'

'We are having a talk about it, aren't we?'

'Apparently not, if you've already turned it down.' Kris was silent a moment, ceding Ton a momentary vindication which he celebrated by getting up to make some tea.

'Look, Ton, I haven't turned it down yet, and the thing is, it's not clear quite what they want . . . '

'That hasn't stopped you before, has it?'

'Again?'

'OK, sorry. But what do you mean—they'll want some music, won't they? Or do they want me to do a DJ set again? Or something else?'

'No, it'll be music, I think.'

'What's the problem then? I can easily bang something out.'

'But I don't want you banging out the same old Tonnetz stuff again and again and it's not what you want, either.' It was true, and Ton knew it, and relished Kris for saying this. 'That's not it, though. This came through the art lot.' Of all the circles Kris moved through, the art crowd were one of Ton's least favourite and Kris knew that. 'They might be interested in the stuff you're doing now, though. The stuff you won't let me listen to.' Ton ignored the dig but saw possibilities. Why not the art crowd? He was done and done with the ravers.

'Find out more about it then we can meet up and have a chat. Yes to the film thing, though—however much it pays!'

'Great.'

'Love you.' Kris didn't reply but only hung up, and Ton instantly regretted saying it. It had been habit, more than anything. It was just what you said at the end of a phone call, wasn't it?

The green tea was already going cold on his desk. He wondered if it might be nearly lunchtime yet, about what was in the fridge, about whether he could afford some new headphones, about the film music, about the murky commission, about anything but starting working. He sat down, closed Logic, ProTools, Cubase, and Ableton Live then went to the video again. He clicked the arrow in the corner of the screen.

TWO DAYS LATER THEY SAT in a café near Görlitzer Park, as it was supposed to be the midpoint between their respective flats though Ton knew it was much nearer to Kris's.

'Let's go ahead with it,' Ton said. 'The art thing.'

'I haven't heard you being so positive in ages.'

'I thought you'd be happy about that.'

'I am. But.'

'But?'

'I'm not sure who's behind it. Who's funding it.'

'That's never bothered you before.'

'I don't want to get cancelled or anything.'

'If someone wanted you cancelled they'd have done it already,' said Ton.

'Thanks a bunch,' said Kris. 'My past, as you very well know, is very complex.'

'Don't worry, they'd probably give you a medal these days.'

'Times have not changed as much as you think. The past is very unpredictable. Anyhow, with your provenance, you're the one who ought to worry.' Being Russian wasn't easy anymore, though Ton had long since given up his citizenship, along with his real name. Tonnetz was his music name; abbreviated to 'Ton,' it had stuck. Most people thought it was his real name, if a bit odd.

'OK. Sure. Thanks. But did you find out more about it anyway?'

'It's some kind of sound sculpture thing.'

'An installation?' Ton liked that idea, working in a public space, a much bigger sense of scale, not having to worry if people could dance to it, a whole different relationship with time.

'I'm not sure. They didn't mention a location, as such.'

'Kris, is this some kind of power trip you're running here? Will you stop being so mysterious and just tell me what this thing is?'

'Why are you trying to make this about us? I honestly don't know much about it. Martin from Kunstkeller told me that Sabine from Reidel's was looking for someone who had worked with sound design, low frequencies, ultrasonics, pitch, someone who knew what they were doing but could be flexible. I thought of you. That's it.'

'That's it?'

'That's it.'

'I don't believe you.'

'Ton, would you stop being so needy, so untrusting? You should be thankful I thought of you.'

'Thank you. I am humbly very grateful.'

Kris had other appointments and left Ton sitting on his own in the middle of a crowded café.

AN HOUR LATER HE WAS back home again watching the video on repeat when he should have been working on the new record. The last one, *Atlas Elektronik*, had done well—the track 'Fluss/Strom' had almost become a minor hit, 'Torus' and 'Kármán Vortex' had been popular with some of the more outré DJs, and when 'Magda' had been licensed by Chain Reaction Ton thought he'd made it, but that had been seven years ago, and there was hardly any money in it, not any more, not with the pitiful amount he got from streaming, and even a vinyl reissue would struggle to break even. Add to that losing live shows for the best part of two years and Ton knew he should be using his time to get to grips with the new stuff, but he hadn't recorded a note of anything he considered worthwhile. It was all in his head, not the sound itself, but the thought of the sound, what the sound should sound like.

The stuff he'd come up with so far was nothing like what he

wanted. It was OK, he guessed, in itself, passable, but not what he'd intended. He wanted to make something that had never been heard before, something that would challenge not just music but concepts of sound itself. Something that would turn the listener inside out, make them doubt their senses. All he was coming out with was drony, echoey techno, something which he could, if necessary, call 'the sound of lockdown.' 'What's it like, Ton?' they'd ask. 'It's the sound of me drinking tea,' he'd say. 'It's the sound of me sitting in my chair.' 'Tell us more!' 'It's the sound of me obsessively watching and rewatching a YouTube video. It's the sound of me thinking about high places.'

He texted Kris: 'Can they give me this commission if it's in a high place?'

Kris didn't answer.

Ton had thought about bidding for some arts funding, but the application process was always a nightmare and the eventual allocations always seemed to be so random, and probably dependent on him doing some kind of collaboration with people he didn't want to work with. The end results were always so bland. So many seemed to be dying to get back into playing live again, but Ton knew he'd lost it, never wanted to go back. The thought of packing into some sweaty club with hundreds of people gave him the horrors. Ton was now over 50 years old and he'd been doing music in one form or another for over half of those and he was sick of it. Going to clubs had always given him the horrors, though he'd loved it too. That was his problem, he'd long since realised, and he hadn't needed an analyst to get there: the things that terrified him were the things that kept him going. His motor ran on the energy generated by the opposing forces of desire and fear. He was an engine of his own destruction.

This new piece would be exactly that, the sound of him losing it but holding it together, powered by the opposing twins of echo and drone. He imagined them asking about his new stuff again, and he would tell them that there are two principles which drove music: not harmony and rhythm, not melody and key, but echo and drone. 'Four to the floor!' they'd say. 'Give us more bpms!' And Ton would think, echo and drone, drone and echo. 'Hi hat,' they'd say, 'more hi hat!' And he'd think about echo. 'Turn up the bass!' they'd say. Prolong the drone, he'd think.

He watched the video again.

The sound of its one minute and five seconds was what kept him coming back as much as what it showed. Ton couldn't work out why there was no wind—there must have been wind there, so why was its sound so muted, almost entirely absent? He couldn't believe this thing had been recorded with a proper mic. He tried ripping the audio track from the video but once he'd cut the voices, there was nothing there, nothing but a rich, thick blank. Not the things themselves, but the sound of the spaces between them: that was what he wanted to create, but that, he worried, was beyond his capabilities. He closed his laptop.

Kris got back to him but not with an answer to his question.

'Franz from Müttli and Dreiss is having a party this evening. Come along?'

'Is that a date you're asking me on?'

'Ton, please.'

'OK. Sorry.' Franz was one of the art crowd. Ton felt the familiar tug of wanting to be part of something and, at the same time, dreading being part of the very same thing. 'Will let you know.'

'Martin or Sabine may well be there. I'll introduce you.'

'OK then.' One part of him had won. 'Let's call it a not-date.'

LATER, TON SAT IN A bar in Kreuzberg, waiting for Kristian to show.

'You didn't reply to my text,' he said when Kris showed up half an hour late.

'What? Of course I did. We wouldn't be here now if I hadn't.'

'Not that one, the other one.'

'Which other one?'

'The one about the commission. The high places.'

'Oh, right. I thought it was a joke. What is it with you and high places, anyhow?'

'I don't know. Just a thing.'

'You're weird, you know that?'

'Better weird than eerie.'

'Come along tonight and you can meet them and ask them yourself.'

'I hate parties, you know that.'

'Don't start being difficult again, please.'

'This is why you're my manager, isn't it? To do the things I don't want to. To leave me free to concentrate on my genius, isn't that the idea?'

'Something like that, I guess. How's the genius coming along?'

'Slowly.'

'Nothing new there, then.'

'How about the film thing? The soundtrack?'

'Oh, yeah. Moritz from Kinetiq was in touch.' Kinetiq had been putting out his stuff for years now.

'Royalties?'

'You should be so lucky. No, it's not that. You know there's that sample on "Fluss/Strom," right?'

'There are a few.'

'The drony, hissy one. Did we ever get a clearance for it?'

'I can't remember. Feels like years back now.'

'What was it, anyhow?'

'I'm not sure. Some field recording. Ireland or Scotland or somewhere. A sound recordist bunged them up on her Soundcloud.'

'If it's not cleared we can't use it.'

'Kinetiq have known that for ages. That record used loads of samples. Why are they being squeamish now?'

'Film, I guess. It's a different world. We'd better try and clear it—have a look and find out where it was from.'

'Sure, whatever.'

'Great. So, are we going or not?'

'Guess I have to.'

Outside the cold air slapped. Ton felt alive again, almost excited to be going to a party. The couple of beers he'd had helped.

'Sorry for being difficult, Kris. You know how I am.'

'I do.'

'I am actually really excited by some of the stuff I'm trying to do now, even though it's difficult.'

'That's good.'

'Here, let me show you something.' He hadn't told anyone about the video, had tried to bury his personal obsessions hoping they'd come out in his work in a new, beautiful form, as though the music had emerged from nowhere. Ton took Kris's phone because it was a newer one and typed in the words he knew by heart: 'Crazy Russian

Kids Climb Old Soviet Tower.'

'You've been watching videos on the internet? That's your work?'

'No, wait, that's just the start of it.'

Kris peered at the screen with interest. A split second, and they got the message: 'This video has been removed for violating YouTube's Community Guidelines.'

'Fuck! Fuck fuck fuck.'

'Don't worry,' said Kris. 'It'll be there somewhere. It always is. Nothing is ever lost once it's on the internet. Just tell me about it.'

'I can't. I need it. I need you to see it to understand.' Ton tried googling it and found hundreds of clips, more. Some of these kids had become famous, got sponsorship deals. There were glossy videos with professional production values, thumping techno soundtracks all over them. Pitches for property companies, product placings for energy drinks, hi-spec cars, climbing gear, go-pros, drones. The original video, at least the one Ton had fallen for, was lost, perhaps there in some form amongst the thousands listed, but cut, clipped, reworked and smothered in horrible music.

He gave up. Ton desperately tried to remember if he'd been smart enough to download it. He was sure he had, hadn't he? He'd been watching it this morning—had that been a download? He'd tried messing with the audio track so he must have downloaded it. Or had he taken that from a stream? He worried. What if it had gone forever?

'It can't be that much of a big deal, can it?' said Kris.

'No. It is. It's a huge deal. You don't understand.'

'No, Ton, you're right. I don't understand. I don't understand at all. There's so much I've never understood.' He stopped walking, flustered, angry now. 'Even when we were together, I felt I knew so little about you. You were such a closed person. As though you had a whole other life going on somewhere that I never knew about, that you'd never let me into.'

'I need to find that video,' said Ton.

'For fuck's sake, Ton—are you even listening to me?'

'I have to find it. Maybe I saved it. I'm going home.'

Ton turned back towards the U-Bahn. Kris stood on the street and cursed, again.

IN HIS CONFUSION TON REALISED he'd been walking the wrong way, and now wasn't sure if he was closer to Kotti or Görli. Even though it would take him a good hour and a half he decided to walk rather than wait for a train. Walking he could stamp out some of this anger. He was sure he'd saved it. He had to have done. It would be OK. Even if it's gone, he thought, memory would be enough. I've seen it so many times. It might even be better this way. I can recreate it from memory. Yes, that'll work, that's the way to go.

This city was so big. Even after thirty years he still found it bewildering. Though he never got lost, he sometimes found himself walking for hours. The place he'd arrived in back then was no longer this one, and he had been trying to live in that place, the old Berlin, not among these towers of swirling capital, cultural or financial. The city where he'd grown up had been a big one too, with its towers, though little in terms of capital.

Perhaps he should move to the country, somewhere smaller. Find a high place. There were so few of them in Berlin. There was the Siegessäule, but the Fernsehturm was best. The old East German television tower had drawn him to this city, he knew, and he regretted that he'd never been able to have an apartment with a view of it. He would have loved to have lived up there, in that slowly revolving restaurant, the warm buzz of it, the old organ player, the view fading ever so slowly then returning. He didn't know how much of it was still there, it was so long since he'd been up.

There'd been that lighthouse on the Rave Fest island. He'd gone out there on the third day, wandered off site in a desperate attempt to get away from the thudding music. Walked for hours, it felt, though it couldn't have been that long because hours would have walked him well into the sea. And there it was, right at the point. The far side seemed to be protected as some kind of military installation, but the place itself had been open. He'd gone in, paid the entry, and begun to climb the spiral staircase that lined the inside wall. Halfway up he'd made the mistake of looking down, and even though it wasn't so far, he'd frozen. He was terrified. He clung on to the railing as tightly as he could, then slowly made his way back down. He'd wanted so much to go up, but couldn't manage it. He'd never forgiven himself for that.

He looked up at some of the high buildings around him now. Nothing that high, but he did see a woman standing in the window of somewhere up on the sixth, seventh, eighth floor, just above the treetops. She seemed to be banging on the window, but then she opened it and leaned forward. Ton knew what she was feeling: that vertigo of possibility. She saw him looking and waved down to him. He waved back then walked on but had become distracted by the tiny, shared moment and—crash—a flurry of metal and dazzle and human smacked him full on. He'd stepped into the cycle lane, distracted by the waving, and some guy had smashed right into him. The guy—who didn't have any lights on his bike—looked at him wildly then picked himself up and sped off again. Phew. No harm done, then. 'Arschgeige!' he shouted after him. Drunk cyclists were a hazard in this part of town.

The adrenaline gave him a buzz. He stopped until the shakes passed.

Kris had been angry, he registered that now. He shouldn't have been like that with Kris. That wasn't right. He thought about texting him then thought better. He wouldn't be able to explain. He should have told him the story instead of trying to show the video, the story about that one time, holidaying at his friend Sergei's dacha somewhere beyond the end of nowhere. The local kids who didn't give a fuck. Back when he'd been Misha rather than Ton.

Kris had known that, at least, but had never called him by his real name, partly because the Misha who'd grown up in St. Petersburg didn't really exist anymore, and Ton didn't like to think of him much.

It had still been Leningrad then, a khrushchyovka building near Plozhad Muzhestva which now would have either been gentrified or demolished, he didn't know and cared less. His schoolteacher mother, liberal enough given the times, had encouraged him to learn the piano, while his shiftless dad, much less liberal and fond of a drink, made him go camping to toughen him up. When he turned teen he'd started smoking Belomorkanal or Laika cigarettes and necking bottles of Zhigulevskoye beer or Solntsedar wine, if they could get it. They used to hang out where they could, climbing up to the rooftops of semi-abandoned buildings, and listened to smuggled tapes of what Sergei called intelektualnaya muzyka, 'intellectual music,' much of it un- or mis-named, which Ton had borrowed and listened to obsessively, only in later years recognising it as X-Mal Deutschland, Dead

Can Dance, Clan of Xymox, Memorial Device. He'd wanted to carry on with the piano, but his father thought he was showing worryingly feminine tendencies so they'd settled on architecture instead. Misha imagined he'd be able to build some of those high places, and though he'd hardly wanted to go his dad had pulled strings and got him a place at Leipzig: it would be better there, they assured him, in their partner country. His whole life was worked out: he'd get a solid degree, go back home, or to Moscow perhaps, or even stay in the GDR and get a state job approving windowsills or stairwells, fire exits or driveways, or—better—lean into academia, get a junior post, then a senior one, collect the wage, collect the pension, collect books, listen to music, marry someone understanding or settle into discreet bachelorship and live the best life he could. The only problem, though they didn't know that at the time, was that it was 1988, and history had other plans.

He'd never told anyone this story.

Ton got home around midnight and made straight for his laptop. He checked all the browser tabs, but it wasn't there. He'd been watching it this morning, surely? Had he been stupid enough to close it? It had been a long day. He ran a search, and it showed up, of course it did, lurking in his downloads folder. Thank fuck for that. He clicked play.

The opening shot: a handheld camera wobbled into focus on scratched metal railings, then lifted, going over the edge to reveal the distance, the vanishing horizon beyond an endless forest, then dipped to the immense drop, so far down it seemed impossible, the trees below on another planet, then back up again, to the girl with long hair, her back to the camera, shuffling out astride a protruding beam, so carefully, her hair so still, not touched by any wind. Then the voices came in—he couldn't make them out—the kids all babbling hysterically, thrilled by their own fear, then a spin away from the girl who it seemed didn't count for so much, past the guy with no shirt on, to the grinning blond boy in the red t-shirt and cut-off jeans, then down again, to the power plant so far below, all distance, all space, the focus going crazy, the sound of the wild terrified laughter as the boy stood and walked along the beam, tentatively at first, right to the end where he stood, proudly, hands on hips, looking out, but he didn't turn, he never turned, he just stared, he didn't speak, even though the others yelled to him, and there it cut.

It was like some fucked up Tarkovsky film. An aerial Zone. And Ton himself, watching them, had become part of that film.

He hit play again.

The intense closeness of the distance. The sound of it. The kids swearing, drunk on the sheer vertigo of possibility. What if I? I could just. Fly. Fear was everywhere but even though it was in them it didn't touch them. No sound of wind, just that of the air itself. The sound of their youth crackling with potential. Their mortality was as nothing to them. It flew distantly above them, giddy, drunken. Death was just another one of their mates, the slightly crazed one who none of them would trust that much, the one with a bit of a cracked look in their eye, the one they all knew was having trouble at home, what with their dad going like that and all, but they'd still make sure he came along. He wouldn't have taken them up there, but he was around, egging the others on.

This was what Ton wanted to create: the sound of space in the world, freed from self, the sound of everything and nothing, always, in its pure wondrous totality.

He tried mailing the video to Kris but the file was too big so he Dropboxed it instead and sent Kris a link. It was a few days before Kris got back to him.

'That's you,' he wrote, 'isn't it?'

AVAILABLE LIGHT

The first sign things were off was when Terry claimed he'd seen an orc.

'Coming down over that hill,' he said, 'on the other side of the marina.' Joe had only been there a couple of days and was still getting to know the crew.

'An orc?' asked Gerry.

'An orc,' Terry replied. 'Something like that, anyhow.' Joe wasn't sure the other guy was actually called Gerry, but he'd never had a good head for names and faces.

'Been on the beers, had you?' They were in the pub now. The question was redundant. They got another round in. It was still raining so they couldn't do any shooting.

Joe looked down at his pint. Head as foamy as a Mr Whippy. He looked at the window. He couldn't see out of it because of the rain. It was only three in the afternoon and dark already, in May. They'd come at this time of year for the light.

The supposed orc hadn't been the first sign. The whole thing had had the intimation of a supreme spectacle of shite before he'd even set foot on the island.

'Do you know who Paul Strand was?' she'd asked. Of course he knew who Paul fucking Strand was. He didn't say this though, that would have been rude. And he didn't want to be rude. He wasn't a rude man, no one would have ever said of Joe Coyle that he was rude, though he could be direct sometimes. And sometimes being direct could come across as being rude, he knew that. But he wanted the job. He needed the job. It might be his last chance. Had they even looked at his CV? Of course he'd know who Paul Strand was. Kind of, anyhow. A photographer. American? German? Something like that. Nice old black-and-white pictures, portraits mostly. Joe had had to do some googling, mind. American, yes—that was OK, he could do accents—Modernist, abstraction at first, all shadows, light and angles, then NYC, the big city, that kind of jazz age thing. Strand had made a film, then moved more into portraits. Socially committed, wanted his work to affect things, to change the world. Joe was on board with that. Strand had remarried, moved to France because he hated McCarthyism. Later in life had taken an ethnographic turn. That was when he'd been there, to the island where Joe was now sitting having a conversation about orcs. Strand had made a book of his pictures from there, *Tir A' Mhurain*, looked amazing but original copies were going for nosebleeding amounts. Joe found a decent reprint for thirty quid, though, ordered it sharpish.

'No, mate, that's a kobold.'

'Tolkien invented orcs.'

'No he didn't—they're deeply rooted in European mythology and folklore.'

'You sure it wasn't just one of the locals you saw?'

Joe had made his own way up there (and, come to think of it, that had been another sign, when he was told he'd have to upfront his travel expenses), flying into Manchester where he'd stopped off to see his mum, then taken a train up to Glasgow after which there was another five-hour train journey to Mallaig, last stop on the mainland,

and only then could he get a boat. It was raining so much when he got there that CalMac ferries weren't sure if they could sail, so he'd settled himself in the Steam Inn drinking Tennent's and playing pool with a bunch of likely lads, and when the message came through that the boat was, actually, about to leave, he'd had to move sharpish to catch it.

'Aren't they, like, part-human or something?'
'Who? The locals?'
'No. Orcs.'
'That's a dragon-bred you're thinking of. Or a half-Elven.'

He'd had to google it, first time he heard the name: South Uist—it was right out there, as far as you could go. Next stop Canada. Even when he was on the boat he wasn't really sure if the place existed or not. He found a seat near a window, squinted through the mist and, once you looked beyond the closer islands, there was nothing there. Nothing at all apart from a grey wall of cloud. The great mechanical drone of the engine cut out. The boat had stopped, he felt sure though it was impossible to tell. A message came through the Tannoy telling them that due to uncertain conditions they would be turning back to Mallaig. He tried messaging Alysson to tell her he was running late several times but there was no reply. He'd been warned the signal out there was patchy at best.

'How do they, like, y'know, get it on? Dragons and people? Or Elves and people?'
'There are complex mating rituals.'

The lounge was permeated by the smell of heavily fried breakfasts so he'd gone up top to get some air. After an hour of being still the deep clunking and whirring began again and another message informed them that they would, in fact, be continuing on to Uist. A small cheer went up. As they began to move the wind battered him like punches, but it felt good, and then, just as the last of the land disappeared, the clouds parted, blue sky revealed itself, a shaft of light hit the sea, and Joe saw a dolphin. A flash, a silvery gleam leaping out from the foam, a dive through the air, then back into the roiling water. An apparition in less than a second. That had been a good sign, surely. He'd turned round to tell someone, to point out the fleeting wonder, but there was no one there.

'Orcs look a bit like Klingons.'

'No they don't!' said Joe, with a vehemence that was admittedly unnecessary, but he couldn't stay quiet a second longer. These two were doing his head in. 'Klingons are plantigrade bipeds with ridged foreheads, bad teeth and a strict warrior code of honour.' The others fell silent a moment.

'How come you know so much about Klingons?' asked Terry, or maybe Gerry, the surprise hanging on his open mouth. Joe stood up, supped the last of his pint and said nothing.

'Orcs are plantigrade bipeds too, though,' he heard Gerry, or maybe Terry, say as he left.

It was a twenty-minute walk up the road to where he was staying. It wasn't dark yet but there was so much rain it might as well have been. He'd be drenched by the time he got back.

AFTER THEIR FIRST CONVERSATION ALYSSON had sent Joe a story to read, 'The Day the Photographer Came,' and it was good, fine, one of those where not much happens, but Joe loved those, he really did, all that atmosphere, that's what he'd remember about it. He couldn't remember who wrote it now, but it didn't matter because she said the film'll be inspired by this, and he thought 'inspired by,' that's always ringing an alarm bell. He'd asked when he could get a script and they said they were still working on it, but she wanted to improvise a lot of the dialogue, and was he up for doing that? He was, he'd done that kind of thing before, he told her. 'There won't be much,' she'd said. 'I want to capture the silence.'

'Of the pictures?' he'd asked.

'Yes, and the land itself.' Joe listened to the battering rain and the buffeting wind around his head right now and wondered if Alysson had ever been to Uist before she'd said that. Not much chance of silence. 'The qualities of those pictures,' she'd gone on. 'Their quiet intensity.'

Despite the alarms he'd thought she was good. 'Quiet intensity.' He liked that; he could do that. At this point in his life, not many people impressed Joe Coyle, but she had. There were funding problems, obviously, there always were, but she had contacts and was confident it'd be alright. She'd made him feel confident too—he'd turned down other offers to do this. And now here he was, trudging up a desolate road in the pissing rain thinking about Klingons.

He'd worked on enough low-budget films to know that you had to be nice to everyone on the crew if there was any hope of it working, and he didn't want to come across as the Great Actor, that's why he'd stuck around for a pint with them, Terry and Gerry the lighting boys, he'd tried, he really had, but all that Lord of the Thrones shite, Game of Rings, whatever it was called, he'd never had time for any of it. They were good oppos for jobbing actors, though, he knew that, and—if he were ever asked—wouldn't deny that he'd put his name forward for one of them. He hadn't got that gig, but they had offered him something else, which was why he did actually know exactly what a Klingon was. It was still on his IMDB page. It was a fucker trying to get that shit removed.

'Joseph Coyle: Jobbing Actor,' that's what it should say on his IMDB page, that'd be enough, a derogatory adjective maybe, but he cared little. He'd been more or less permanently engaged in the thirty-odd years he'd been working which wasn't bad for any actor, especially not one his age. Fed up with the late-80s gloom in Britain and depressed in the second year of a geography degree, he'd chucked everything in to go and live in a squat in Berlin, months before the Wall came down. At the time he'd thought it would only be for a few months, a year at most, but then he'd fallen in with an arty crowd who were impressed by his capacity for mimicking accents and got a role in an experimental production of Hamlet (playing the gravedigger, naturally), and so the rest of his life had unfolded. He'd only had a few dry spells which he'd spent working as a builder or a delivery driver and, once only, in a call centre. He could have had a nice life, a quiet life, settled somewhere, a wife, two kids. That kind of thing. To be fair, he did have a wife, but he didn't see that much of her these days, and a kid, too, and he saw even less of her.

Joe looked around and realised he was lost. Fuck. How could he have done that? There was one road. A straight line. There were no sideroads he had to take, no forks or bends, no snickets or shortcuts. All he had to do was put one foot in front of another and he'd managed to fluff it. It wasn't unusual. It happened all the time. Along with names and faces, directions were his downfall, especially if he got distracted by thinking. He was lucky he'd made it here at all.

WHEN THE FERRY EVENTUALLY DOCKED the crew member who removed the chain to open the gangway looked at him, the only foot passenger, and asked if he was one of those film people. Joe was obscurely flattered.

'I am, actually. There should be a few of us here.'

'Aye, there are that.'

He'd been told there would be someone to meet him, but seeing as they were now hours late he had no idea. The few cars waiting all drove off without so much as a glance at him, then the ferry unloaded and the place emptied. If there's no one there, the message had said, go and wait in the hotel. He looked around for a hotel but couldn't see anything apart from the CalMac ticket office. The only thing he could see through the rain was a rambling building a few steps up the hill. Looked a bit like a hotel, he reasoned.

He walked up and tried to find the door. What looked like the main one was locked so he walked round to the side and found another. With a bit of a pull it came open but he thought he'd walked into a store room. A pair of wellies sat next to the door, accompanied by bulky objects hidden by waterproof covers or old tarps. No one was around. He walked further in. A chandelier made from stag horns hung from the ceiling, bare lightbulbs on top of the points. A handsome wooden rack with an enamel sign on it saying 'Fishing Rods' stood against the wall, but there were no fishing rods. A thick tartan carpet led up a narrow wooden stairway. There was something like a reception hatch, so he leaned in and saw two desks piled with ring-binders and an old-fashioned VDU monitor, switched off. No one was in the office. He thought he could hear movement somewhere, but that was probably mice. He walked on, through a lounge with a worn leather sofa under a ceiling sagging from an invisible weight, wallpaper drooping from the walls. A young woman with a full face of makeup walked past him, taking no notice.

'Excuse me...'

'Sorry, we're full.'

'I thought I might be booked in here.' She shook her head.

'Full.'

'Doesn't seem to be anyone around.'

'You could try the Borodale. In Daliburgh. Three miles to the road.' She walked off.

Seeing the rain had stopped he went back out to the car park and leaned against a wall. The wind hadn't stopped. Eventually an old Vauxhall Vandal pulled up and its window rolled down.

'Joseph?'

'Alysson! Thank god!'

'Sorry about that,' she said as they drove away. 'Wasn't quite sure you were due to get in. Or even if you were coming at all.' Someone whose name he didn't catch but seemed to be the sound tech was sitting in the back seat.

'All the hotels are full,' she said. The crew and actors were all staying in different places. Maybe for the best, thought Joe.

'How come they're all full? There's hardly anyone here. What's going on?'

'Not sure,' said Alysson. 'A birdwatching convention? Fishing expeditions? I can't really work out what anyone does here.'

'Leaves as quickly as possible,' said the sound person.

They'd got glamping pods on the small bay to the other side of the port. The rest of the crew—there were seven of them in all—were staying in a B&B further up. Joe would have his own place, they told him, not far from there. They turned off the main road and drove along a narrow track before pulling up at a stolid one-storey house with pebble-dashed walls. It wasn't pretty but it looked warm and sheltered. An RV was parked in the garden next to it.

'Here we are,' said Alysson. It took Joe a couple of minutes to realise it wasn't the house he'd be staying in, it was the van.

And it was to the van he now returned, the place appearing from the dark like an apparition. Joe had hardly been lost at all.

ALYSSON HAD WANTED TO MEET up later, after he'd got himself settled. 'Come over to the pods!' she said, handing him a shooting script. 'A few things to run through.'

Later that day, Joe made it to the pods without getting lost. 'You can't lose yourself here,' said Alysson. 'Very flat, over this side of the island. You can see everything.'

'That's the problem,' said Joe. 'I can't tell one place from another.' The tiny pods were built into a low hill.

'Chemical toilets!' said another new face, Andrea, who seemed to be the assistant director, or director's assistant. They sat around a firepit between the pods, the wind hitting them in sudden baffles, then disappearing.

'We're changing the working title.'

'Not *The Day the Photographer Came*?'

'Too Hugh Grant.'

'Early Hugh,' Andrea added.

'What is it now?'

'I'm not sure yet. I'm leaning toward *The Land of Waving Grass*.'

That's what Tir A' Mhurain means. The book? You've seen it?' Joe nodded. 'And the black-and-white thing, too. I wanted it to look like the pictures, but since being here, well, there's so much colour. Feels wrong to waste it.'

Joe looked out at the water, the other low islands, the hills looming behind. He could only make out various shades of one colour. If he concentrated, maybe there was some green amid the grey.

'Give it time,' said Alysson. 'Let it reveal itself slowly.'

'And the funding?' asked Joe. 'Is that revealing itself slowly, too?'

'Don't worry about that,' said Alysson, but Joe was worried. He'd been through entire real-time reboots as investors stuck their oars in. He'd had such a clear idea of what he wanted this film to be, had seen it already in his head: slow, the power of the silence of those Strand photos, that quiet intensity. It was a role perfect for him: older British actors were where it was at now. In other fields he'd be done, but he could still make it at 58. Brian Cox, Bill Nighy. That was who he wanted to be and this film would get him there: a pivotal role in a difficult film, almost a one-hander, the camera close up on his face as craggy as the rocks. A few festival screenings, critical acclaim in the right places, one of the more discerning prizes, and he could book his ticket to LA, one way.

And now it'd be sunk by some billionaire know-nothing who'd insist on a Celtic fiddle-dee-dee soundtrack, a charming cast of local yokels, super-saturated colour and—god help him—an inevitable plot detour which would see him fall in love with a flame-haired Scots maiden. No sex scenes. There was no way he was going to do any fucking sex scenes.

'I want to start tomorrow,' said Alysson. 'We've only got ten days.'

'What about Lydia? I haven't even met her yet.' Lydia Morton was playing Hazel Kingsbury, Strand's wife, who'd accompanied him here.

'She's been held up. Should be here in a couple of days. It's not a problem. We can start without her.'

The weird thing was Joe's wife had the same first name, only with an i. He didn't see Lidia that much these days. They hadn't split up, but they weren't exactly together. Work often took them away from home for long periods, and—with differing degrees of awareness—they scheduled trips so they'd rarely meet. He didn't entirely blame her; he knew he wasn't always an easy man to be around, and it had always been a bit bumpy. He'd first seen her at a party in a Kreuzberg basement, sometime in the early 90s, black hair and green eyes, half-Irish half-Sicilian with the wit and danger of both, the kind of woman who'd tattoo her own name on your leg and show you how to hang on the back of a truck while cycling; he stood no chance. They were on and off for a couple of years until she got pregnant and, claiming that family on both sides would murder her if they didn't, they'd got married. He was delighted, besotted; she less so, and strayed, he knew, but tried not to know. They'd balanced, though, until she'd taken off to London a couple of years back, claiming she was visiting an old friend who wanted to see some kind of art exhibition. He didn't hear from her for a month, and didn't see her for six.

He said goodbye to Alysson and Andrea and the sound woman who'd also appeared, then headed off to have a good look at the shooting script and ready himself for what it might hold. Despite nearly getting keel-hauled by a massive truck which roared up the narrow main road, he found the way back to his van and settled in for an early night.

He hadn't been too worried when Lidia disappeared. He knew

what she was like. Luckily Elena had left by then, started her own life, but she told Joe that she'd heard from her mum, nothing more. It was almost more difficult when Lidia did show up again. Always moody, now she was off the scale: hardly speaking at all, continuing to disappear for a day or two then turning up again with no explanations. She seemed to have quit her work as an interpreter and translator and spent her time doing intricate drawings of towns and cities, baroque in their complexity, then started making tiny models of them from papier-mâché, buckets of which he'd find strewn across the floor of their small apartment. He didn't ask; knew not to. Strand's wife Hazel would have been very different, he thought as he fell into an easy sleep. She was a photographer, too, Joe had seen a picture of Strand she'd taken when they were here: it was sunny. He was kneeling down, cigarette in mouth, looking at something out of the frame. There was a wooden pole there, the leg of a tripod probably, as if he were fixing his camera into place. The focus wasn't on him as much as flowers on the foreshore. They looked like daisies. Joe hadn't seen any daisies yet.

The next morning rain pounded on the metal roof and leaked into a dream in which the clouds had become sentient and weren't happy. Their incessant needling and hissing turned into a heavy thump which, thankfully, woke Joe when he realised it was someone hammering on his door.

'Sorry to wake you. Thought you'd be up by now. I'm Graeme.' The lad had forearms like tree trunks and was wearing only a t-shirt and jogging bottoms. 'I'm helping youse out with stuff. Alysson told me they can't start this morning. The weather, aye. The other guys are having breakfast in the pub. I'll drive you there.'

They'd sat through breakfast then opted for lunchtime pints when the weather refused to stop.

'It'll be clear later,' Graeme told them. 'I've lived here all my life, on and off. I know the weather.' That was when Terry had arrived announcing the orc.

Pub abandoned and now back in the van, Joe looked through the new script for the changes he dreaded but was relieved to find his worst fears unconfirmed. It was thin though and that set him worrying. There wasn't much of a story. His initial trust in Alysson was dented—all that art school background looked impressive, but this was her first feature, and he wasn't sure she had a clue what she was doing. You couldn't just improv a whole film.

He had no phone signal. He was bored already. Boredom was always part of making a film, but it was unusual for it to set in so early. He could have sat longer in the pub, arguing the toss with the boys, but that wouldn't have ended well. He found himself thinking about what the German word for 'midges' was—Mücken probably, though that wasn't quite right. Having lived much of his life now between two languages, he often ended up considering the relative inadequacies of each. Gemütlich wasn't quite the right word for this trailer, though it certainly wasn't 'cosy,' either. Langweile was good for 'boredom'—the 'long while' of it, but didn't have the solid smash of those two English syllables which weighed on him right now. Having lugged the Strand book all the way up here with him, he'd thought he'd better read it—so far he'd only looked at the pictures. He rarely bothered with the blathering verbiage in art books, but this time he was glad he did.

There was hardly anyone on the island, he found, because they'd all been shipped off. A good while back, but nevertheless. Three thousand of them, put on a ship and sailed off to Canada where they were dumped and left to sort themselves out. Sheep were more profitable than humans. A few came back, but not many. As if that wasn't enough, there was the rocket range. Rockets, it turned out, were even more profitable than sheep. Built in the 50s—exactly the time Strand was here. How much did Strand know about that? And why didn't Joe know any of it? He'd never heard of the military base, the missile site, didn't even know if it was still there.

There was always something dodgy going on in Scotland, he thought. Best place to hide it. There were places like Diego Garcia, but that was just so bloody far away. Well, to Joe it was far away, though if you were one of the poor sods who'd lived there it wasn't. But in Scotland you could do dodgy things and have them be relatively close to home. Faslane, nuclear submarines. Perfect place to hide. *Edge of Darkness*—that was in Scotland, wasn't it? Or was it the Lakes? Bob Peck. He was good. Joe would have liked to have been Bob Peck in *Edge of Darkness*.

NEXT MORNING IT HAD CLEARED up.

'Told you it would,' said Graeme, banging on the door at 6 am. And then, as soon as Joe stepped out of his trailer (as he'd decided to refer to it), a plane swooped over their heads. Immense. And low, so low that if Joe had jumped he could've touched it.

'What the fuck was that?'

'Cargo plane. I think. It happens sometimes.'

'Where's it going?'

'Dunno.' It was grey, not camo, so grey Joe couldn't really tell what shape it was, other than generically huge-plane-shaped. Its edges seemed all wrong, yet impressive, as if some mad modern architect had designed an enormous fuck-you plane. 'It'll like be the military base, top end of the island. It's something to do with them.'

'The rocket range?'

'Test-firing site, I think it's called.'

'Can we drive up there?'

Graeme looked worried.

'Ach, not now, y'know. Alysson.'

'How long will it take?'

Twenty minutes later they were heading up the road looking for a military base. To the right, Joe spotted a large grey industrial shed, newer than any other building, squatting as if trying to hide from the horizon.

'Is that it?'

'No. That's where that artist works.'

'What artist?'

'Can't remember the name. Some artist.'

'It's massive.'

'I know, right? Must do some huge paintings.'

The land flattened, the sea came closer on both sides.

'They have raves out here sometimes,' said Graeme.

'Good place for it.'

'I know right? Turn it up as loud as you want. No one can hear a thing.'

The road narrowed until it was only concrete on grass.

'Here we go.' Graeme nodded at some blue signs by the road. They looked like signs for a hospital but read: 'Range Head,' 'Testing Area,'

'Launch Area.' Joe was disappointed: he'd hoped for something far more sinister than this. 'They've got like, drones, flying in there now.'

'Drones?'

'Y'know. Unmanned things. Huge fuckers, some of them.'

They drove on as far as a scattering of small buildings that looked like public toilets, utterly forgettable in their sheer ordinariness. Beyond one clump, a flat cemented area rolled out, making Joe think of a supermarket car park, but populated by a careful arrangement of low aerials, like old TV antennae. Further still, a newer building, prefab slabs and a grey corrugated plastic roof, and another cluster of signs, this time more interesting: 'Carousel,' 'North Vedette,' 'Aerial Targets,' 'Explosives Department.' It felt like the perimeter road of an airport. There were wire fences, but those like he'd seen around primary schools, nothing barbed, nothing you couldn't hop over if you'd wanted to. Eventually they came to a portacabin by the roadside, flanked by a barrier. In the distance Joe could see a scaffold tower about twenty feet high, some lower white buildings, and a shipping container.

'What's that tower?'

'No idea. A viewing platform or something?'

'And why's there a container there?'

'Ach, they're everywhere, those things. Ask my brother. That's what he does—sails those things around the world for a living.'

'Never tempted to join him?'

'I get seasick.'

They couldn't get any closer but followed the road until it met the sea. There was a farmhouse and a couple of cows, then the ocean.

'This is where we stop.' Joe felt empty. He'd quite hoped to be flagged down, followed, security checked down to his pants. He'd expected armed guards, masked troops, sinister SUVs on mysterious manoeuvres. This had been nothing more than mildly interesting.

'There's nothing there, really.'

'Not much to see, no.'

TWO HOURS LATER, AFTER HE'D stopped to get suited, Alysson was waiting for them.

Lydia still hadn't arrived. Tomorrow, she hoped.

They did some B-roll: shots of him walking along roads, then across an empty field, then around the small bay where Alysson's pod was. They had to keep modern buildings out of it, but that wasn't too hard. There were none of the old crofts with their turf roofs left on the island. They filmed him up close. He had to do lots of looks. There was no sound: the sound person, who was called Rachel, was having trouble with her equipment.

'It's OK,' said Alysson. 'We'll do that in post.'

Joe wasn't happy. They were two days down now and still hadn't really made a start. His feet were wet and he was getting bitten to buggery by the midges. He knew they'd be able to use the pick-up shots they'd done that morning, work it in somewhere, but.

'It's not right, is it?'

'I don't know what you mean.'

'Strand was making a deeply political piece,' he told Alysson. 'He was responding to the military-industrial complex. To a people facing the imminent threat of expulsion, of extinction. We need to show that.'

'We are showing it!'

'We're not—there's nothing here, a guy comes to an island, takes some photographs and goes home again. Is that it?'

'That's never it. And you know that.'

'It's too subtle. It should be about people losing their homes. About human capital.'

'Are you the director now?' He was surprised to hear Alysson with that line already. He didn't normally get that until well into the second week.

Before Joe had a chance to reply, Gerry appeared and claimed he'd seen Tom Cruise.

LATER, BACK IN THE PUB, Gerry went into more detail. 'Range Rover Bludgeon GLS. Three of them in convoy. They stop, bald bloke gets out of the front one, opens the door. And there he is—Cruise!'

'How'd you know it was him?'

'Short. He's short.'

'He's not the only short guy in the world.'

'You're forgetting that I worked on *Mission: Impossible – Ghost Protocol*. Ray-Ban Aviators. That was the key. He was wearing them. That was Cruise I saw. I know it.'

A huge TV screen hung on one wall showing Spanish boxing from some dodgy feed. A group of solid blokes stood beneath it, not really watching but not talking to each other either. There was a sign by the door which read: 'Be kind (and bugger off).' Two girls sat at the bar nursing berry ciders and checking everyone who walked in.

'So if it was him, and I'm still far from convinced by the way,' opined Terry, 'what in the name of fuck would Tom Cruise be doing here?'

Four orcs walked in.

'Told you,' said Gerry. Worse still, Joe knew one of them.

'Joey Coyle!' the lead orc said. 'What the fuck are you doing here, mate?' He stretched out a black-gloved hand. 'Hang on,' he continued, hastily withdrawing the offer of a handshake. 'What am I saying? How did I not know? You're in on this too!'

'In on what?' said Joe, still trying not to shrink too far from Kev Whealdon, who he recognised despite the ludicrous hat and had last seen when he'd been dressed up as a Klingon.

'On what? *The Portal Keeper*, mate. You playing it close to your chest? I get it, lot of secrecy still.'

'I don't know what that is, Kev, but whatever it is, I am most definitely not in on it.'

'You're shitting me. What the fuck are you doing here, then?'

'Filming.'

'What?'

'It's a small thing, low-budget. About Paul Strand. Sort of.'

'Paul who?'

'Never mind.'

'I do not fucking believe it. Two crews here at the same time.' Joe couldn't believe it either, especially not one containing Kev Whealdon, who'd always got on his tits.

'So, to settle a debate,' asked Terry, 'are you orcs?'

'Of course we're not fucking orcs,' said Kev. 'It's a post-apocalyptic thing we're doing.'

'We're a mutant breed,' said a second not-orc. 'Genetically developed to be a security force. But then we go rogue.'

'Who's Cruise playing?' asked Gerry.

'Cruise?'

'I saw him today.'

'Can't say anything about that, mate. A lot is still under wraps.'

'We don't have a full script,' said another mutant.

'God no. Nothing like. Even we're not sure what's happening half the time. We're doing combat scenes and we have no idea who we're supposed to be fighting. Being an actor's crap sometimes. You know that, don't you Joey? It's all mo-cap and green screen now. AI shite. Directors are wankers.'

'How long are you here for?' asked Joe.

'Couple more weeks, probably.' Joe finished his pint and left. He'd been hoping Kev and his mates would be gone far sooner than that.

ONCE OUT, IT WAS STILL raining so Joe zipped up and hit the road. Why wasn't there a German word for endless, insistent, driving rain? Why wasn't there an English one, for that matter? Maybe there was a Gaelic one. He'd have to ask Graeme. A great sweep of light at the far end of the bay lit the rain-thick air. It was the opposite direction from his van, but what the hell. Despite knowing he'd get lost, he had to know what it was. The drink helped and the wind had at least died down a bit. It looked like a lighthouse. For reasons he never really understood, Joe loved lighthouses. He didn't remember seeing a lighthouse there before, it must have been a small one, not really visible until the night called it to do its work. Joe followed the road down past the harbour to the new marina they were building. A few smaller boats moored, the usual grey corrugated industrial barns for repairs and fish. No sign of a lighthouse, though the light was growing stronger. Now it looked more like arc lights, but they still had that sweep, as though searching for something. It'd be the other bloody film crew, he thought, doing some night scenes. He paused for a moment, listened to the sound of his breath until he caught it, then the rain on the hood of his jacket. Standing there, watching the light swing through the darkness, a couple of pints in him, Joe thought he might actually be happy.

He carried on a little further, to where the road ended and the rocks and bracken began. He really shouldn't be doing this, he knew, could easily slip and fall and then he'd be the twerp they'd had to call out the rescue for. A semi-pissed English actor would probably get short shrift from the services who'd be more concerned with drowning mariners. He went on.

Then, as if emerging from an oil slick, shapes formed. The shine of light on black steel, the bounce of rain from glass. One car, then two, then three, all silent, rolled forward to meet him then stopped a few feet down from where he stood. Joe couldn't even see a road down there. Though the rain hammered, there was no other sound. Each car switched on its headlights, dazzling Joe until he turned away, then the lights went out again. Were these the lights he'd been seeing? He thought not, the car lights were trained on him, and not strong enough to reach out into the sea. They came on again, then off again, plunging him back into the dark, then again a third time.

He got the message, turned carefully and headed back the way he'd come. He looked back only once, and could still see the massive light casting across the water.

That had been scary. What were they doing down there? Joe had been on one or two high-security sets, but nothing ever like that. This was like Strand again, he thought as he trudged back, his brain overstimulated by the night, the booze, and the decidedly threatening cars. Strand was being followed, too. The CIA would have been onto him, worrying he was going to make some propaganda, crashing the chances of their missile site, or at least drawing unwelcome attention to it. He'd suggest this to Alysson the next day. That would get the film going.

JOE WOKE THE NEXT MORNING with red blotches all over his face. He looked like he had the plague.

'Midges, eh?' said Graeme.

'I walked out to find that lighthouse last night. Not a great idea.'

'What lighthouse?' said Graeme. 'No lighthouse here.' Joe didn't say anything else and concentrated on trying not to scratch the midge bites.

They were shooting at an abandoned house Alysson and Andrea had found. A stone sign above the door said '1890.'

'What happened to the people who lived here?' Joe asked.

'No idea,' said Andrea. Joe had a very clear idea, but didn't want to get into that now.

'I want to linger on it,' said Alysson. 'So many textures here.'

'Textures?' asked Joe.

'Yes, if you look around—it's all the textures. There's peaty and boggy and rocky and sandy. Floral. Herbal. The bracken. Then this house among them all—the permanence of its stone. The walls have great texture.'

'Lots of texture,' agreed Joe.

'Yes, texture,' said Alysson. The word 'texture' got weird then so Joe decided to shut up.

He walked into the place and looked around. Grass had started growing through the floor, but other than that the place looked like it had been lived in up until recently. There was still a gas range fixed to the wall, and an old sofa with its stuffing spilling out. Some mugs and plates, all chipped, all dirty, sat beside the sink. A painting of a seascape on the wall. Chunks of plaster had fallen from the walls revealing the brickwork beneath. A wooden chair sat in the corner, almost inviting someone to sit on it and recount an old tale.

Gerry and Terry got busy with some lights and Rachel crouched next to them fiddling with a mike. Alysson decided she wanted natural light so sent the boys away.

It was eerie in there. Joe felt like he'd walked in on someone else's life, or as if he'd been there before, though the memory was so distant it couldn't be trusted. He stored the thought to use it for Strand when they started filming.

'So, we're setting up this shot with the kids,' Alysson told him. 'Those pictures in the book, you know them? Strand rehearsed them first, framed and posed them very carefully. Like making a film. This'll be easy.'

They'd found some local kids and dressed them in fifties clothes, all wool mufflers and heavy jackets, but they could have been the ones from Strand's pictures. The faces hadn't changed.

'Do you know who used to live here?' Joe asked them.

'Sorry sir.'

'Dunno.'

''S been empty for an age.'

'How long's an age?' he asked again.

'Dunno. A long time.'

Rachel was having some trouble with her sound equipment, so they had to do it again. The echo was strange in there, Joe noted that. It was no better after the third and fourth takes, but Alysson said it'd be OK and they could fix it in post.

'And, oh, by the way,' she added. 'Looks like Lydia might not be able to make it after all. I've had a think, and it's not a problem. Most of her scenes can be interiors. We can do them later.'

For a second, Joe had thought she was talking about his wife.

'YOU'LL BE DOING A LOT of work when you get back, then?' Joe asked Rachel as they were packing up.

'How do you mean?'

'Alysson keeps on saying you can fix everything "in post."'

'Yeah. Maybe.' She was difficult, this Rachel, thought Joe, but he didn't mind. He was used to difficult. Joe knew that films were made in post-production. The actual filming was only a sketchbook, the notes, the pieces with which to knit the thing together. When it eventually came out, how much of his experience here would it hold? Not much.

'The sound's important, though, isn't it?'

'Yeah. Very.' Despite not getting much out of her, Joe decided he liked Rachel. He detected northern flint in her monosyllables, admired her self-sufficiency. One of Alysson's friends, he guessed, hauled in and willing to do the job for little or nothing. Some of the best things he'd done were like that. People working for the love and not the cash.

'What was the problem?' She looked offended, then softened.

'I don't know, to tell you the truth. Everything's working fine, but—the sound wouldn't come out.'

'How do you mean?'

'I mean, nothing was recording. Or rather, only noise. Here, have a listen.' She handed him a pair of headphones. There was a crackle, almost like static, but softer, which resolved itself into a kind of hiss or drone. It wasn't unpleasant, but there were none of the voices. He'd be getting called back in, too—sitting in a sound booth for ages, not to mention the scenes he'd be doing with his on-screen wife. 'I had a colleague, once,' she said. 'Well, someone I worked with. He'd been somewhere like this, Orkney I think it was, doing a film about trout fishing, and he'd tried to record running water there—the sound of a brook or stream or something. When he played back what he'd got it was off, like this, and he realised it wasn't water he'd managed to record at all, but thousands of tiny fish leaping up to catch bugs.'

'Lots of bugs here. Have you seen my face?' She looked at him briefly.

'Yes, but there are none in there.' She gestured to the house they'd just left. 'Or at least none that I can see. I'm having trouble distinguishing signal from noise. It's all noise at the moment. Even if they are bugs, or fish, or something I can't even recognise. Tell me the truth,' she asked, 'did you get spooked in there?'

'Only by those kids,' he said. He had been spooked though, but he wouldn't admit it. It was just the weirdness of the previous evening, he thought. He was about to tell Rachel about it, but then—finally, the first time since Joe had arrived—the wind stopped.

The silence became present. Nothing became something.

'There's fuck all here,' said Rachel, 'but you could spend a lifetime discovering it.'

THAT AFTERNOON THEY WERE FILMING outside the hotel with the bar attached. Strand had stayed there, some sixty years earlier. Joe wondered if he'd stopped for a pint in the bar.

'Not a drinker, I don't think,' said Alysson, 'and the place must have changed a lot since then, so we'll just be doing externals.' Joe looked at the crumbling walls and doubted it had changed that much. It was probably because Alysson couldn't get permission to film inside.

'Am I just standing around again? Looking moody?'

'You're good at that.'

'You know the CIA were following him, right?'

'You want to turn this into a thriller?'

'There's no tension, no conflict.'

'I'm not interested in tension and conflict. I want texture, atmosphere, suggestion. This is experiential.'

Joe shut up and looked moody for a bit while they filmed. It was too static, even Alysson saw that.

'How about some dialogue?'

'I've got no one to talk to.'

'You're having a conversation with Hazel, only she's not there.'

'She's not there?'

'She's not there. Andrea, can you stand in? Joe—talk to Andrea, bounce off her.'

'This is ridiculous,' said Joe.

'It'll work, trust me.' Alysson leafed through a script, highlighting some of the text. 'Here, these are your lines.' Joe read for a minute. 'OK, are we ready?' He looked at Andrea; the camera looked at him.

'Photography is a record of living.'

'Good—but again, and a bit slower.'

'Photography,' said Joe, as slowly as he could without being ridiculous, 'is a record of living.'

'Another.'

'A photograph is ink on paper. Anyone can take a photograph, a portrait. The trick is to make someone care about a stranger, by showing the core of their humanness. To show their humanity.' That, he thought, was a good one. Make someone care about a stranger. He liked that. He went on.

'No matter what lens you use, no matter what speed the film, or how you develop or print it, you cannot say more than you can see.' He wasn't quite sure about that last bit—can you say more than you can see?—but let it ride: it was Strand, after all, not him.

'The decisive moment is when I see something that I choose to photograph.'

'I need to find form that adequately represents reality.'

'All art is abstract.'

'This is a record of life.'

'All light is available light.'

'I WONDER IF WE COULD do this all the way through,' said Alysson, later. 'Have Hazel in as an almost phantasmic figure, only seen in flashback or imagination. That way we can do all of Lydia's parts back in London.' It had worked, Joe knew, and not so different to his real life: he spoke; she wasn't there.

'You can't be a feminist film-maker if you cut the main female role.'

'Yes I fucking can,' said Alysson. 'Anyhow, I'm not cutting her. I'm actually giving her a more important role. Just because she's not actually here doesn't mean she's not the centre of it all.' Joe could see her patience with him was running out, along with the money, probably.

'Did you manage to get the sound for this?' he asked Rachel after Alysson had stormed off.

'I did. Have a listen.' Joe put on the headphones and heard his own voice hanging in the silence, as though he were there and not there at the same time. When he took them off, the world had changed, by a degree. The sound he heard around him now, the wind gently buffeting, some distant gulls, the sigh of a car engine maybe, or the drone of a ship in the distance, all took their place in a panorama of near silence, a symphony of almost nothing. For a moment, he forgot all his fears of the film failing, of being followed, of the long trip home, and of being home again.

Then the car noises grew louder and Kev Whealdon and his genetically modified friends turned up again.

'Still here, are you?' he asked. 'Looks like you'll be outstaying us.'

'How d'you mean?'

'We've been given our cards. Time's up. They reckon they've got enough, or something. We were contracted for two weeks at least. I'm going to make fucking well sure we get paid for it.' Kev wasn't happy. The rest of them marched into the hotel. 'Time to get packing lads. Can't wait to get the fuck out of here to be honest. I've been bitten to death by midges.'

'Being an actor's crap,' said one of the others.

'They'll probably just AI us now,' said another.

'Film-making is dead,' said a third.

'Film-making has been dead for ages,' said Joe. 'It's always been an art of disappearance.'

'What are you on about?' asked Kev.

'We don't make films anymore,' said Joe. 'Well, we do, but not in the old way. There's no capturing and recording light. It's projecting. It's an intricate and complex action based on and built of algorithms and perceptions. The camera constructs an image for us.'

'What the fuck got into you?' asked Kev again. Joe didn't know. 'Always the pretentious git, you were. Any road, good luck with whatever it is you're doing,' he said. 'See you at the premiere, eh?'

NEXT DAY, THEY FINALLY GOT to the beach. The two cars they had only got them so far then they had to lug the equipment the rest of the way. Luckily there wasn't much of it. Gerry and Terry, Graeme the fixer, Rachel with her sound stuff and Alysson and Andrea with their cameras and computers all trudged across the soft, spongy grass to where they could see an end. Hills held up the land behind them, the stretch before them lay flat, as though the island was sliding slowly into the sea. The beach, Joe had heard, ran all along the western shore and was supposed to be magnificent, if they could see any of it through the rain. Rabbits darted back and forth.

'That's a hare, actually,' said Gerry.

'No it isn't,' said Terry. 'It's just a massive rabbit.'

'They used to have raves out here,' said Graeme.

'I thought that was further up, by the Deep Sea Range,' said Joe.

'Ach, yeah. Maybe there too,' Graeme replied. 'There's some neolithic burial ground around here, you wouldn't want to be dancing on that.'

'Such great landscape though,' said Alysson looking around. 'It's like that Balzac quotation—"Here there are gods without men."' It was a good line Joe thought, but he also knew it untrue: there were all kinds of human traces here, and few gods. He thought about pointing this out, but didn't want to risk upsetting Alysson again. 'It's the rock, the grass, the water,' she went on, undisturbed and un-upset. 'That light! It's elemental. No spirits here, no fairies or folklore, only raw elements, but in the grass, the rocks, the wind—there's everything.'

Joe knew what she meant, but wasn't going to openly agree with her. There probably had been ghosts here, but they'd left too. Humans had driven them off. Any wandering spirits out there would still leave it well alone.

'We've got our stories,' said Graeme, marching on ahead, his voice trailing back to them. 'Not so many, but there are some. Shapeshifters, in the water. Eich-usige. Water horses, but not nice ones like the kelpies. They'll come as a handsome man, or a horse, or an eagle or something. Watch out for lone strangers by the shore. They'll drag you down and drown you.'

Joe was astonished when they finally reached the sea. The beach was as long as promised, disappearing into the mist to the north and south of him, and could well have been endless, but it wasn't the length which amazed him as much as the colour: not quite white, nor grey, but with a near-luminous bluish quality. Joe had never wanted to paint anything more than a bedroom wall, but he wanted to paint this. It was like the moon.

There was a lone stranger there, too, but he seemed friendly enough, out walking his dog. Joe eyed the dog carefully. They asked him if he wanted to be in a film, but he politely turned them down and walked off down the shore until he vanished.

'Costume was all wrong anyway,' said Andrea.

They got going on the usual shots: Joe had to stare, to walk, to brood.

He had to be quietly intense. He was bored. He was rarely bored while they were actually filming. He sat down and looked out at a ship on the horizon while the crew fiddled with their equipment and Alysson and Andrea muttered in a huddle. Rachel was having sound trouble again. Slowly, as he gazed out, Joe began to see as Strand might have done: he saw a frame, then a composition, then a picture emerge. And once emerged, it lived: the clouds became slow-moving mountains, the grass quivered, a stick lying in the sand became a snake, the light itself was made of guillemots, razorbills and fulmars—darting and swooping from the water to the land, never still. He was on the edge of somewhere, and about to fall.

But it was the sound most of all—everything became a roar: the wind, the rain, the shifting of the sand and the singing of the marram. He thought he could hear the rocks, that ship far out. The cries of the seabirds bounced wildly, pinging and howling off the sea, their continuous echo a counterpoint to the huge swell of the air and water.

'Sound's fucked again,' said Andrea. Joe returned to himself.

'I'm not sure we can do more today, anyhow,' said Alysson. 'This rain's too much. We did some good work there, we've got enough.' Joe sat, mute for once, adrift, watching the ship on the horizon while the others packed up. Rachel trudged over.

'That's a funny-looking boat, isn't it?' she said. It was like the plane Joe had seen: all angles and shadows, and though graceful, not quite ship-shaped.

'Yeah. Not a container, I don't think. Same problem with your recorder?'

'I don't know what's going on. I think there's too much rain, that's all.'

'You should just keep it all. Let whatever you've got be the soundtrack.'

THAT EVENING ALYSSON HAD HER usual debrief at the pods. The rain had slackened enough for them to sit around the fire pit and poke vegan sausages into the embers. Gerry and Terry had some cans and Joe helped himself.

'Guys,' said Alysson, and Joe flinched. It wasn't only the word 'guys' that bothered him, but his knowledge that any time anyone began a sentence with 'guys,' it wasn't going to be good. It wasn't good. 'I know we were hoping to stay on for a few days, but with the weather and everything, and our tech problems, I think we're going to wrap at this point. I'm not worried, I think we've done some great work and that we've got enough to make something really special. I want to thank you all for your work.'

'Thank fuck for that,' said Gerry, or Terry. Joe opened another can.

'Was this just some kind of tax dodge? A write-off?' he asked.

'Joe...'

'It's nothing but a hobby for you, isn't it? You like to think you're making art but all you're doing is faffing around so you can impress your mates. Has the money run out?'

'Joe, come on. I am—we are—making art. You know this—this is only the beginning. There'll be VO work to do yet. Lots.'

'It's not what it was supposed to be.'

'It never is. Films get made in their making. I'm seeing this as much less linear now, more a curve, or spiral.'

'Listen—is someone chasing you off? First that other lot, now us—what's going on?'

'I've no idea what you're talking about, Joe.' Joe stood up, stuffed a can into each pocket of his jacket, and walked off.

He must have slept at some point, but by dawn the next morning he felt like he'd been walking all night. He did remember going back to the trailer at some point, having got lost on his way there, to change his boots and fill up his hip flask, and also seemed to remember going in search of the lighthouse, or whatever it was, but had found nothing there, or perhaps not even managed to find the place at all. After that he'd had the great idea of finding the place where he'd been happiest, and heading for the beach again. That must be why the sun was rising and his legs ached so much. He realised that he was now the lone stranger on the shore and wished he could turn into a horse and dive into the waves and swim away, and was at least glad that his appearance might dissuade anyone from coming near him. Didn't happen though: he saw someone else sitting at the top of the ridge which led down to the beach and recognised Rachel, there with her mic and recorder. He didn't want to approach her, but she saw him first, and waved.

'Out for a walk?'

'Something like that.'

'When are you off back?'

'Don't know. When's the next ferry?'

'There's one in a couple of hours. I'm supposed to be on it. That's why I came out here early, to see if I could get anything. I thought it might be quieter now, but if anything there's more sound.'

'It's strange isn't it—it's so quiet here, but as soon as you listen it's noisy as hell.'

'Maybe you're right, and that should be the sound. I really wanted that silence, though. When the wind stops.'

They sat, and listened, and waited for the silence.

'Is there a German word for it?' asked Rachel.

'What?'

'That silence.' Joe had to think for a moment.

'I don't think so, no.'

'I thought they had a word for everything.'

'Not everything.' There was silence again.

'Have you heard from Alysson?' asked Rachel.

'Since when?'

'Last night.'

'No. Why? Has she changed her mind?'

'No. Not at all—her computer's fritzed.'

'What?'

'Yeah. Water got into it, or something. Completely frazzled.'

'For fuck's sake. Can she salvage anything?'

'Seems to think she's got enough back up, and tech people in London who can save something.'

'Thank god for that.'

The wind dropped, and for a moment, that silence embraced them.

'Did you get that?' he asked, when the wind rose again.

'I think so. I've no idea what it'll sound like.'

'Can you listen back to it?'

'I think I'll wait until I'm somewhere else.'

Without speaking, they both noticed the ship from yesterday, still there, much closer now, but still as indescribable.

'It's the same colour as the sea,' said Rachel. 'That's why it's so difficult to make out.'

'It looks like the rocks,' said Joe.

'Only man-made. There's nothing natural about it.'

'It's been a whole series of weird encounters, these last few days.'

'That's true. This is another.'

'You mean . . . us?'

'I meant that ship.'

'Ah. Wait a minute—is that smoke coming out of it? It's not a steamer, is it?'

'I don't think so.'

'Yep. That's smoke.'

'Jesus. Those are flames too.'

'Should we call someone? The Coastguard?'

'Probably. Your phone work?'

'No.'

'Mine neither.'

So they just sat there, the actor and the sound recordist, watching the ship burn. For a second, Joe was reminded of the dolphin he'd seen on the way out, and thought how this was its opposite—not a momentary flash, a glimpse of something other, but the slow process of decay. They both knew the sound would be roaring, but they could hear nothing. After some time had passed, the ship gently imploded on itself. Joe waited for something else to happen, but there was only the wind, and then even that died away.

CONTRACT

Some time back, Jen had worked the night desk at a private members' club. The little she had to do bored her, but she didn't sleep. She arrived each evening at seven, logged in to the computer, checked her messages, then the booking system, then moved the pens on her desk and rearranged the dried flowers by the door. If guests ever came it was her job to welcome them, but this didn't happen often. Once she had checked her messages again, she had nothing to do but avoid sleep until seven the next morning. There was no reason for her to be there, but they wanted a human presence. When avoiding sleep she watched YouTube videos of cats falling off tables, freak weather events, assembly-line conveyor belts, or free climbers scaling vertiginous construction cranes in China. She wanted to read but wasn't supposed to when on duty; they said it would make her look distracted. People didn't want to disturb someone who was reading. She'd been there a couple of months and didn't not like it but didn't like it either. The work was straightforward and boring but the regular deposit into her bank account was enough to keep her arriving each evening and not sleeping until she left the next morning.

She rarely saw anyone. The cleaner had gone by the time Jen arrived and didn't come again until after she'd left. There was no handover, which was strange. She guessed her daytime counterpart must leave shortly before her and arrive shortly after, though whoever it was left no trace. There were seven rooms for guests, but they were seldom occupied. The Pearl was an international chain, an exclusive society, a new concept of 'club'—whenever you were staying in London, or Berlin, or Rio, or New York, there would be a bar, or a sauna, or a conference suite, or a room, waiting for you. Jen didn't know where the bar or sauna or suite were; they hadn't told her, she didn't need to know. She worked the rooms. At any time of night, the idea was, someone could simply rock up and—provided they were an associate (never merely a 'member')—enjoy restful sleep. In reality, it didn't work that way: there was a strict list of who was allowed in and who wasn't. People not on the list were always to be told that the rooms were full, which they usually weren't. Some nights, when avoiding sleep, Jen scrolled through the listed names to see if she recognised any of them.

The Pearl where Jen worked the night desk was on the top floor of a new tower. The lift opened directly into an atrium with a sofa, the dried flowers and her desk. Jen couldn't tell if the flowers were real or not, if they'd ever once lived or had been manufactured. A corridor lined with three rooms on each side ran from the atrium and Room 7 sat at its end. Room 7 was to be left permanently empty. The only person to be allowed into Room 7 would introduce themselves as an 'Executive Associate' and already have an access code and a passkey. Two months into the job, Jen had never met an Executive Associate.

She hadn't met anyone really. The few times when permitted guests had come, they'd arrived late and tired, and Jen knew that her job was simply to open doors for them, to smile and be invisible. It seemed to work. No one tried to flirt with her, not even the single men.

No one looked at the art, either, apart from Jen. There were seven pieces on the walls, six of them next to the rooms. They were part of a rotating collection, she'd found, should anyone ask. The pictures in the corridor were portraits, Jen couldn't tell if they were photographs or paintings, of people who had had their faces removed, or blacked out, or whitewashed. She found them disturbing, but not uninteresting. They were a strange choice, she thought, for a place like the Pearl. The seventh work hung in the atrium, a huge video screen which showed a slow-moving image of a ship coming into dock, then leaving again, repeatedly. The names of the pieces and of the artists who'd made them were somewhere on the Pearl intranet, but she'd never got round to checking them.

There was a garden too, accessed through the few steps which ran up to each side around Room 7. It was called 'The Deck,' and it was only after Jen had been there a few days that she realised the whole place was supposed to have a nautical theme. Very subtle, thankfully, no anchors, barnacles or portholes. There were no windows at all, in fact. Maybe like a cruise liner. That would explain the current choice of video art (though the portraits remained baffling). Two months into the job, she still hadn't been out onto the Deck. It was winter, dark, cold and rainy enough to stop anyone from going out, especially this high up.

In order to check her messages and the booking system, Jen had to log in to the intranet each evening when she arrived. She had a password for the VPN, then she'd get sent a code before she could access it. That was how she'd got the job in the first place—she'd never actually met anyone who worked for the Pearl: the advert had come to her through her daily jobsearch update. She'd followed the link, clicked 'apply online,' sent off the usual CV, supporting statements, covering letter, then received an email within hours. Usually there was no reply at all, so this was a definite plus. They sent her an access code to the Pearl site, where she did an interview with what she assumed was a bot.

The day after the interview she'd been sent another code to a Workspace Application where she found a contract with a request for a digital signature. Approval, the message said, was dependent on her responding to the Task Description. She checked the Task Description: 'Completing Induction Process.' The Induction Process required nothing more than watching a video and clicking the answers to some multiple-choice questions. 'Welcome to the Pearl World,' the video began, high-resolution graphics and a generated voice, neither male nor female but utterly reassuring. 'Get comfortable and take some time to become part of our exclusive family.' Some work had gone into it, though it was largely standard corporate hokum. 'This film has been designed by our creative team to facilitate smooth onboarding.' Every few minutes the screen froze and asked her to choose an answer to a question. How many Pearl hubs are there in the worldwide network? What are the most desirable outcomes of service-user interactions? Which phrase best describes the workflow procedure? How does the Pearl integrate user activity and data management to optimise needs projection and incentive alignment? Her attention had been flagging so she clicked at random. Ten minutes later, as soon as the video had finished, the Task Manager of the Workspace Application informed her that the task had been completed and the start date was immediate.

Jen signed but didn't read the contract. It was a job and she needed one and this would be better than tending bar in a chain pub, carting a Dyson around deserted office workstations before dawn each morning to remove crumbs from packaged sandwiches, grinning to get commuters to donate 10 percent of their incomes to a dubious charity while hanging around a draughty train station or slinging overpriced coffee-based froth to sullen university students who never even took their earbuds out while ordering. Her CV was not looking good. This could only be better.

There'd been a second training film, about post specifics for the Evening Session Host, which, it turned out, was her new job title. It didn't say she couldn't go into the rooms (apart from Room 7), but it didn't exactly encourage it, either. The first time she did it her cheeks flushed with excitement and her pulse raced. She ran the passkey, which wasn't a key but a card, across a shiny black pad and a green light pinged. She felt the cold of the doorhandle keen on her fingertips. Once in, though, the feelings subsided. She didn't know quite what she'd expected, but it hadn't been this. As she sat on the edge of the hard, high bed, she realised she'd imagined a den of louche and opulent decadence, a secret boudoir rich with bosky perfumes and the potential for debauchery. Instead she found the executive suite of a mid-range ring-road hotel, somewhere you might stay if your cousin was getting married and you'd been coerced into being part of the bridal party, perhaps, or a rendezvous for a sad 50th birthday party. The candle was Diptyque, the pods for the Keurig were Illy and the bottles in the bathroom were Jo Malone, but still. Was that it? Pleasant enough, serviceable, larger than average, certainly, but little more. To have the kind of money she imagined a Pearl associate had, and this is what they aspired to?

She tried the other rooms and they were all the same, identical apart from the fact that they had windows on different sides. At least there were windows. She drew back the blinds and peered out but couldn't see anything other than her reflection in the glass. There had been no reason to imagine anything other than this, given that everything she had learned about the Pearl was distinguished only in its blandness, but the sleepless night did its work and her imagination had spun. Her imagination, she decided, was crap. It always led her to hoping for more than what existed.

Even after the disappointment, she did it again. There was always a thrill in sliding the passkey across the pad and slowly opening the heavy doors to rooms where she certainly wasn't being advised to go and where, she knew, she'd end up let down. The log would tell her if a guest was present or not, and if one was she wouldn't enter, as that would feel too much like a violation, but that meant she could go in most of the time, as guests were so rare. It was partly the relief from boredom that lent it the thrill, she knew, as much as the idea that she was doing something forbidden.

Jen never went into Room 7, though wondered what was in it, and if it would be the one her imagination had insinuated. It would have to be different in its layout, at least. Two months into the job, racked by boredom and unwilling to sleep, she stood in front of its door, exactly the same as all the others, and held the passkey in her fingers. What could Executive Associates have that ordinary ones couldn't? What did Executive Associates do by night? What attracted or aroused them? She touched the pad with her passkey. A red light blipped. The handle wouldn't move. Jen turned on her heel and almost ran back to her desk.

She'd have been tracked. Her attempt to enter would have been reported, to someone, somewhere. Everything here was recorded. There were security cameras watching her—she couldn't see them but knew they were there. A signal would have been sent out. She checked the messaging system. It was hesitant at first—instead of the usual circle, an infinity symbol wound its way back into itself while the screen loaded. It looked like a hexafoil or daisywheel, there to seduce and trap demons. Only a second, maybe two, but long enough for her to think something was off. She was right.

>Sender: workflow
>TASK
>Task Name: Unauthorized entry attempt
>Task Description: Respond to Unauthorized entry attempt
>Reply to this task in the Workspace Application
>Task performer: Jennifer Wise 1760036
>Task owner: Security Manager 850834
>Required: Yes
>Status: Initiated
>Start date: Immediate
>Due date: Immediate

SHE ACCESSED THE WORKSPACE APPLICATION and wondered how to respond to an Unauthorized entry attempt. She could deny all knowledge of it, or admit to her curiosity and blame her rampant imagination. Neither option was good. 'A suspicious noise was heard in Room 7,' she wrote in the box in the Workspace Application. It warned her that she only had 162 characters left. 'Checked door,' she continued. 'No further noise detected.' That'd do. 'No further action taken.' She'd shown herself to be conscientious, at least.

CONTRACT

Jen worried about losing her job. She had nothing else. Although she didn't want to sleep, she needed somewhere to sleep. She thought she probably ought to check the intranet for the code of conduct. It told her to look at her contract. First up, she noted that the contract guaranteed Jennifer Wise the status of a legal entity. She didn't know if she should feel different now she was a legal entity. She didn't really know what that was. Things like this were the reason she hadn't bothered to read it in the first place. She went on. 'Zero hours,' it said, but she was working twelve every night. She knew what this meant: they could sack her at any moment. The ship around her rocked and tilted. She was precarious.

She carried on scouring the Ts & Cs and there was the stuff about presenting professionally, not reading, not sleeping, but nothing about access to the rooms. She let herself relax. She was fine with all this, apart from the reading. Jen liked reading, but didn't like sleeping.

She didn't sleep not because she wasn't tired, nor less because she wasn't supposed to. She didn't sleep because sleep scared her. Sleep was the province of dreams, and dreams were supposed to be good, but Jen's weren't. Though never exactly nightmares, her dreams were disturbing enough to bring her back to wakefulness uneasy and riddled with non-specific dread, even though she could rarely remember anything that happened in them.

Night was waking time for her. Days meant nothing. She could hardly remember them. And though the existence here was boring, at least it was an existence. She wasn't sure if her daytime outdoor self existed anymore. It had only been two months.

By 4 am it was the sheer intensity of the boredom which kept her awake; 4 am was the strangest time, the very dead of the night, when it was both too late and too early. Jen always went a little mad around 4 am. The dark; her imagination; sleep deprivation. This place, she thought, was more like a submarine than a ship.

The next evening she arrived as normal, logged on and checked her messages. There was nothing more about the security incident. The booking register, though, was full. This had never happened before. The few guests there had been had arrived in ones or twos, turned up late and left early, barely causing a ripple. Now there were twelve.

They all arrived together and seemed to know each other, at least by name. Jen picked up snatches of their conversation. They'd all come for the opening of the Sigismunda Conrad show. Jen took an interest and knew the name but not much about the artist's work. It must be something quite big if they'd all come this far, Jen thought. They were all staying for two nights. She checked them in smoothly, no problems, and they all ignored her. Not even a question about where to eat near here or how to get to where they were going. Jen assumed they all knew that anyhow. Some dropped bags and went out again, others closed their doors and went quiet.

It wasn't until midnight when the extra arrived. The lift door opened and there he was. Jen thought she'd be advised about anyone coming, but there'd been no message about this man. The really strange thing was that she thought she recognised him, though she couldn't quite place him. Even though he was a resolutely bland-looking individual (white, short brownish hair, nice if undistinguished suit, buttoned-up shirt with no tie), Jen thought that she had definitely met him somewhere before, but could not remember where. More than that, Jen knew that this man had done something in the past that he shouldn't have done. She could tell by his face, or it was her memory that told her, or both of these things. This was a man, she thought, who had done something he wished he hadn't, something he hoped other people would not know about, or have forgotten, but was not entirely sure they had. She looked at him, and he knew this, and he smiled, then produced an Executive Associate card.

'I'll be in Room 7,' he said. 'I can let myself in.' As he walked up the corridor he paused to look at the pictures. 'These new?' he asked. Jen smiled and shrugged.

'I've only been here a couple of months,' she said.

'You don't know them yet, do you?' he said, then went into Room 7.

The obscure challenge in his words distracted Jen so much she didn't even get the merest glimpse into the room. She went back to her desk and looked for the information about the pictures. It was there somewhere, in the tech specs section, but she couldn't find it. She ended up scouring every part of the interminable website, each page leading her onto another. The few people who'd gone out returned scarcely acknowledging her, as if she had become invisible. None of the men even bothered flirting with her, and she was relieved about this. Somewhere under 'Mission,' she got completely lost. 'Outside,' the Pearl Mission Statement said, 'we are required to live with a constantly harried sense of time. At the Pearl, we live in a no-time, a state of atemporality.' This was strange, even by the standards of corporate bullshit, but Jen found herself warming to it and wondered what kind of imp had smuggled itself into the copywriting team. 'Digital technology can involve a dilation of time,' it went on, and Jen was no longer sure about the mischievous spirit and wondered if there wasn't, in fact, a clear ideology at work. 'At the Pearl, motion can cease.' Was that an invitation to relaxation, or a recasting of Newtonian laws?

'At the Pearl we own nothing, but we possess everything.' That one sounded like an anarchist call to arms, but it went on to contradict itself: 'Possession is not about laws and contracts, a matter of movement and circulation.' But wasn't the Pearl a site where motion ceased? She was confused; it was late. The last one she read convinced her she was hallucinating: 'At the Pearl, technological upgrades have replaced the need for cultural development.' It was 7 am, time to go.

At 7 pm, she was back. No one else was, though. The entry log showed everyone had left at some point in the day and hadn't yet returned. This wasn't unusual—they'd be back later and possibly very late. Meanwhile, the place was full, yet empty. Jen was tempted to enter each room but worried she'd be caught by a returner. She wondered about Mr Room 7. There was no log for Room 7. It might be occupied; it might not be. His presence was unpredictable.

She spent the evening trawling the company website again but couldn't find the pages she'd read the night before. The browser history auto-deleted. By 1 am she wondered if she should report the absences, but there was no procedure for this, and at this point they still weren't even absences.

At around 4 am, Jen staring down sleeplessness, Mr Room 7 turned up. He smiled and asked if she'd found out about the pictures.

'I haven't managed to trace that info, I'm afraid.'

'No worries,' he said, and went up the corridor and into his room. Jen had forgotten the pictures and thought of investigating again but instead found herself trying to place the man. He was uninterestingly handsome, a face you'd notice then quickly forget or, at least, be unable to discern from other early middle-aged white men with average height and features. She tried an image search but his face was too bland.

CONTRACT

It was soon 6. It wouldn't yet be light outside, thought Jen, not at this time of year, but it still qualified as morning and none of the others had come back. She was almost worried, though couldn't understand why. Those people were nothing to her, and were quite probably still out partying. She shouldn't peek in their rooms, but she could.

The first two looked undisturbed, as if no one had been in there at all, and it was only when she entered Room 3, where a small suitcase lay by the bed, that she noticed what was different. The room was smaller. She checked Room 4, its counterpart, to see if she had merely been mistaken, if these rooms had always offered less space than the first two. Two bags lay between the bed and the door, blocking her way. Perhaps it was the bed that was larger in here. Room 5 was smaller again, though, its exterior wall seeming to have moved several inches inward, pushing against the bedside table. She could hardly open the door of Room 6. The furniture was piled up on itself, as though the cabin of a ship which had sailed through a great storm. There wasn't enough space in it for her to walk through. She closed the door behind her and left, glad that it was nearly 7 am and someone else's problem.

The next night, at 7 sharp, she was back and checked the log before her messages. No activity. No one had returned. She checked her messages. Nothing. She should file a report. She went into the Workspace Application and opened an incident. There was no protocol for this. 'Guests not returned,' she wrote. 'Please advise on procedure.' She waited for a response.

She didn't know about Room 7. He might be in there; he might not be. The room was in an unstable state of being, both either/or and neither/nor. She went and knocked and there was no answer. This didn't necessarily mean anything. Perhaps he was in the shower, or otherwise engaged, or simply ignoring her. Jen wondered about going out onto the Deck. If she went out she could at least see if there were any lights on in the room. The door pushed against her as she tried to open it: the wind was strong. Once out, it was a gale. Black rain blew sideways across her. She had to hold on to a railing to stop herself from being blown away. The weather roared. She was drenched within a minute. And yet, a few steps on, and everything ceased: the rain became mere drizzle, the wind stopped completely. She let go of the railing and looked around. Save for a few city lights which she could not identify, it was black as far as she could see. She took a step forward and hit the wind again. It only existed in certain spots, strange eddies and vortices. A step back and it was calm again. She'd seen a video about this somewhere. It was terrifying. Once in the wind she could hardly hold her footing. She could swear she felt a nip of salt in the air.

The strangest thing, though, was Room 7. It wasn't there.

Where it should have been, there was only a wall. It should project out—Jen had imagined it with windows on three sides, giving a view from the top of the building over the city, but there was nothing. Had she misjudged? Was her spatial awareness that off? She risked the wind and walked around the deck, thinking it lay to another direction. There wasn't even a window.

Back in, she went to Room 7. Its door was there, but now she knew there was nothing beyond it. What could it open on to? Maybe there were stairs, or an elevator, but she had seen no stairwell, no elevator shaft. It must be an architectural trick, some clever play of line and structure, surface and appearance. Somewhere on the intranet she'd seen a plan of the building, she was sure, and made to find it again.

Back at her desk, two things hit her. First was the response to her incident report.

> Action required: none
> Incident: closed

THE SECOND WAS A CARD lying there. Black and shiny, a slice of obsidian. The only words on it: Pearl Executive Associate. The man in Room 7 had left, and had left her his card. She picked it up and it was cold to her touch. As she walked back along the corridor to Room 7 she told herself it had probably expired, or was only single-use, or faulty, and that if it was some kind of an invitation, then it was one best left unanswered. She considered the man, the occupant, and realised what was strange about him: not so much the thought that she had met him before, but the feeling that somewhere, sometime, she would meet him again.

She brushed the card over the pad and the door sprang open.

The room was filled with soil. Jen walked in and felt it give beneath her feet. It grew so deep she almost touched the ceiling as she walked into it. She felt herself beginning to sink. A cloud appeared above her, thick, dark and curling, and then it began to rain. The soil turned to mud which became a vortex, which then became a cloud and swirled around her, then away. There was someone sitting on the edge of the bed with their back to her. She knew that the person must not turn around. Before they could, the room began to fill with gas, and Jen was relieved. She knew this wasn't anything poisonous. She breathed it in until she was so light she began to float, then fly. The room was on fire, and she was above it, powerless to do anything. She brought herself down, slowly, and found the room was now filled with water, but she didn't get wet. The water grew and swelled until there was an entire tide in the room, a whole ocean battering around her.

The room was filled with everything Jen dreamed about and was afraid to return to. The room was filled with the reasons Jen didn't sleep, and it was getting smaller, the seawater deeper and louder. She turned and left.

Back at the desk, two messages appeared on her screen. She checked the first one.

TASK

Access this task in the Workspace Application.

Sender: workflow

Task Name: Exit Interview

Task Description: Please complete Exit Interview

Task Performer: Jennifer Wise 1760036

Task Owner: Identity Manager 990828

Required: Yes

Status: Initiated

Start date: Immediate

Due date: Immediate

She checked the second one.

TASK

Access to Workspace Application denied.

Sender: workflow

Task Name: Exit Interview

Task Performer: Jennifer Wise 1760036

CONTRACT

Task Owner: Identity Manager 990828

Task Description: Exit interview (completed/terminated)

Action required: Delete any corporate ID, apps, passwords from personal devices. Please access our corporate health and wellbeing site. Please post pictures of favourite pets, hobbies, crafts, etc. to this site. Note that post-termination you no longer have access to this site. Return identity and company property.

THE SCREEN WENT BLANK SAVE for that symbol again, slowly feeding itself. It was night in the Pearl. It was night, thought Jen, all over the world. Jen put her card on the desk she no longer worked and wondered if the desk, and the computer on it, and the fake plants, and the pictures on the walls, and all the rooms would still be there after she had left. She turned to close the door behind her and the place, she knew, was already smaller.

ALEATORIC OUTCOMES FROM AN INTERACTION OF CONFLICTING FORCES

In the beginning Silas found it easy. Once the cash started coming in it got more complicated. There wasn't that much, at first, but more than he'd want to keep stashed in the box room of the flatshare in Stoke Newington where he was currently living. He had a bank account but worried that making frequent deposits of small-denomination notes might attract attention. He could claim he was a busker, if anyone asked, but even buskers had card readers these days.

He'd had Jaz for herbal and Pav for chemical but then everyone started on Adderall, Ritalin and Xanax so he needed a dodgy medic. Jaz fixed him up with Ren who was a pharma postdoc and had the necessary, but then it got griping. Like, seriously griping. Silas tried to use his commercial inflow as his investment outflow but was then left with stashes in half a dozen places: it looked like he was setting up an off-brand pharmacy but with bags full of foul-stinking bushweed piled up in the hallway. He moved the jazz cabbage to the food recycling caddy but then someone put it out and the bin men had a field day, no doubt. He shouldn't be holding much—that was always a flaw. It'd be worse getting caught with twenty-odd grand's worth of prescription medications, odoriferous resins and murky leaves than it would with a stack of greasy notes. Not that the notes were greasy

ALEATORIC OUTCOMES FROM AN INTERACTION OF CONFLICTING FORCES

these days: that plastic finish kept them clean, at least, though if ever tested for traces of anything, Silas suspected they'd set off alarms from here to Istanbul.

The flat where he lived was used by their never-seen landlord as a repository for off-brand 1990s furniture. The guy hadn't even bothered with Ikea but sourced everything from charity shops and house clearances. There was a lamp in the shared living room, scratched matt black surfaces and chrome tubing. Silas posted it on eBay marked as 'vintage' and asked 250 quid for it. No one bid, so he bought it himself.

Next up was another lamp (broken), same deal, then an ethnic-style CD rack, then a pint-sized wine glass with 'Wine o'clock!' written on it. That was the plan: keep it circulating, make it look legit. When a wall clock made from the case and insert of Oasis's *Be Here Now* CD actually sold to a real punter and he had to bother posting it out, Silas realised he was now running a shadow business, an echo company, one which replicated his most lucrative line in the purveyance of actual as opposed to metaphorical junk (though he'd never touch heroin—he had some scruples).

The things he sold to himself could stay where they were, but when more people actually seemed to want the stuff resources soon began to run low. He considered the sofa but worried his flatmates might start to notice. The only thing to do was to become both producer and consumer. It was easy to call anything 'art,' so he figured he'd make some pictures, jack the prices up to ridiculous levels then buy them with his own surplus.

He got some black-and-white sketches of David Bowie, threw glitter all over them then stuck them in clip frames and asked for seventy-five quid a pop. They went, so he did some more and this time asked for two hundred. They still went. He couldn't roll them into their cardboard tubes quick enough. He was worried they'd get to know him at the post office. This wasn't how it was supposed to work; now he had even more excess income. The thought that he might have to do a tax return didn't stop him carrying on with his Rock Icons series, asking five hundred, seven-fifty until some photographer got arsey about copyright on one of his Joy Division pictures, so he had to deprioritise that line. He thought about the stuff his on/off girlfriend Kasha worked with, and reckoned he could knock out something similar so got himself some fancy paper and proper paints, did some smudges and some lines. This stuff would be worth a grand. Only one of the dozen he put up sold: so much the better, he could buy the rest himself and get back to his original aim of cleansing that grubby cash. Silas relaxed for a bit.

Problem was, the one that sold came back to him. He was sitting with Kasha one day, getting slightly stoned, and she was working like always, scrolling through her various feeds looking at pictures and their prices.

'SV,' she laughed. 'That could be you, couldn't it?' Silas had (stupidly) put his own stylised initials in the corner of the picture, thinking it would look more like proper art.

'Ha!' he said, peeking over her shoulder to see his own picture staring back at him, but this time from some swanky art website. The fucker who'd bought it was selling it on. Three times the price, he noted.

'Didn't know you'd moved into the art game,' she said.

'Ha!' said Silas, again. 'As if!' He didn't not tell Kasha things, but he didn't tell her them, either. Once she'd gone he went to the swanky art site and registered, carefully not using his own name. He put the pieces up there, decided he'd wait a week then buy them himself.

A week later they'd all gone. He was now making more money with the art than with the drugs; the shadow enterprise had taken over the real one. He thought about going legit, though that would throw up various problems: firstly, the shadow enterprise wasn't exactly legit to begin with; secondly, he'd have to face up to the tax man; thirdly, he didn't know how quickly he could bang out new art.

He dealt with problem three by nicking stuff from Kasha. Even though she preferred to have other people move the art around, and her job was merely to make this happen, Silas knew she kept some things she hadn't managed to palm off on anyone else stashed in the spare room of her flat. He had a nosey next time he was there—there wasn't much, a few things he thought might be sculptural works but you could never tell: a collection of spindly wires and pieces of cracked plaster, gaudy orange rubber tubes, some polythene bags scrunched up into balls. It was one thing when you saw these things in a gallery space, but outside of that they were nothing. There was an A2 portfolio of scratchy pencil drawings which looked vaguely promising, so he waited until one morning when he'd slept over and she'd had to leave early, then slipped off with them.

Once home he looked at them more carefully and found drawings of places which he partially recognised but couldn't identify, places he might have been once, but couldn't remember when, or where. He didn't know if they were pencil or charcoal or whatever, some grey substance etched and rubbed into the thick paper. They were odd. When he thought 'places' he wasn't quite sure if they were internal or external, but whichever they were, there was something off about the perspective, as though these places couldn't really exist. They unsettled him, they gave him the ick, they were hectic; he'd be glad to get rid of them.

He still had problem two, the tax. Pav told him he should be getting into crypto, an opinion backed up by Ren, but Jaz told him to leave that stuff well alone. Silas tended to side with Jaz: he didn't want to add scam to scam and risk getting caught for something he wasn't doing which would inevitably entail him getting caught again for something he was doing.

Which led him back to problem one. Was this actually legal? He decided to deal with that one by adopting his usual MO which was to do nothing at all, tell himself that it wasn't a problem, redefine it, then ignore it, hide if necessary and hope that it went away. It had worked so far, mostly.

At that point the pandemic kicked in and Silas actually breathed a sigh of relief. At least he didn't have to worry about it anymore. Everything would go quiet for a while. He didn't know how long; tried not to care too much. Only, it didn't. Contrary to his predictions the work picked up. More than picked up; it went crazy.

'Logical,' said Jaz. 'People got nothing else to do.'

'NFTs,' said Pav. 'That's what you want to be doing.' Silas spent hours trying to work out quite what an NFT was but ended up none the wiser and decided he wouldn't bother. It was the same as the crypto thing: the idea was brilliant, but the practice gave him the ick. Besides, he didn't need any new slang, his flow was doing fine. Those weird drawings had moved slowly at first, then all started to go in a rush. He'd had to use a courier to come and pick them up as he didn't think he could get away with a cardboard envelope for this stuff, and

ALEATORIC OUTCOMES FROM AN INTERACTION OF CONFLICTING FORCES

anyhow didn't want to risk picking up anything nasty in the post office, but the amount of insurance they wanted when he told them it was 'original art work' was nose-bleeding. Still worthwhile, though. When he got down to the last one he wondered if Kasha had any more. He hadn't seen her for a bit and she'd never trusted him with a key.

He got a message asking him if the pictures were Conrads. He didn't know who Conrad was. He'd left a blank for the name of the artist thinking that it would make them like Banksy, or something. The name rang a bell though—was Conrad one of Kasha's exes? That'd explain why she had the stuff lying around. He'd be happy to lose them if it was one of her exes. He was doing her a favour, really.

The messenger said they'd have them if they were Conrads but would need a signature or certificate of authenticity. Silas thought he could probably fake that, but then got worried again, so ignored the offer. He'd grown to quite like the pieces anyway. They'd crawled under his skin, become part of his own vision, or world, somehow. He got some proper art pencils and tried to make his own versions. A few lines at awkward angles, shade in some parts, a smudge here and there. He did some tiny ones, postcard-sized, and others much bigger. They weren't bad, but they weren't right. They had nothing of the originals but it didn't matter; he knew he'd be able to fob them off.

He wasn't wrong. The last genuine piece sold with two of Silas's own attempts. One of them was A2-sized and Silas knew he'd have to ship it properly. The address was down in Chelsea, Belgravia, somewhere in that area. It was a fair walk, but he could do it by hand.

'You need a cargo bike,' said Ren. Silas looked them up online but they were massive clunky things that would have made him look like a butcher's lad. He wanted something sleeker but there was a bicycle shortage so ended up with an 80s three-speed. It was rusted to fuck but he still had to pay well over the odds. He strapped the art to his back and pedalled off. Cycling was harder work than he'd remembered and he was knackered by the time he got there.

No one answered the buzzer so he left it on the doorstep. It was definitely the kind of neighbourhood where people wouldn't steal things, he thought.

'Dropshipping,' said Jaz, who was doing an online course in e-commerce. 'That's what you want to be doing.'

'What's dropshipping?' asked Silas.

'You advertise the merch, but you're not actually holding it,' said Jaz. 'People come to you 'cause you're the man, but the orders go through you, directly to your content producers, who also ship.' Silas would become the perfect middleman, pure portal. 'I can set you up a bot.'

Once the bot was up and running Silas passed days in the flat, quiet now as all his housemates had gone AWOL during the pandemic, with nothing much to do other than count the money and think about not calling Kasha. Everything felt empty. The merch was circulating and he had become part of the flow. He was a unit of exchange, part of the process. A token. He watched the prices of the pictures he'd sold go up and up on the swanky art site. At first he thought he'd sold them too cheaply, but realised how such things worked: prices would spiral then collapse. He'd set the process in motion.

It wasn't the fact that he could have got more for them, though. He missed them. He didn't know why. When he'd first seen those drawings they'd left him almost physically unwell. They'd hurt his eyes and tiptoed round the edge of his nightmares. He'd been happy to see them go. Now he wanted them back. He had enough money, he could do it. Even if not the ones he'd sold. Just one or two maybe. He reassured himself that this was back to the original scheme: buying stuff he himself had put up for sale in order to cleanse his inexplicable income. He began looking for anyone dealing in Conrads. There was very little out there, and thankfully the artist herself (who he now remembered that Kasha had once worked with, or something) had made herself properly scarce.

He went for two smaller ones first, originals mind, not one of the rubbishy copies he'd done, and kept them covered up on a shelf, looking at them once or twice a day, gradually becoming braver, working his way up to leaving them uncovered. Then, though, he felt them looking at him, or rather, like small holes in his world, opening out onto somewhere else, but nowhere he knew or could even imagine. He wanted more.

Even with his current surplus there was little else he could afford but he set up an alert and kept checking until 'Work #246' popped up. It was a small black box, nothing more. Made of metal. Nearly two thousand dollars, but he went for it.

Three weeks later it arrived. It came in cardboard bound with packing tape, which disappointed him. He'd been hoping for a wooden crate, even though it wasn't much bigger than a shoe box. Once he'd opened the cardboard and thrown out the biodegradable foam packing peanuts, the work itself wasn't much bigger than a thick laptop. It was heavy, though, far heavier than something of that size should be. He put it on the shelf between the two pictures. At first it looked black, like, really black, so black it seemed to suck light into it, but after time, and when Silas looked more carefully, he saw how it changed colour throughout the day, and wasn't actually black, but rather a very dark grey with a pearlescent sheen where it caught the light, and reflected it, rather than eating it up. He spent a long time staring at it. It was closed with two sunken sliding metal clasps, like an attaché case with no handle. He didn't know if it actually opened, or if he was supposed to open it, or if he wanted to open it. While it was fascinating to watch, it felt too ominous nestled between the drawings which had their own strange qualities so he cleared the little desk in the corner of his room and placed it there, all on its own. Now, though, the room felt as though it were being pulled in different directions so he left the room, closed the door and didn't go back in for a good while.

After a week of kipping on the sofa he'd convinced himself it was nothing more than the fact that he'd been smoking too much, and went back in. The dregs of tea in a cup he'd left by the side of his bed had dried into a thick glaze, but nothing else was wrong. Everything was still there, just as he'd left it. It was ridiculous, he knew. It was just a metal box, mildly interesting in itself but not worth the two grand he'd dropped for it. He could resell it, probably at a profit, but that would mean leaving himself back where he'd started, with that emptiness.

It didn't exactly disturb him, but it didn't give him any peace either. The only thing to do was open it. He picked the box up then put it down again, finally admitting to himself that he was scared. His housemates still hadn't shown up so he was on his own. He wanted to call Kasha but knew he couldn't: he was supposed to be her rock, the one with the good advice all the time. Asking her to come and watch him open a box would not be a good look. Besides, he'd have to tell the whole story of how he'd got it. He texted Jaz, and Ren, and Pav. Ren didn't respond but Jaz and Pav came over.

'What's up?' asked Pav.
'I've got to open this box,' said Silas.
'What's in it?' asked Pav.
'I don't know,' said Silas.
Pav looked at Jaz. Jaz looked at the box. The box looked at Silas.
'Go on then,' said Jaz. Silas took a step forward and placed his hands on the metal clasps. The box felt cold, or hot, he wasn't quite sure. He snapped the clasps and they sprung open. He lifted the lid of the box.
'Fuck,' said Pav.
'Fuck,' said Jaz.
'Are those . . . ?' said Pav.
'Yeah,' said Silas. 'Yeah, I think they are.'
There were two guns in the box. Silas had never seen a gun before, not in real life.
'Is somebody sending you a warning, mate?' asked Jaz.
'Nah,' said Silas. 'It's an art work.'
'Are they real?' asked Pav.
'It's an art work,' said Silas.
'Ah, OK,' said Pav.
'Art,' said Jaz. 'Not a warning.'
'Yeah. Art,' said Silas, but he wasn't entirely sure.
'Chicago typewriters, they used to call them,' said Jaz.
'What?' asked Silas.
'Guns. In the prohibition era. Gangsters and that. Al Capone.'
'Right,' said Silas.
After Pav and Jaz had gone, Silas picked one up. It was heavier than he expected. He turned it over carefully, not wanting to set it off, to

see if it was signed anywhere. There was no signature, no writing at all, not even a brand name. Though he couldn't be sure he thought they were real, working firearms. He worried they might be loaded and had seen people on TV and in the movies unload guns just by clicking something on the handle. He couldn't see how to do it and didn't want to click anything in case he set it off. The box was now properly malevolent.

He told himself it would have been fine if it weren't for the guns. There'd been no mention of them in the description. Were you even allowed to ship guns? Surely not, that had to be in contravention of something or other. Where had the thing, in fact, come from? He'd bought it from one of the swanky art sites, went back to the order. It had no address on it. He'd thrown the packaging away. It had almost certainly been dropshipped.

He wondered if he'd been scammed. Not a traditional scam—he had no reason to doubt the authenticity of the thing—but if he'd somehow got mixed up in an arms dealing ring. Perhaps it had just gone to the wrong address? His order had been mixed up with someone else's? There was probably some hitman out there, right now, with an empty art box, looking for him.

But no, of course not. It was art. Of course it was. The guns weren't real. He tried to think how Kasha would spin this—there'd be some artspeak way of describing the work. It speaks to the nexus of power, violence and money through a representation of cliched imagery. Something like that. Ultimately questioning the possibility of human agency by interrogating the real. Not bad.

He checked the window. There was a massive Range Rover Oppressor parked outside. It had been there all day.

ALEATORIC OUTCOMES FROM AN INTERACTION OF CONFLICTING FORCES

All agency was human though, wasn't it? Inanimate objects had no power. Had he been dealing with forces beyond his control? Oh god. Now he was just a bit part in a bad film. He wished he could escape, run away to sea. Maybe doing nothing would be the best thing, as ever.

The car was still there. Silas knew this was a lame trope from a lazy movie but couldn't help squinting to see if there was anyone in it, watching him. It was too dark now and there was a reflection coming off the windscreen. He double-bolted the door, pushed a chair up against it, and slept uneasily.

Next morning the car had gone, at least, though now he was troubled by the space that it had left. He went down to have a look at it and of course there was nothing there, no tell-tale pile of cigarette butts or mysterious forcefield. When he went back up again the door was closed. He was sure he'd left it open. Luckily he'd thought to bring his keys with him so opened up and walked in very slowly. He should keep his back to the wall, check each room, move as silently as possible. There was no one there, of course. He went to find the box. It was closed. Had he left it closed? He couldn't remember. He didn't want to open it again and risk seeing if it was empty. He lifted it up and could have sworn that it was lighter than before.

He had to get rid of it. He could dump the guns and keep the box. But better to have done with the whole thing. The river or canal or whatever it was, by the park. He'd wait until dark then chuck it in there.

When it was safe he carefully put the box in his backpack then got the bike out. He wasn't quite sure exactly where the river was, had never really bothered to notice it, but knew the general direction, over on the other side of the park. He set out onto the quiet streets. He'd find his way, be there in no time.

He heard a car behind him, going slowly. He hated that. Maybe the driver thought they were being safe and respectful, or were going to beep at him for having no lights. Silas waved to get the thing to go past but it refused. He turned his head, trying to get a look at it but then swerved and nearly fell off. That gave him an adrenaline rush which made him grip the handlebars more tightly and speed up but the car kept the same distance. It was tailing him. Had to be. He pushed the pedals harder, heaving the old bike as fast as he could, but it was no good. The car stayed where it was, quietly droning behind him.

He pulled a sharp left without signalling, then turned to see the car (a large black Lexus Persecutor) sail on. He laughed; he'd shaken it. He turned back to meet two headlights, full on, in his face. Slammed brakes. Fuck. The headlights, white holes in the blackness, hooted at him. It must be a one-way street or something, and he was going the wrong way down it. This was hectic, griping. He pulled to the side, got off and pushed the bike up the rest of the street. He couldn't risk jolting the box; his cargo was unpredictable, dangerous. The car that had almost face-slammed him sat there, its lines emerging from the darkness. He waited for the window to roll down and someone to lean out and begin haranguing him, but nothing happened. It just sat there. He tightened the straps on the backpack, grabbed the bike and started to run.

The street ended on another main road, this time one with a cycle lane. He'd be OK here. He got back on the bike and sped off, unsure quite where he was going, but still thinking he was heading in the right general direction. The road went on for miles. He no longer knew where he was. There had to be a river or a canal or something near here. He could dump the box and its contents anywhere. He could just put them in a bin. Someone might find it in a bin, though, and he didn't want that, nor anyone to see him disposing of it. There were still people around and there'd be CCTV everywhere, not to mention one of those cars being after him again.

Then—crash—the slam of metal against warm soft human, with bone in it. Some dickbrain had stepped right out into the cycle lane, and Silas was now on the pavement. The fucker got up, dusted himself off then walked away without so much as an acknowledgement, leaving Silas with his ass on the ground, his jeans torn, his knee bloodied and his bike halfway across the road.

'Asshole!' he shouted. The backpack—thankfully—was still in place, and unexploded. His front wheel was a bit bent but still worked. He got back on and hit a steady pace, trying to watch for everything yet not be distracted from the road. He couldn't risk another crash. He carried on for hours, no longer sure where he was, turning every while so he wouldn't get too lost.

He was afraid to go back home and afraid to stop. He kept on cycling, going round and round as though he had been kicked into an elliptical and shaky orbit by a force that he himself had set into motion, and over which he no longer had any control.

CHICAGO TYPEWRITER

Everyone was there. Oreste Lauro was there, Kasha Hocket-Baily was there, Franz from Müttli and Dreiss was there. Che Horst-Prosier was there. Anders Laerp was there. Chloe from Brown's was there, as was Dan from Aster's. A rumour went round that Thomas Vyre was there too, though no one was sure about that. They all drifted in, through the main doors, the side ones, or even the ones at the back. They came down the stairs or out of the lifts, and some appeared as if from nowhere, emerging from the ripples and folds along the side of the main hall. Moritz from Kinetiq was there, Carolynne Fox and Howie Brennan were there. JJ Wilson and Guy Perotta had already been there when all the others began to arrive. Everyone was there, and the place was getting fuller.

'It's the first time he's spoken in years,' said Carolynne.

'I thought there was going to be a show,' said Howie.

'A show?'

'Yeah, you know, like music or something. At least some pictures to look at.'

'There are supposed to be some dancers somewhere. Haven't seen them yet though.'

'Dancers?'

'I heard Beata Baum was doing a promenade piece. In response to his work.'

Howie looked around, trying to work out if any of the people he saw (Olivia Forshaw, Elaine Chang, Lukas Remment) might be dancers. He didn't think they were.

'So it's just a talk?'

'Just a talk? No, it is not "just a talk"—it's the first time Lukas Lemnis has spoken for years.'

'Who?'

'Lukas Lemnis.'

'Oh, OK.'

'Is that a real person?'

Carolynne rolled her eyes. 'What the fuck are you doing here, anyhow?'

'I don't know really. I just thought everyone would be here.'

Everyone was there, Martin from Kunstkeller and Sabine from Reidel's were there, Bernhard Ulbrich was there, Jalal Saba was there, and people were still arriving.

'Actually,' Dan butted in, 'there are a lot of stories that say he isn't.'

'Isn't what?' asked Howie.

'A real person.'

'Who?' asked Carolynne.

'Lemnis. He's a group of people.'

'A group of people?' asked Howie.

'Yeah,' said Dan.

'That would tally with his ideas about the self,' said Carolynne.

'I didn't know he'd written about the self,' said Amy Lai, who'd just arrived.

'In his first book.'

'Oh, the early stuff.'

'I prefer the early stuff,' said Dan.

'Of course you do,' said Amy.

'Can you get a phone signal in here, by the way?' asked Dan. 'Mine doesn't seem to be working.'

CONTRARY TO CERTAIN RUMOURS, LUKAS Lemnis did exist, though right now he was in his hotel room wishing he didn't. Every time he had a paper to give, or a presentation, or a speech, even just an introduction, Lemnis was gripped by an anxiety so strong it made him want to cease to exist. There was no reason for it, he knew. His audiences were—on the whole—unfailingly engaged, attentive, polite. On the occasions he had managed to deliver his talks they were usually followed by applause, some intelligent questioning, heartfelt thanks. But it was no good: the fear was there, and the fear had him.

'**I THINK THEY'RE SHOWING A** film, too. That was what I heard.'

'A film?'

'Yeah. Based on his work.'

'Based on?'

'Inspired by?'

'I don't know how his work could be filmed.'

'No. Me neither, to be honest.'

RECENTLY IT HAD GOT WORSE. On a few occasions Lemnis had feigned illness, although 'feigned' wasn't the right word—his illness was real, though he'd said it was just a stomach bug or a bout of Covid, something, anything other than say what it really was. He could have simply told the truth, or said that he no longer wanted to give public talks, but this would have meant letting down so many people, and Lukas wanted to please people. He wanted people to like him. He meant so much to so many.

'HE'S THE ONLY PHILOSOPHER WHO could pull in a crowd like this.'
    'You think he's a philosopher?'
    'He's an artist.'
    'A poet.' Someone who may have been a dancer shimmied past.

LUKAS LEMNIS KNEW HE COULD have asked someone else to deliver his speeches, but it was never enough. No one wanted a substitute, a stand-in, ersatz Lemnis. They wanted the man himself, his flesh and bones in the room with them, his presence, the original, authentic voice. He could have done it online, zoomed himself in, but that wouldn't have helped. Given that he hated having his photograph taken almost as much as he hated public speaking, few pictures of him existed, and even those that were in circulation were old. This meant that hiring someone else to speak his words without directly acknowledging the fact had been a perfectly plausible plan, and had worked smoothly on more than one occasion. He didn't think he was defrauding anyone, merely using a speaker. He had thought about making it a point, about philosophising it, making it some great statement about identity or speech or truth or some such, but that would have been banal, and Lemnis loathed banality. There was no great point to be made: it was simply that Lukas Lemnis had terrible stage fright.

Bryon Vaughan and Tyrone Gaunt were there, and were both embarrassed when Ryan Vaunt turned up too. They'd both been wondering how Vaunt had managed to get the Laerp commission, despite both of them being far more established in the field of corporate portraiture.

'Can you get a phone signal here, man?' asked Tyrone.

'No,' said Ryan. 'I can't.'

'Have you seen your piece yet?' asked Bryon.

'No,' said Ryan, 'I haven't.'

'Do you want to go take a look?' asked Bryon and Tyrone.

'Yes,' said Ryan, 'I would.'

THIS TIME LEMNIS HAD MADE it as far as the hotel, but the evening before had once again succumbed to the fear. There was no way he could do it, he knew, so asked his PA to discreetly find someone who could. They'd got hold of an actor who'd seemed confident and could drop everything at short notice. The man hadn't shown up yet and Lemnis was growing increasingly anxious as he'd done a last-minute rewrite and needed to go through it carefully. They only had an hour at most.

THOMAS VYRE WAS THERE, THOUGH he wasn't sure he was actually Thomas Vyre.

'Hey,' said JJ Wilson. 'You look like Thomas Vyre!'

JOSEPH COYLE WASN'T THERE YET but definitely would be shortly, as soon as he found the place. The problem wasn't his usual poor sense of direction. Something was happening, a parade or demo, maybe. There were roadblocks, and big black cars lined up on the pavements. They couldn't all be for the talk. Perhaps this thing was bigger than he'd thought.

REN, PAV AND JAZ WERE there. Silas was almost there, but was looking for somewhere to lock his bike.

'SO WHAT'S IT ALL ABOUT, then?' asked Howie.
'"About" isn't the right word,' said Dan.
'His work's ... difficult,' said Carolynne. 'Sometimes.'
'He covers so many areas,' said Amy.
'That's because he's not one person,' said Martin from Kunstkeller.
'But there's something that unites it all, isn't there?' said Sabine from Reidel's.
'Angles, obliquities,' said Ebba from the Moderna Museet.
'Spirals. Hubs and pods. Spokes and tines,' said Rima from SIMA. 'Making the invisible visible. The alchemy of film and photography. The metaphysics inherent in representation. The effects of sound on the body. That kind of thing.'
'He writes about helixes, curves, and corkscrews,' said Cora from ARCO. 'Spiral dynamics.'
'Flow. Flow is big. Pipelines. Clouds as circuits. The autotelic. Csikszentmihalyi has been an influence, I think.'
'Pallasmaa's *Eyes of the Skin*. Bachelard's *Psychoanalysis of Fire*.'
'Kittler's *Gramophone Film Typewriter*. Moretti's *Graphs Maps Trees*.'
'Berlant's *Cruel Optimism*. Stiegler's *Symbolic Misery*.'
'He's as important as that.'

'Bauman's *Liquid Modernity*. Virilio's *Dromology*.'
'Ngai's *Gimmick*. Irigaray's *Speculum*.'
'Sloterdijk's *Bubbles*.'
'I heard that SunnO))) wanted to collaborate with him, but they thought he might be too heavy.'
'Ha!'

JOE WAS GETTING WORRIED. He had a print of the speech in his pocket and all he had to do was read it out, but if he didn't understand at least some of it, there was no way he'd be able to read in any way convincingly. He'd been trying to learn the opening section by heart. 'What is in the container?' it began. That was easy enough, even if a little baffling. 'The container is empty' was the next line. Joe thought he'd make sure there was a big pause between the question and its answer. Problem was the next line: 'Then what is the container, if the container is empty?' He worried it would sound like comedy if he made the pauses too big, but there again, it could imply gravitas. Yes, he thought, lots of pauses, lots of space. He'd have to make sure that was OK with the guy, if only he could find him. The hotel had to be around here somewhere. 'I would like to posit three questions' the paper went on. Joe had more than three.

TWO PEOPLE WHO NO ONE else knew and were both wearing sunglasses were there and joined in.
'His work is elliptical, recalcitrant, rhizomatic,' said one.
'His work is dynamic, unfixed, aleatory,' said the other.
'His work is monadic, gnomic, aphoristic.'

'His work is para, meta, poly.'

'His work is post, proto, con.'

'His prose is luminous, sublime.'

'His prose is lapidary, lambent.'

'Oh please,' said Rachel Noyes. 'Enough, now.' Rachel Noyes was there and she'd already had enough. The few pages of Lemnis she'd read had given her eyestrain.

'Everything's always "addressing," "interrogating" or "mediating,"' she said to Alysson, who was also there. 'I just want something to be what it is.' Alysson nodded.

'No one really understands his work,' she said. 'That's why it's so fascinating. Endlessly interpretable.'

Kev Hewes was looking at Egidio Panebianco who was looking at Ton and Kris, who were also there. Ton was telling Kris that he was making a tune called 'Crazy Russian Kids in High Places.'

'That's a really shit title,' said Kris.

'How about "Psychic Return" then?'

'Worse.'

Everyone was doing the art look. No one was looking at each other. They were looking for someone who might be more interesting.

JOE WAS LOOKING FOR THE hotel, which was part of a newly developed complex, or something, an old factory or warehouse around a freight terminal. His phone wasn't working for some reason and he was lost without a map, not that maps always helped him. He looked for railway stations. Ich verstehe nur Bahnhof. That's what the Germans said when something was all Greek to them.

SEEING THE TIME DRAWING ON and still no sign of the actor, Lemnis decided to disappear. He couldn't face the crowd, so he wouldn't. He'd leave right now, get on the first train out of this place, pick a destination at random. Absence would make the point itself. The stage would be empty and he would be blissfully far away. He put his papers and his toothbrush in his bag, slipped his coat on then made for the door.

'WHAT IS IT THAT'S STRANGE about this building?'
'I know what you mean, but I don't know the answer.'
'It's an old factory.'
'A warehouse, I think.'
'For arms.'
'But completely rebuilt.'
'Not completely.'
'Recommissioned, perhaps.'
'It's part of a rail terminal, too.'
'Isn't the upper part a hotel?'
'Short-let luxury apartments, I think.'
'It's a hub.'
'A pod.'
'More of a spoke, I'd say. In a wheel.'
'It all belongs to the Laerps.'
'The Laerps?'

ZINNIA LAERP WAS THERE IN a finely tailored grey woollen suit and a pair of patent leather lace-up shoes, and being filmed. 'Up until now,' she was saying, 'we've worked with non-static location, a kind of body without organs—or, maybe, organs without a body!' She laughed at her joke, but no one else did and Zinnia worried the Deleuze reference was too passé. She pressed on. 'We were very much against physical space but then we realised we had to rethink space, territory, consider what it could be, project it into a future—I mean, it's like space, isn't it? And you can't give up on that? On the body. We all have bodies, don't we?' The question didn't fall right: it didn't sound like she was inviting assent as much as genuinely unsure.

'WHY LEMNIS, ANYHOW?'
   'He's our greatest living thinker.'
   'Is he, though?'
   'You don't think so?'
   'It's pronounced Lem*nis* by the way. Stress on the second syllable.'
   'Are you sure?'
   'How can anyone ever be sure about anything?'
   'They were supposed to open with Sigismunda Conrad's comeback show.'
   'Why didn't they?'
   'She didn't deliver on time.'
   'I thought she'd quit art.'
   'I heard she'd disappeared.'

ZINNIA CARRIED ON, EVEN THOUGH the film crew had stopped filming her, having been distracted by something else. 'I mean,' she said, 'we thought this was the way to go, to inaugurate this . . . space'—she laughed there—'with some words from our finest living thinker.'

Joe found the hotel, finally. There were police, or private security, or something like that in the lobby. He had to show his passport to get in. What was it, another country? He checked the room number, took the lift, looked at the speech again while it was going up. 'We are in the midst of three crises,' he read. As if three weren't enough. 'That of representation, that of evidence, and that of temporality. I would put it that these are one and the same.' Temporality was Joe's main one at the moment. He was over an hour late. At least he'd solved his spatial crisis. 'Reference, data, causality, perception, belief: all are falling around us. But where to? What of space?' Joe hated rhetorical questions. He always worried some smart-arse heckler would pipe up an answer. 'Space is not static, but in constant movement. Space is a dynamic, relational force-field in which objects and actions must be seen in constant and contingent relation with other objects and actions. The words "interior" and "exterior" cease to mean. New techne enable us to emerge from unexpected places. All material is now materiel.' Joe knew the words and appreciated the pun, but couldn't think how it would work when he read it out aloud. 'We can move across space, time, through walls, like a worm that eats its way forward, emerging at points and then disappearing.' The lift stopped and the doors slid open and Joe felt very much like a worm appearing. The corridors on the twelfth floor were endless. 'Every territory is a border territory.' There were little signs pointing him in the right direction but he was sure he was going round in circles.

LEMNIS COULDN'T MOVE THE DOOR handle. It was locked. It wouldn't open. He needed a keycard or something—it was right there, in the little slot beside the door. He removed it and the lights went off but the door still did not open. He put it back in, and still nothing. He pushed hard until the handle moved up, then pulled it down, but the door would not open. He banged on it and shouted, but no one came. He was locked in.

By the time Joe found the room he was breathless and sweating. He knocked on the door but there was no answer. He knocked again. He thought he heard a sound inside and pushed the door but it didn't open. He checked the email again. This was definitely the right room, or at least, the number that he'd been given. Maybe he'd been sent an update that hadn't arrived. He didn't know what to do now. He paced the corridor and read on. 'When two, or more, conceptual spatial networks overlap—there lies conflict. Possession is not about laws and contracts, but about movement and circulation.'

KADY FROM *ABÎME*, **FINN FROM** *Ogive* and Yue from *Grey Noise* were all there and watching images moving on the wall. A man walked along a remote road, his back to the camera. The image faded and was replaced by a close-up of his face, then the cycle repeated. They weren't sure if they were watching a film or a monitor glitching. They were interrupted by a group of four people walking in a line, very slowly. The people stopped, then turned, then walked at the same pace back through the hall.

'Beata Baum,' said JJ Wilson. 'She's studied the movement of people in working environments, then recast them as dance.'

'I hadn't noticed it,' said Guy Perotta, watching the figures file away.

'But had you noticed me?' asked Beata Baum, who was also there.

BRYON, RYAN AND TYRONE STOOD in front of a picture which Ryan had no memory of ever having made.

'I ended up abandoning the commission,' he told Bryon and Tyrone. 'I never did this. This isn't mine.'

'SO IF IT'S LEMNIS, WHAT'S the adjective?'
 'Lemnisesque?'
 'Lemniscian?'
 'Lemniscate.'
 'That's good.'
 'Yes. The Lemniscape. That's where we live now.'

'"THE ISO 6346 INTERMODAL CONTAINER is the greatest work of art of the 20th century." That,' said Kady from *Abîme*, 'is one of the most beautiful sentences I've ever read.'
 'Poetry,' said Finn from *Ogive*.
 'There nothing human in it,' said Yue from *Grey Noise*. 'That's my problem. Where's the empathy? Where's the soul?'
 Kady, Finn and Yue were all there to write pieces about Lemnis, or his talk, or art, or architecture, or whatever.
 'Nothing human?' asked Kady. There were a lot of humans there. People kept on appearing. Three versions of Thomas Vyre were having a polite but animated conversation.
 'It's all about the human,' said Finn from *Ogive*, but wasn't sure if anyone heard them because there was a loud noise. It might have been coming though the speaker system, but it might have been coming from outside. No one could really tell.

JOE SLUMPED AGAINST THE DOOR. The guy would show up in a minute. He'd probably just nipped out. There was a weird noise that came from outside, or downstairs, he couldn't really tell. He sat himself down and thought he could do some more reading while he waited. 'I have been asked to talk about art, but I know nothing of art.' Great. 'But we know that automated images stored and distributed across discreet surveillance systems, hidden labour, logistics, infrastructures, and networks, make up technical conditions of perception and operate upon the very material fabric of the world.'

ORESTE WAS HAVING PROBLEMS WITH the material fabric of the world. This wasn't unusual, but he didn't want to get hit by lightning again. There were no windows in this building, which he was glad about, because he didn't want to see any clouds right now. They were outside, he knew. He could feel them.

'THESE OPERATIONS ASSEMBLE NEW UNSTABLE arrangements of relations, politics, and feelings, scaling them out of sync,' Joe read. 'As such fragile realities risk degradation and collapse, what role can the techne of art—if it is such—play in altering what is mapped and measured, what is perceived, experienced, and known? How far can the boundaries of our interpretation be stretched?'

In the main hall the loud noise continued to grow until it found a form, swelled then balanced. Rachel thought the sound familiar, though she couldn't place it, and then it died away again before she could listen more carefully.

'Did that sound familiar to you?' Ton asked Kris.

'What?' asked Kris.

'That sound.'

'I don't know. Maybe?'

'IT HAS BEEN ESTABLISHED THAT the invention of any technology is also the invention of its own new disaster.' Joe was trying to commit this to memory, but there was no way it would stick. 'The invention of the ship is the invention of the shipwreck, the invention of the train is the invention of the train crash . . . and so on. But the invention of art, and its practice—what catastrophe does that bring into being?' At that point, a fire alarm went off, hammering Joe's eardrums. It was so loud it made him dizzy. He got up and looked around but couldn't see any fire. No one seemed to be coming. It was late; he had to leave. The lift wasn't working due to the fire alarm so he found the stairwell and started running.

DAN WAS TELLING SABINE THAT everything was in the cloud now. 'It's all there,' he said. 'Everything. All those images, all that information, swirling around us, if only we could see it.' Sabine disagreed.

'There's the cloud, but you need things. Massive server farms, in polar deserts. Cables. We need cables. It's all in the cables.'

'No one needs cables anymore. It's all in the aether.'

'Aether,' said Sabine. 'That's a good word.'

'Is that a fire alarm I can hear?' asked Dan.

'Probably just a test.'

'Strange time to test the alarm.'

'It's probably just that music again.'

'Was that music?' They looked around to see if they could see a fire, or any signs of one, but no one else seemed to be bothered.

JOE MADE IT DOWN THE stairs and through a doorway which opened up into the main atrium. The place was packed. Everyone was there. Some people he hadn't seen for years were there, and many more people who he'd never seen at all. He couldn't believe how many people were there, and they were still arriving. They were coming out of every doorway, through the windows, from spaces in the walls. Thing was, while it was packed, there was still space in there, as if the building was growing to accommodate all the people who continued to arrive. He tried to find his way to the stage, but there didn't seem to be one. He wished he had a lanyard saying who he was.

'Imagine,' said Lydia Morton, who was there, to no one in particular, 'all the voices, all our sound, leaving the world, reverberating until they hit the edge of the universe, and then returning.'

Carolynne Fox was telling Howie Brennan why Riga was the new Berlin. Howie told Carolynne that it wasn't Riga, it was Ljubljana. Rachel was telling Alysson and Andrea that the sound of running water was complex. Kev Hewes was asking Franz from Müttli and Dreiss if this was all going somewhere, if there was actually going to be an event, a point to the evening, or if it was all going to be rambling without a conclusion or revelation. Bernhard Ulbrich was telling Lukas Remment about epiphylogenesis and object-oriented ontology. Lukas Remment was telling Bernhard Ulbrich that quantitative analysis, simulation modelling and probability were new ways of making. Che Horst-Prosier was telling Kasha Hocket-Baily why a container ship was the perfect exemplar of a Foucauldian heterotopia. Moritz from Kinetiq was asking JJ Wilson if he'd heard Tonnetz. JJ said he hadn't. Ton was telling Rachel that while you could see seeing, you couldn't hear hearing. Rachel told Ton that's what her work was trying to do. Oreste was telling Olivia Forshaw about how he'd been struck by lightning. Elaine Chang was telling Egidio Panebianco that cities had been completely reconceptualised as hubs for property development and consumption, with culture a distant third. Egidio told Elaine that the city was for investment, which made cities the ultimate piece of capital, and that art was the glue for the movement of capital. Elaine said movement didn't need glue. Yannis Makris and Jānis Balodis were telling each other that they didn't know what they were doing there. Andrea was telling Alysson about how trout are so energy efficient they get turbulence to do their work for them, taking energy from eddies and using pressure drops in wakes to propel them forward. She said that it was so effective that it worked even if the fish was dead. Silas was telling Anders Laerp that financiers were moving from crypto into eco. Anders Laerp was telling Guy Perotta that he was considering moving from eco into crypto. Perotta asked Laerp what had brought him along. 'I wanted an explanation,' said Laerp. 'I wanted to know what was going on here.' Joe Coyle found a slip of paper in his pocket and tried to read what was written on it, but it made no sense to him. Someone who no one else seemed to know was telling Ren, Pav and Jaz about how they'd travelled on a cargo ship. Howie Brennan was telling Oreste how NFTs were the perfect realisation of relational aesthetics.

'NFTs,' he said, 'cut out the middleman. It's all about the circulation of capital. No art is, in fact, necessary. It's like poker I mean. Poker isn't a card game, it's a game of money, using cards.' Oreste wasn't sure what Howie was on about.

'Do you think I should get in early on the NFT revival?' he asked, but Howie had gone.

Moritz from Kinetiq was telling Ton and Kris that the CIA had funded junk art. 'Stuff that looked like art, but was just rubbish. They did it to flood the market, push up prices. It's all still out there,' he said, 'circulating.' Ton and Kris didn't understand what he meant. Joe Coyle was telling anyone he could that he was Lukas Lemnis and he needed to make a speech, but no one was listening to him. The fire alarm was still going off in Lukas Lemnis's room, so a security guard knocked. There was no answer so the guard went in with a passkey, and found the room completely empty. Kris was telling Martin and Sabine about hyper-objects.

'They're things which we can't possibly understand,' he said, and Martin and Sabine didn't understand. Oreste was looking for a way out. Ryan Vaunt was telling Bryon Vaughan and Tyrone Gaunt that there was no space between anything, because everything was space. 'Nothing is solid,' he said, but they didn't understand. They could hear the words he was saying but they made no sense. Jen was telling Rachel about perfect forms, Klein bottles, and spiral arrays. Rachel said all that was fascinating, but she still needed a thing to be a thing. 'That thing you want things to be,' Jen told her, 'it's not there anymore.' Rachel couldn't hear what Jen was saying.

The images on the wall returned to the man walking along the road, then shifted to an empty seascape. The sea, or its image, expanded until it covered the entire wall. No one could tell what was image, what was wall, and what was sea. People kept appearing but they couldn't understand each other. Silas was sure that there were at least twelve versions of his uncle Thomas. Zinnia Laerp was in three different places at the same time. Outside, a fleet of large black cars pulled up. A cloud snaked into the building then hung over the heads of everyone there, slowly gaining mass.

'It's dust,' said Moritz.

'Dry ice,' said Kris.

'It's steam,' said Ton. 'Water vapour. Rising and gathering. It'll start to rain soon.'

'It's a fire!' said Amy Lai.

'It's not a fire, don't worry,' said Oreste, but no one could hear him. 'It's part of the show,' he tried to say, but then the noise, or music, returned, louder than before. It was exciting; it was terrifying. People kept on arriving. No one knew what anyone else was saying. Someone got up on a stage, or stood on a chair, or something, and said they were Lukas Lemnis, but they clearly weren't. 'What is in the container?' they said, but no one could hear, and even if they heard, they couldn't understand. A Thomas Vyre was telling everyone that, according to Thomas Vyre, a cloud was both metaphorical and metonymic, symbol, sign and referent, both condensation and its displacement, but no one could hear him, or understand him. The sound around them was that of hundreds of voices, chattering, babbling, sparkling, rising then slowly falling as though shards of weightless shattered glass. Lukas Remment thought he saw a drone flying in, but Guy Perotta said it was only a projection. Mary, Mani and Vinod were having flashbacks. There was the sound of champagne corks popping, or fireworks cracking, or a typewriter going faster than any human hand could propel it. Oreste told anyone who could hear or understand him that it was the sound of gunshots. Some people started laughing. Other people started trying to leave. 'Does anyone know the way out of here?' asked Jalal, but no one did, or no one heard, or no one understood. A ship, on fire, appeared on the wall. Some people, dressed in black, were dancing. More people arrived.

KLEIN BOTTLE: THE COMEBACK

by Che Horst-Prosier

It's difficult to know where to begin with a piece like this. Let me propose a question: What do you remember, now, about Sigismunda Conrad? It seems straightforward enough, doesn't it? But try answering.

Go on. Have a think. What have you got? Not much? A few factoids, a couple of memory-scraps? Anything at all?

It's been roughly a decade since Conrad was last definitively sighted, the same amount of time since her last—abandoned—show. Not so much time, perhaps, in any greater scheme of things, but a long time for a practising artist, poised on the brink of greatness, to effectively disappear. So, reader, imagine my feelings when I received an invitation to *Klein Bottle*—Sigi Conrad's 'comeback' exhibition.

I'm using the words 'disappear' and 'comeback' tentatively here, as Conrad has never left us, not really, has she? Rumours of such a return had been mooted for a while, but while nothing ever appeared (and here I'm including the strange events surrounding the Laerp-sponsored Lemnis presentation), and over time her name might have grown fuzzy and vague through disuse, dropped out of conversation and been shunted to that grey zone at the side of the mind, Conrad and her work, I feel, have always been here.

You may well disagree but I'm not here to listen to you. I could go on to make a good case for the continuing relevance of her work, but what would be the point? If you've read this far, you probably care enough to carry on.

So, here we are. There are a good few of us. We know we all received the invitation, but—and this is the first strange thing—we cannot remember quite how. Some of us say they received the full gilt-edged envelope, others merely a postcard or an email, others still only a WhatsApp message with a rendezvous point. Quite a few simply found a slip of paper in their pocket. Some of us hadn't actually been invited at all but knew someone who knew someone who had heard something.

Thing is—and this is the second strange thing—although we know we are here, we are not sure quite where we are. Nor can we remember how we got here. Were we ferried in a fleet of shiny black cars? Did we walk? Have we come far, by air or sea? Everyone seems to have a different idea, and none of us are sure. I seem to think I came by train, but I'm starting to doubt that.

'We've probably been here all the time!' jokes one of us, and we all laugh, though none of us are quite sure why.

The show, as noted, is called *Klein Bottle*. A Klein bottle, we find out, is, informally, 'a one-sided surface which, if travelled upon, could be followed back to the point of origin while flipping the traveller upside down.' If that doesn't quite make sense, then a more formal definition might help: 'a two-dimensional manifold on which one cannot define a normal vector at each point that varies continuously over the whole manifold.' To us, a Klein bottle looks like a fancy vase in which it would be impossible to put any flowers, or a trick wine glass from which you are tantalisingly unable to drink, or a Murano version of a twisted donut, or a Möbius strip, or the universe itself, crafted by a particularly talented glassblower.

That, however, doesn't help us much as we stand here (wherever here is), waiting to be let in. The atmosphere is friendly. There is camaraderie among us. It is unlike any other opening I have been to. There are none of the usual gawkers, influencers or hangers-on. It feels like everyone is here to see the work, and not each other. But there is excitement, yes, and it is palpable. This is an exciting moment, the point where the work is there, waiting, but not yet quite existing. An unorganised flux waiting for our senses to experience it. Only once it is experienced will it come into being.

Once in (we don't really know—the doors opened, that's all) the first thing that strikes us is that unlike Conrad's previous shows, this is a collection rather than a single work. Or, it is a single work, but a single work made up of many smaller ones. They could, we think later, be seen in any sequence.

First up, we all walk out onto some kind of plaza. Yes, we know that's not a great word, but it's the only one that seems right here. It's not a space which may have formed or risen out of the natural flow and meeting of people, but rather something imposed, constructed, artificial. There are buildings around us but they are distant and look like facades only, AI-generated architectural maquettes, de Chirico rebooted for a CGI age. But all this is merely background we think, as we walk further out. Pools of sound appear like puddles, only invisible, then loiter, sometimes staying and forming small lakes. We walk through them, seeking their sources but there is nothing to be seen— no speakers, no amplification devices. They're just there. We walk through the sound of rain showers where there is no rain, through hubbubs of conversation although there are no other people, through bursts of music, through deep, clanking mechanical sounds which pass after a few steps. We turn and go back through them and notice they have shifted, only inches perhaps, but are still there. At one point we hear an opera singer rehearsing, a beautiful mezzo soprano, and we gather there and listen to the practising of scales through various keys for some time until it fades and we move slightly, and find it still there. Further on, there is some hardcore breakbeat techno banging out, and a few of us start dancing, having a little rave, until our eardrums are tested too strongly and we take a step to our right, and it stops.

We're not sure if this is the main piece or focus here, or if it's only background to the other things taking place on the plaza. Most notably, we are presented with a bicycle going round in large circles, or maybe a figure-of-eight pattern, pursued by a car. The bicycle has no rider, and the car no driver. As with the sound pools, there is a certain amount of wonder among us at the sheer technical virtuosity of this (how is that bicycle being powered, and how is it staying upright?) but as we watch, and realise that it is unclear exactly who is pursuing whom, we become entranced, and let our questions drop. The chase, or pursuit, will go on forever, so we move away and notice that there are other people on the plaza too. (Have they just appeared, or have they always been here?) Some of them greet us, tentatively, as if they think they know us from somewhere but cannot remember from where. They are polite, but seem unwilling to engage in conversation. Though friendly, they have an undeniably eerie quality which leads some of us to ask if they are holograms, or actors unsure of their roles.

We watch them carefully as they in turn greet each other in the same fashion, and note that some of them are performing some kind of action, or—at least—a repetitive sequence of movements. One man, much like the car/bike combo, seems to be walking in circles, only stopping at certain points, perhaps dictated by the sounds. As we watch, we note that he is not walking in a circle at all, but in some other pattern which we cannot define, and that others are following him, each one at a different speed. Some overtake him, while he laps others. The work is extremely boring and intensely comic. It has a quality that is almost slapstick, absurd, yet we found watching these agents going through their cycles, coming into and going out of phase with each other, to be utterly hypnotic.

We've been working as critics for as long as any of us can remember, we agree, but we don't know what to say about any of this. 'Where are the themes?' we ask. 'What is this work about?' And then we realise that we're asking the wrong questions.

'What questions should we be asking?' we ask each other, with increasing desperation. 'Are we critics at all?'

That question leads us to a discovery. We cannot, it seems, remember what we were. Were we all critics? Or something else? Philosophers? Novelists? Playwrights? Painters? Or chemists, physicists, biologists or astronomers? Though none of us are sure we feel we would have liked to have been musicians, even if none of us could remember playing an instrument. They were all just words, after all, names, categories. It wouldn't have changed who we were, would it? Already, we feel ourselves blurring around the edges.

'What is it that brought you here?' we ask each other, and we find out that we all had a dream about a burning ship. We all had the same dream.

We move on and find ourselves in a long corridor with a locked room at its end. Only, perhaps not.

'Perhaps this is the room, and the corridor is on the other side,' one of us says. We look around and note that the corridor, while certainly long, is wide and spacious.

'So, we're in a locked room?' we ask.

'Yes. Maybe?'

'Perhaps it's a thought experiment,' says another of us, remembering that we are, after all, putative critics.

'A puzzle, certainly,' says a second.

'A conundrum, definitely,' says a third. We all ponder the word 'conundrum' for a moment then try the door again. This time it opens.

One of the actors/holograms/characters stands on the other side, but we are not sure they see us. We are not sure if we have entered their room, or if they have entered ours. We walk on through what, in fairness, does seem to be a corridor, which turns into a gangway and then becomes a bridge. We look down and see that we are hundreds of feet above ground, and rising. We are so high up we feel we can see the curvature of the earth, the tip of the troposphere, what we think might be electrical and magnetic fields. We have, we think, reached the Empyrean. It is beautiful. (And yes, we are aware that is not the kind of word that critics are supposed to use, but there is no better one here.) We can hear each other's thoughts. Others appear, climbing up the scaffolding, then leaping off with abandon, diving into the vast emptiness only to resurface, as if from a swimming pool, climbing up again to again dive off. The thin air around us crackles. In this Olympian frequency domain, we too feel ourselves immortal. We stay there long enough to catch the flickering green ray before the sun sets then turn and head back. Some of us linger, and when we chide them they tell us they want to remain there, and perhaps try a dive or two into the infinite, so we bid them farewell.

'There are no "themes" here,' we say on the way down, remembering again that we are critics who have to file reviews. 'Nothing we could say the works are "about."'

'It's experiential,' says one of us.

'Of course it is,' we reply, 'but what is experience?'

'Is it only that which is presented to our senses?' we ask. 'Is experience only ever fleeting and unrecordable? Or is true experience, that is, an experience which can be learned from, something which engages with memory?'

'Yet memory, too, is an experience,' we say, and feel this debate may go on for some time.

As we walk on we talk about what this work may represent, or mean, or signify, and none of us have any clear answers. We talk about mimesis and abstraction, about impressionism and expressionism, about the modern, the postmodern, the altermodern and the metamodern. We talk about formalism, materialism and deconstruction. We talk about semiotics and affect. Some of us appreciate work that is compelling, propulsive, direct, clear, with a strong narrative; others value that which is sprawling, messy, and digressive.

'We need work that is replenishing, reparative,' we say. 'We do not need work that is extractive.'

'We are against extraction,' we agree.

'We need reparative readings, not extractive readings.'

The next space we come to is, initially, one of the most delightful. It is an empty cinema, possibly abandoned we think, looking at the worn velvet seats, the spent 'Exit' signs, the dusty and crumbling mouldings, their cheap gilt paint chipped and faded. We sit down and a film begins. We see a man walking along an empty road, his back to the camera. This goes on for a while. It's not very interesting. But then something happens, and we realise that we are not watching the film, but we are in it. We are now part of it, simultaneously observing and participating. We are on a small, remote, rainswept island. We're not sure where, but we know that on the way to the island we were stuck for some considerable time, beleed by fog. Our boat stayed where it was for days, gently rocking back and forth, side to side, sometimes higher, sometimes lower, with water around as far as we could see, which wasn't far, given the fog, which in itself was a thing to see, a pearly cloud, the gently billowing surface of a satin robe. When we finally arrived on the island we realised that everyone had gone. There had been others with us, we were sure, though we could scarcely remember now who they were. The man, a photographer, was alone now, as were we. We remember that he stepped out onto the land and we followed him.

As we spend time with him we learn more. We have a mission, but we are unsure what it is. We can only record traces of what is around us. We like the pictures we take, but are also frustrated by them, feeling that something is missing. We begin to feel that the camera we carry is useless, not fit for the obscure task we have. We grow nervous; we are far from home. Someone, we think, is following us. (We turn around every few minutes, but never see anything or anyone.) Over time we adopt the sound of the land and the sea around it and learn to speak its language. The whip of the wind and the slap of the water become our new friends. We display the pictures we have taken on the walls of an abandoned house. They are portraits of people in all the fullness of their humanity, people doing people things, falling in love and dying, being born and beaten by the wind, working, walking and dreaming, staring out at the sea. We are, almost, content with our work. No one is following us anymore.

Meanwhile, a man whose name no one can remember wakes up one morning in a small hotel room then wanders out into the snow where he sits on a bench in a small park and awaits the arrival of a friend or lover. That's it, that's all there is. We are dreaming this man's dream, only to find that it is real.

After all this, we think, we need a breather. We wonder where the white wine is. We wonder if there are any canapes. (This is, after all, the opening of an exhibition by a major, if neglected, contemporary artist.) Then we remember who we are: we are serious critics (or something similar), here to experience the work and not be distracted by such fripperies. And yet, we continue to wonder if there is a bar anywhere, and head off in search of one.

We do not find a bar. Instead, we find what some of us think may be the intellectual heart of the show, though others of us disagree. Some of us experience the control room of a nuclear bunker or power station, others that of a complex rail network, while others still feel that it is nothing but a dreary call centre.

'Are we supposed to be here?' we ask, looking at the serried banks of control panels, the screens, the flashing lights, the switches, dials, knobs and levers. 'Or have we managed to wander off-limits, into somewhere from where all this is being orchestrated? Will we get in trouble? Will someone come and stop us, move us on?' No one appears. There are chalkboards on each wall bearing complex diagrams, glyphs and equations which none of us can decipher. We wonder if we press the right button if someone will bring us glasses of champagne. We doubt it.

'Have we gone behind the curtain?'

'Is this where the human operating the Mechanical Turk is supposed to sit?'

'Are we, in fact, the humans controlling it all?'

'If so, are we supposed to do something here, to reinstall or restore the complex equilibrium of this unstable homeostatic system?' We understand and we do not understand. We are part of this and this is part of us, though we do not know which part. We do not understand what we can control and what is being controlled.

We start to think about numbers, number theory and numerology, the natural refuge of apopheniacs, compulsives and conspiracists, but also of musicians, artists, geometers and physicists. We try to count but our usual system has lost all meaning. We find another way of seeing numbers. We lose our nerve and think we need to be getting out of here. As we make our way out, some of us tarry.

'We're OK,' they say. 'We like it here.' The rest of us leave and do not bid farewell to the remainers, because we know that they are always with us.

Once out we realise that we have been on the bridge of a massive ship that had once been used as a prop in a film, but is now totally burnt out. It is, perhaps, the ship we all dreamed about. We wander through its scorched and empty metal corridors until we find a door, half-open, which leads into a cabin, a large one, more like a small apartment.

'Is this the luxury suite?' we ask, though realise that while it is above the standards of many sea-going craft, it is quite far from luxury. It's much bigger than we first thought, though, and we take our time to walk around it. Though empty, it is noisy, but not with ship sounds: we can hear someone running around the place, maybe two or more people, very quickly. If we strain we think we can almost hear music, as though some kind of party is going on here. The strange thing is that some of the sounds are moving very quickly (we can tell by the pitch shift) and others very slowly, as if they are being played on an old tape machine which is running out of battery. The place feels haunted, obviously, but in a pleasant sort of manner.

A picture hangs on the wall. We all immediately assume it's by Conrad herself, which would be unusual as she has rarely shown her graphic pieces. It could be an objet trouvé, which would make it more in keeping with the rest of the show, but short of a more careful analysis there is no way of knowing. A small plaque on the lower edge of its frame tells us the picture is called 'The Arms Dealer's Beautiful Daughter.' It shows a young woman in reverse three quarter, so we can see the back of her head as she slowly turns. It's difficult to tell if it is a painting or a photograph. The image is pristine yet also dreamlike. As we observe it, like the film we watched before, we become part of it and know that the woman is, in turn, looking at a portrait of her father, though the father is not present in the picture she is looking at and it is instead a representation of the room in the house where he spent so much time. We feel we are intruding on a private moment and move on.

The ship, we think, as much as it is anywhere, is in some kind of a holding pattern, waiting to dock at a free port somewhere. We are in a marine storage department where we both exist and do not exist. We need to get out, we tell ourselves, to get to somewhere we can trust our senses again, and trust them to tell us that we do indeed exist. Fortunately, at this point, the ship—though still seriously damaged, and not in fact an actual ship at all—heaves into dock and slows alongside a busy harbour. One day, we think, people will sing songs about this ship, but for now we are more interested in what is happening portside.

A group of people wait for us on the quay. They seem pleased to see us, though also somewhat wary.

'Who are you?' we ask, and hope that they speak our language.

'We're the survivors,' they laugh. They have the same quality as the ones we came across before in the plaza, though are perhaps better defined. We ask them what they mean and they tell us the following story.

'Once, some time ago, we went to see an art exhibition. Some of us didn't come back. Others did, though, only changed.' (Throughout the story they interrupt and contradict each other, constantly backtracking and clarifying, asserting then modifying their claims. What I report here is a synthesis, and the substance of their communal tale.) 'Some of us, that is, came here immediately, while others left the exhibition and tried to go back to their old lives, but many were not successful. In some cases it didn't manifest for months or even years. One of the difficulties in the diagnosis was that the symptoms were varied and difficult to spot. For some it was only a withdrawal or a growing silence, for others a complete refusal to speak. Relationships broke up, some went to live alone. All of us began to sing in languages we didn't recognise, or build complex models of systems we didn't understand, or write screeds of text so tiny the letters were hardly legible even to ourselves. Some made huge dioramas of empty towns. Many of us began to paint or draw, forms and shapes of things which could not possibly exist. Space became challenging for us. We lost track of time. Eventually we found ourselves here. Some of us are still there too, but here as well. It's complicated. We all made each other welcome, though, whenever we arrived. We worked out who was best at doing what, how we could help each other. We all have time to pursue our projects. We put on shows and organise readings. It's not really a commune, and definitely not a colony. We don't like that word. It's like a retreat, or an escape—though some of us don't like that idea. We're not retreating or escaping: this is the real thing.'

They show us around their not-commune. They are happy here, we can tell. Some of us consider staying here. Stray animals wander around, they too seem to have made their homes here. We ask the not-colonists if they want to return, but they don't seem to understand the question.

'Who are they?' we ask each other, and come to an agreement that they are impulses and symptoms of the world of primal forces, and that their behaviours both reveal the world, and attempt to resolve it. We are pleased with this line, and make a note to ourselves to include it in our eventual reviews.

As we are leaving they tell us about another encampment, a few miles down the road. 'But watch out,' they say, 'the ones over there are really crazy.'

We walk on, following the road which soon becomes a dirt track, then a mere pathway across a desert landscape, marked by stones. On the horizon we see a shanty town, shacks, huts and tents held together by rope and string, planks and rusting metal beams. A man wearing a faded military uniform greets us as we arrive.

'Glad you made it!' he says. 'Long journey, eh? Are you from the Commission?'

We tell him we don't know what he means, and he seems disappointed.

'We're waiting to be commissioned,' he says. 'They keep on telling us they'll send someone out, with the right contracts, but we haven't heard from them for a while now. Comms aren't very good out here, I'm afraid.' He shows us around the encampment. Some of the tents and huts have been made into homely dwellings, brightly if roughly decorated, with pots of flowers attempting to grow in the thin sandy soil. Others look like small workshops with a few power tools sending out showers of sparks. They have rigged up their own electricity supply, he tells us proudly. 'Some very ingenious people out here with us,' he says.

As we go around, the other inhabitants regard us with weary and impassive faces.

'Some of us have been here longer than others,' the man says. 'All still waiting for that commission. Meantime, we're making a go of it, though there's a lot to do.' It is very hot here. We are uncomfortable in our critics' clothes, our good suits, sharp shoes and clean shirts. 'The contracts'll be arriving soon!' he shouts at a group of men sitting sullenly on a shaded porch, drinking home-brewed liquor.

'We like it here, on the whole, we've built up a solid little community,' he tells us, 'but some cope better than others. That's the way it is, I suppose. One of us went mad from the heat, another from the drink. Another one of us got God, for a brief while. Some of us got bitten by mosquitoes, or some such bug, and contracted a disease that made all of our lips turn black, though fortunately only one of us died.'

He offers us food, which we gladly accept, though we are unimpressed by the greasy meat and pallid vegetables served up on tin plates. We drink mugs of what he describes as the 'local brew,' which tastes of grapes and petrol.

'We were told we would be commissioned shortly,' he goes on, 'and that everything was going according to plan, although there were localised delays, significant in some cases, and severe in others. We were told there were some procedural issues, or contractual issues, and that these were holding up the commissioning process. They still send us their communiques, though, official bulletins and gazettes, that sort of thing. It's good to know they're still on board, even if no one has shown up for quite a while now.' He swats a fly away. 'There's a lot of damn admin we have to keep on top of, though. We have to file interim reports and complete update progress checklists every week.'

He takes us to see the communications mast they are building. It is far from complete. 'We don't have the necessary expertise,' he tells us. 'That's the problem. Don't suppose any of you could help?' We try to help as best we can, and pass several years there, helping them to rebuild their world, even though we do not like these people much.

At one point we speak to one of the inhabitants, a very tall man who seems shorter than he is. 'I never signed a contract,' he tells us, 'but even so, I knew they'd taken something from me. I'm smaller than I used to be, and I used to be quite something, I can tell you. I had money, riches even. I had a wife who worked for many good causes. I had a beautiful daughter. But mostly, I remember how cold it was in the factory where I grew up, and my father's beard. I once saw a painting of my father's beard, blowing in a terrible gale, and I tried to buy it, because I could buy anything I wanted. Once I'd bought it,

I realised I already owned it. It was part of my collection. It did not make me happy.'

When we eventually leave we worry about what we are leaving behind, not just here, but everywhere we have been, and in everything we have seen and experienced. Our absence from the exhibition will surely leave its trace.

'Are we part of the show?' we ask. 'Or is it part of us, now? Where does any of this begin or end?' We aren't ourselves anymore, but we are not yet sure who we have become.

As the few of us who are left slowly return we see that the show is being dismantled. Crews of technicians in hi-vis tabards and hard hats are taking everything down and storing it in shipping crates.

'The work's not easy,' one of the men tells us. 'Some of this is very complex. It'll take us a while.'

'Added to that,' says another one, 'there are a lot of contractual issues to get around. Tax stuff.'

'NDAs. Penalty clauses.'

'There'll probably be a few sweeteners getting chucked around at some point.'

'We're in choppy legal waters,' says the first. 'Mind you, a lot of this will just go into storage.'

'Some of it will be recycled. Used for other exhibitions.'

'But we'll be leaving the unmanned systems. They'll carry on much as before. Nothing ever ends, really, though I suppose we'll end up leaving some detritus around. Unavoidable.' They tell us they are already at work building another museum, one which will be filled with works of art which may no longer exist, stacked up in shipping containers.

We finally arrive at a place we do not recognise though we know we have been here before. It's where we began.

'Have we learned anything?' we ask. 'Is that even important?'

There is noise and its interpretation, we agree, that interpretation being a signal or sign upon which we confer form, and value, and beauty. The problem is, we may never recognise it.

'Too abstract,' we say. 'Too difficult. Some of us are writing for the general reader. What can we tell them?'

Not much, we think. We try to draft something else, and come up with this: 'Everything that is broken can be fixed. Everything can happen again, but in a different form, one you may not recognise. Everything will find its form, its home, its resting place.'

We see our lovers again, for the first time, but knowing what we know now, and our lovers are even more beautiful. As we embrace we wonder who is holding and who is the held. We form a spiral, a current of running water, then pure sound. We are the portrait, its sitter and its painter, the dancer and the dance, the singer and the song, the tale and its teller. The drone becomes an echo which continues spiralling outward forever. Everything is connected, we tell ourselves, and nothing ever dies.

ACKNOWLEDGEMENTS

I would like to thank New Writing North and the International Writers' and Translators' House Ventspils, Latvia, for their assistance during the writing of this book. The work of artists Jill Gibbon, Trevor Paglen and Thomas Demand provided some of the book's starting points. Texts consulted include Hito Steyerl's *Duty Free Art*, Laleh Khalili's *The Corporeal Life of Seafaring*, Marc Levinson's *The Box*, Rose George's *Deep Sea and Foreign Going*, Grégoire Chamayou's *Drone Theory*, Nick Dyer-Witheford's *Cyber-Proletariat*, Eyal Weizman's essay 'Lethal Theory,' and Paul Strand's *Tir A' Mhurain*. And thanks, as ever, to my first reader, Michelle Devereaux.

ABOUT THE AUTHOR

C.D. ROSE was born in the north of England and has lived in a number of countries, including Italy, France and the USA. He holds an MA in Creative Writing from the University of East Anglia, and a PhD from Edge Hill University. Though he currently lives in Hebden Bridge, West Yorkshire, he is at home anywhere there are dark bars, dusty libraries, and good second-hand bookshops.